"YASMINE GALENO...
—Jayn...

continued...

Dragon Wytch

"Galenorn cleverly reveals her plot threads in the latest Otherworld offering... Action and sexy sensuality make this book hot to the touch."
—*Romantic Times*

"All great stories must have great heroes and heroines. [*Dragon Wytch*] is no exception. In her books, you enter a world of wonder, danger, whimsy, suspense, sensuality, and action... This book is a great ride, and the destination is well worth the wait."
—*Bitten By Books*

Darkling

"The most fulfilling journey of self-discovery to date in the Otherworld series... An eclectic blend that works well."
—*Booklist*

"Galenorn does a remarkable job of delving into the psyches and fears of her characters. As this series matures, so do her heroines. The sex sizzles and the danger fascinates."
—*Romantic Times*

"The story is nonstop action and has deep, dark plots that kept me up reading long past my bed time. Here be Dark Fantasy with a unique twist. YES!"
—*Huntress Book Reviews*

"Pure fantasy enjoyment from start to finish. I adored the world that Yasmine Galenorn has crafted within the pages of this adventurous urban-fantasy story. The characters come alive off the pages of the story with so many unique personalities... Yasmine Galenorn is a new author on my list of favorite authors."
—*Night Owl Romance*

Changeling

"The second in Galenorn's D'Artigo Sisters series ratchets up the danger and romantic entanglements. Along with the quirky humor and characters readers have come to expect is a moving tale of a woman more comfortable in her cat skin than in her human form, looking to find her place in the world."

—*Booklist*

"Galenorn's thrilling supernatural series is gritty and dangerous, but it's the tumultuous relationships between all the various characters that give it depth and heart. Vivid, sexy, and mesmerizing, Galenorn's novel hits the paranormal sweet spot."

—*Romantic Times*

"I absolutely loved it!"

—*Fresh Fiction*

"Yasmine Galenorn has created another winner…*Changeling* is a can't miss read destined to hold a special place on your keeper shelf."

—*Romance Reviews Today*

Witchling

"Reminiscent of Laurell K. Hamilton with a lighter touch… A delightful new series that simmers with fun and magic."

—MaryJo Putney, *New York Times* bestselling author of *A Distant Magic*

"The first in an engrossing new series…A whimsical reminder of fantasy's importance in everyday life."

—*Publishers Weekly*

"*Witchling* is pure delight…A great heroine, designer gear, dead guys, and Seattle precipitation!"

—MaryJanice Davidson, *New York Times* bestselling author of *Swimming Without a Net*

"*Witchling* is one sexy, fantastic paranormal-mystery-romantic read."

—Terese Ramin, author of *Shotgun Honeymoon*

"A fun read, filled with surprise and enchantment."

—Linda Winstead Jones, author of *Raintree: Haunted*

Legend of the Jade Dragon

❦

Yasmine Galenorn

BERKLEY PRIME CRIME, NEW YORK

THE BERKLEY PUBLISHING GROUP
Published by the Penguin Group
Penguin Group (USA) Inc.
375 Hudson Street, New York, New York 10014, USA
Penguin Group (Canada), 90 Eglinton Avenue East, Suite 700, Toronto, Ontario M4P 2Y3, Canada
(a division of Pearson Penguin Canada Inc.)
Penguin Books Ltd., 80 Strand, London WC2R 0RL, England
Penguin Group Ireland, 25 St. Stephen's Green, Dublin 2, Ireland (a division of Penguin Books Ltd.)
Penguin Group (Australia), 250 Camberwell Road, Camberwell, Victoria 3124, Australia
(a division of Pearson Australia Group Pty. Ltd.)
Penguin Books India Pvt. Ltd., 11 Community Centre, Panchsheel Park, New Delhi—110 017, India
Penguin Group (NZ), 67 Apollo Drive, Rosedale, North Shore 0632, New Zealand
(a division of Pearson New Zealand Ltd.)
Penguin Books (South Africa) (Pty.) Ltd., 24 Sturdee Avenue, Rosebank, Johannesburg 2196,
South Africa

Penguin Books Ltd., Registered Offices: 80 Strand, London WC2R 0RL, England

This is a work of fiction. Names, characters, places, and incidents either are the product of the author's imagination or are used fictitiously, and any resemblance to actual persons, living or dead, business establishments, events, or locales is entirely coincidental. The publisher does not have any control over and does not assume any responsibility for author or third-party websites or their content.

LEGEND OF THE JADE DRAGON

A Berkley Prime Crime Book / published by arrangement with the author

PRINTING HISTORY
First Berkley Prime Crime mass-market edition / May 2004

Copyright © 2004 by Yasmine Galenorn.
Cover illustration by Julia Green.
Cover design by Lesley Worrell.
Interior text design by Kristin del Rosario.

ISBN: 978-0-425-19621-2

BERKLEY® PRIME CRIME
Berkley Prime Crime Books are published by The Berkley Publishing Group,
a division of Penguin Group (USA) Inc.,
375 Hudson Street, New York, New York 10014.
BERKLEY® PRIME CRIME and the PRIME CRIME design are trademarks of Penguin Group (USA) Inc.

PRINTED IN THE UNITED STATES OF AMERICA

10   9   8   7   6   5   4   3   2

*To Wanda Thompson,
my beloved sister
and one of my biggest fans.*

ACKNOWLEDGMENTS

My thanks and gratitude to my husband, Samwise, for his love, belief in me, and incredible support. To Carolyn Agosta, my critique partner extraordinaire. To the members of Writers Will Be Warped, who always inspire me and encourage me on. To Edith Worsencroft, my mother-in-law, who disproves all the myths about terrifying in-laws and who is a wonderful "second reader." To Tara, for drooling on my keyboard, and to Luna, Meerclar, and Pakhit—all my fuzzy feline children.

And again, to my agent, Meredith Bernstein, and my editor, Christine Zika, for helping me make this series a reality. I am having so much fun with it! To all of my readers, both old and new. And of course, to Mielikki, Tapio, Ukko, and Rauni, who keep me on my spiritual path.

Bright Blessings and thank you!
The Painted Panther
Yasmine Galenorn
Galenorn En/Visions: www.galenorn.com

The glories of our blood and state
Are shadows, not substantial things;
  There is no armor against fate;
Death lays his icy hand on kings.

JAMES SHIRLEY (1596–1666),
Contention of Ajax and Ulysses

One

———✦———

AS I STARED at the cards, I had an overwhelming desire to fold them up and tell the man sitting opposite me to forget it. It wasn't like I needed the cash. Ever since the news broke a few months back that I'd managed to catch a two-time murderer thanks to the ghost of one of his victims, my china shop was packed with customers. The tearoom was full every afternoon, and my appointment book for tarot readings was crammed. *Emerald O'Brien,* I'd told myself as I looked myself in the mirror that morning, *you've got it made. Life's sure turned around, so count your blessings.*

And count them I did. Every night I gave a little nod of thanks to the universe for letting me spend another day with Kip and Miranda, my peculiar and brilliant children. I loved my life, my cozy house, my thriving business, and my family of friends. I also tried to be grateful for the two men who both wanted me in their lives, but it was hard to smile at the same time I was the prize in a determined, if good-natured, rivalry. So this was what it felt like to be a love goddess.

Yep, things had turned around, all right. But as I laid out the reading for the man sitting on the opposite side of my table, I felt a flicker of apprehension. When I studied the cards, that flicker turned into a cringe. The Tower, Death, the Five of Swords. Great. Just great. A tidy prediction forecasting the breakdown of everything in this man's life, and I was the one destined to tell him about it. The phrase *Please don't kill the messenger* ran through my head as I tried to gauge whether or not he would be able to handle the reading. My clients trusted me to be honest, and I never fudged, regardless of what I knew they wanted to hear. Nine times out of ten, I was dead-on accurate.

The man, who had introduced himself as Daniel Barrington, came into my shop carrying a suitcase that looked like it had seen better days and wearing a black raincoat faded from too many storms. He set the suitcase down by the table and asked if I had time to read his cards. Something about him whispered *worn out* and, even though I didn't particularly feel like dragging out my deck, I sensed an urgency in his demeanor, so I motioned for him to sit down. As he took his seat, a flash of fear grazed my intuition. He wasn't a dangerous man, I could tell that right off, but his presence unsettled the energy in my shop. It was almost as if something had shifted when he walked through the door, and I felt as if I was standing on the edge of a cliff and the railing protecting me from the long drop had suddenly disappeared.

I shook off the feeling and studied the cards, looking up after a moment. Daniel met my gaze with a tired glint of resignation, and I could tell that he already knew things weren't hunky-dory.

"Have you ever considered taking some time off? Maybe get away for a while?" I searched for the right words. The cards only showed the most likely events to come. There was almost always the chance to change the future, but this time, I drew a blank. Everything seemed so bleak, so full of trauma and turmoil, and then the reading *really* disintegrated into chaos.

"I hear Bermuda is nice this time of year." I grinned. Hey, a little humor couldn't hurt, and maybe it would ease some of the tension.

He shrugged and, with a short laugh, leaned back and let out a long sigh. "You don't have to pussyfoot around the truth." His accent was clipped, British, but as faded as his overcoat. "It predicts bad luck, doesn't it?"

"I'm afraid so." Bad luck, my ass. Doomsday was more like it.

"How bad?"

What should I tell him? Some clients took every word I said as gospel. I didn't want to discourage or scare him. "Well, I don't recommend investing at this time or trying out for the X-Games. Watch out for speeding trucks and the IRS. Airplanes, too, so I guess you'd better forget that trip to Bermuda. The reading gets a little jumbled after that." It was like trying to focus on a collage; every time I looked at the cards, the images seemed to shift and change. Usually, when this happened, I wasn't supposed to interfere in whatever was going on. Karma at play, or perhaps destiny. I decided to forget my fee; the cards weren't clear, and he looked like he didn't have any money to spare. "This one's a freebie. The cards aren't being cooperative."

He tapped the table with his fingertips and cleared his throat. "Don't worry about it, I know what they're telling me. Believe me, the confusion is par for the course and bad luck, my constant companion." He reached for his raincoat and proceeded to empty the pockets as he searched for his wallet. First a balled-up handkerchief, then a Greyhound bus ticket, then his keys and a pocket-sized notebook. He finally found the calfskin trifold and pulled out two twenties, tossing them on the table. "Don't feel bad, please. I think I'm beyond help at this point." As he stood up, his coat caught on the edge of the table, and he tugged at it. The material had snagged on the hinge of one of the folding legs and, before I knew what was happening, the table tipped—cards and all—and everything spilled to the floor.

"Damn it! I'm such a klutz." Daniel knelt down to help me clean up the mess, hurriedly scooping up his keys and other items. "I'm so on edge that I've been tripping over everything. I hope I didn't break anything. If I did, I'll pay for it."

"Don't worry about it," I said. The poor man had enough to deal with, without me fussing over a pack of spilled cards. "Please, it's okay."

He hesitated, then picked up his suitcase. "Then, I'll say good-bye. I've got one final leg on my journey, and then maybe it will all be over."

"Where are you going?" I asked, mesmerized by his resignation.

He stopped at the door to give me a half-wave. "The Pacific. I have one more errand to do before I can rest. Destiny has a way of forcing you to see things through to the end, you know." Then, without another word, he turned and walked out the door.

I watched him leave. The poor man was surrounded by a nimbus of despair. What could have happened to make him so depressed? I shook my head. Most of my customers were locals who just wanted to know about their upcoming party or whether it was a good time to invest a little extra in the stock market, but sometimes tarot clients came into the shop who I never saw again, who stuck in my mind years after I met them. I sighed as I gathered up the cards. Daniel would be one of those. He would remain a mystery, and I'd probably never hear from him again.

As I reached for the last card, I saw something white peeking out from behind a nearby cabinet. I fished it out; it was the linen handkerchief from Daniel's pocket, and it was wrapped around something. It must have rolled behind the shelf when the table tipped.

Curious, I unfolded the cloth. Wrapped in the thick kerchief was a dragon, little more than four inches tall, and it was incredibly exquisite. I hesitantly turned it over in my palm. No Made in Taiwan labels here. Possibly hand-carved. As I examined the figurine closely, I realized that it had been sculpted from a single piece of jade. This was no sweatshop-produced tourist crap designed to be sold at WorldMart or the Import Emporium. No, I had the feeling it was incredibly old. What had Daniel been doing with this?

Daniel! I had to catch him before he got on the bus and disappeared. He might not remember where he'd dropped it, and the dragon looked like some sort of heirloom. I raced out the door. A throng of shoppers strolled along the sidewalks, but I managed to dart my way through them just in time to catch sight of him as he started into the cross-walk.

"Daniel! Wait! You forgot something!"

He glanced back. I held up the dragon; he clasped his hand to his mouth, nodded, and began to move in my direction. Before he could take another step, the sound of screeching tires filled the air as a beige van came hauling ass around the corner, speeding along at at least forty miles per hour. Daniel jerked, trying to get out of the way, but then it hit him, and he bounced off the hood. He flew into the air, twisting as the van shot away and disappeared down the road before anybody could even react. His suitcase popped open, and clothes scattered across the road as a hush settled over the crowd. Daniel came to rest in the middle of the crosswalk with a thud. He didn't move.

A scream from one of the passersby shattered the silence and jolted me out of my paralysis. I shoved the dragon in my pocket and raced toward Daniel as the crowd surged forward. As I pushed my way through the knot of people gathered around him, I saw that Doc Adams—our doctor—had already reached his side.

I knelt beside the doctor, and he glanced around as he felt for Daniel's pulse. "Does anybody know this man? What's his name?"

My stomach lurched as the blood began to pool, trickling from Daniel's mouth down the side of his cheek to form a puddle on the asphalt. "His name's Daniel Barrington. He was just in my shop. He forgot something, and I called him back, and the van—the van—" And then it struck me. If I'd been a moment earlier or a moment later, Daniel would still be alive, but I'd caught his attention at the exact moment that the van wheeled around the corner. I stared at the broken man lying in front of me as Doc Adams motioned to a man with a cell phone.

"Did you call 911 like I told you to?" he asked.

The man nodded.

"Okay, somebody give me their coat; he'll go into shock if we don't get him warmed up." The man who'd called the paramedics offered up his long wool duster.

Just then, we heard the high-pitched keen of sirens in the background, and a medic unit pulled up. Numb, barely able to stand, I started to back away to give them room, but a strangled gasp made me turn around. Daniel had regained consciousness. He focused his gaze on me and weakly lifted his fingers. I dropped to his side and took his hand. His breath raggedly puffed from his lungs, torn as if he couldn't catch enough air.

"The dragon . . . the dragon . . ."

I leaned down, looking in his face, making certain he could hear me. "It's safe, so please don't worry. I'll keep it for you until you get better. Now, save your strength. The paramedics are here to help you."

He blinked, pain flooding in his eyes. "The dragon! Please . . . you mustn't . . . don't . . . get rid—" Abruptly, he choked on his words and slumped. As I moved aside to give the medics room to work, I knew it was hopeless. A white flicker hovered above Daniel's body. I could see it as clearly as I could see Doc Adams, who was staring at me with a puzzled look. Then, like a breeze gusting past, the spirit vanished. Daniel had passed through the tunnel, and all the work the medics were doing wouldn't bring him back. Silently, I looked down at my shirt. Speckles of blood clung to it where I'd leaned close to his battered body.

Doc Adams was talking to the police; I recognized one of the officers. Deacon Wilson had worked closely with my friend Murray before she got her promotion. Deacon motioned me over and asked me what I knew about Daniel. I told him about Daniel's visit to my store and the forgotten dragon and how I'd run out to stop him and what he'd said at the end. Deacon jotted everything down. I was about to ask him if he wanted to take the dragon back to the station when one of the paramedics hailed him, and he gave me a quick nod before joining the EMT. He came back after a moment. "We've got his wallet and his identification." He looked at the dragon. "Looks like just a bauble to me. Since he asked you to keep the dragon, I'd say go ahead for now. Just don't lose it, in case we need it for some reason."

I grimaced. "If I hadn't called to him, he'd still be alive. Daniel turned around to see what I wanted, and that was just long enough for the van to clip him as it barreled through."

Deacon patted my shoulder. "Emerald, that van was doing a good forty to fifty miles per hour from what everybody says. I don't think a few seconds would have been

enough for Daniel to get out of its path. Damn bastard
didn't even slow down. I'm not sure if we'll be able to
catch them, but we'll try. I just don't know what gets into
some people."

I wiped my eyes and smiled wanly at him. Maybe Deacon was right; maybe the accident would have happened
even if I hadn't called out at that moment. Maybe when
Daniel said that he had to see things through to the end, he
knew something was going to happen.

The paramedics gently loaded Daniel's body in the
ambulance and drove away, their sirens no longer necessary. With nothing left for me to do, I headed back to the
shop. Lana was dishing up soup for a pair of customers
who were weighed down with bags and boxes from an
active morning of shopping, and Cinnamon was restocking
shelves as I came in. My shirt was spattered with blood-
stains, my face tearstained, red, and puffy. Cinnamon set
down the packet of water biscuits she was holding and
cleared her throat. At her questioning glance, I shook my
head and whispered, "My tarot client was just killed by a
hit-and-run driver."

I kept a spare outfit in my office, just in case I ever
needed it. I gathered up the clothes and headed into the
bathroom. I closed the door behind me and leaned against
it, shaking. How could this happen? One minute he was
alive, the next he was dead. I closed my eyes, but images of
Daniel flying through the air instantly sprang to mind, so I
opened them again. I could do without the instant replay.
After taking a deep breath to calm down, I looked in the
mirror. Mascara streaked down my cheeks, and my lipstick
was smeared. I scrubbed off my makeup and washed my
face, splashing cold water against my skin. The chill helped,
bracing me as I coughed. I wiped my nose and faced my
reflection.

"Emerald, you sure do attract trouble," I said. My

reflection shrugged along with me, green eyes flashing against my paler-than-usual skin. I absently brushed my hair back into place, binding it into a quick ponytail to corral the wayward curls as I thought about Daniel's last words. "The dragon ... don't ... get rid ..." Well, that was a no-brainer. He wanted me to keep the dragon.

Okay, I thought. I could do that much. Deacon had given me permission, so I assumed that I wouldn't get in any trouble with the police, though I decided to check with Murray just in case. She'd always been smarter than her buddies, and now that she was a detective, I trusted her more than the average cop on the beat.

I pulled the dragon out of my pocket and examined it closely. Beautiful. Lustrous. Old, but I couldn't speculate just how old. And now Daniel was dead, and the dragon was in my keeping. A shiver ran up my spine, and once again a wave of guilt swept over me. I took another deep breath. Deacon was right; I knew he was. Daniel's death wasn't my fault. So why did I feel like I was to blame?

I flipped the statue over in my hand. Yep, I was certain it had been some sort of family heirloom. Well, I would keep Daniel's dragon until I found his next of kin and then return it to them. It was the least I could do for the unsettled man who had been so resigned to his fate. But an odd fluttering in my stomach whispered that there wouldn't be anybody to find. I had a feeling Daniel was very much alone, as alone in life as he now was in death.

The dragon stared up at me, cool eyes gazing into my own. For a moment, I could almost swear I saw them flash red, but then I blinked, and they were the pale milky jade as before. "Little guy, do you know something about Daniel that I don't?" I asked. "Do you know where I can find his family?" The dragon remained silent, but I had the uncanny feeling it heard me and understood everything I was saying.

Two

❖

WHEN I RETURNED to the alcove set aside for my readings, I sat down and stared at the wall, wanting nothing more than to get away. Thank heavens I'd reserved a cabin out at Tyler's Resort for next weekend to celebrate Kip's recent release from being grounded for three months. The kids were really looking forward to this getaway, and after today, I needed to get away for a while, too. I'd put down a hefty nonrefundable deposit, but it was going to be worth it.

Finally, I picked up my deck and rapped it on the edge of the table to align the edges. As I slid the deck into its velvet pouch, I pondered Daniel's accident. Was there anything I could have done to prevent his death? Any chance I could have read the signs clearer? But then, a thought hit me. Maybe I hadn't been able to read his future because maybe Daniel didn't *have* a future. Maybe he'd been doomed before he walked into my shop. Shaking, I stashed the cards in my office, hiding them in my bottom desk drawer. As I forced myself to return to the front counter, Cinnamon asked if I wanted to leave early, but I told her no, I'd probably just brood if I sat around the house. At least here I could keep busy.

Busy. That was an understatement for the pace we'd been running lately. Ever since Susan Mitchell's ghost showed up, begging me to prove she'd been murdered, my shop turned into a shrine for those wonderful old ladies like Mrs. Halcyon Maxwell, president of the Psychic Occult Society of Rachel in *The Ghost & Mr. Chicken*. All they wanted was a little taste of adventure, a chance to contact the "other side," and tarot readings now appeared on the menu next to the daily tea selections. I'd been able to hire Cinnamon full-time and Lana part-time and relegate myself to the background, managing, organizing, helping customers with special orders and—of course—reading the cards.

The shop bells jingled as Kip wandered in, carrying a backpack full of books. He'd become very studious the past few months. Back in December, Kip had managed to set loose a tidal wave of trouble with a nasty ghost right before Christmas. During the three months he was grounded, he somehow got the idea that the more he studied, the better my mood. I wasn't about to break the spell.

His face was ashen. "There's a police car out there, and they're cleaning stuff off the road. What happened?"

How could I explain what had happened? My children knew about the realities of death, but I didn't want them to dwell on it. I opted for an honest yet simple answer. "A man got hit by a car and died. The driver didn't stop."

"People shouldn't run away from what they do," Kip mumbled. "I guess he just didn't want to get in trouble."

"You're right; he should have stopped and tried to help." I gave him a hug and a gentle shove toward the tearoom. "Now go have some lemonade and cookies. Only two, though. Remember, Miranda's making dinner tonight." He grimaced, then his eyes lit up as he spotted Lana. Oh, those little-boy crushes that were both terribly sweet and sad at the same time. Lana thought he was adorable, thank God, and endured his attentions with the utmost grace.

Cinnamon asked if I would watch the till for her while she took a break to go drop her paycheck in the bank. I waved her off and peeked into the tearoom to see who was there. Mabel Jones, with her daily cuppa and slice of pound cake, saw me and nodded, then went back to the romance she was reading.

The only other person in the tearoom at this point was Ida Trask, the best baby-sitter this side of the Pacific. I poured myself a cup of tea and joined her when she motioned me over.

"You look tired, dear." She put her hand on my arm.

I shrugged. "Tired isn't the word for it," I said and plunged into the story about Daniel. She let me ramble on until I finished, coming to an abrupt stop.

"How sad," she said.

I nodded. There wasn't much else to say. Destiny, fate . . . no matter what you called it, the man was dead.

Ida took a sip of her tea, frowned, and added more hot water. "So, the police let you keep the dragon?"

"They know who I am and where I live. If they find any family he might have, they know I want to give the statue to them." I tasted my orange spice tea and let the warmth stream down my throat. "Truth is, I'm really shook up. Do you mind if we talk about something else?" I had to get the vision of his body, sprawled on the pavement, out of my mind. "How about you? Has your nephew arrived yet?"

She leaned back against the chair, her starched linen dress crinkling with that *scrunchy* sound good linen always makes. Ida always dressed up when she went out; it was just her nature. She adjusted her glasses, making sure they were still attached to the chain that looped around her neck. "He's due in on the bus this afternoon. I'm hoping to introduce him around this weekend, if he's up to it."

"Why don't you start by bringing him over tonight? I'd love to meet him." I knew vaguely that her nephew had been in trouble but wasn't sure just what he'd done.

She smiled at me, obviously relieved. "Thank you, I was hoping you wouldn't mind if I started with you. He's only been out of prison a couple of days, you know, and there are bound to be adjustment issues." She toyed with her cup. "I'm just sorry Caroline died before she could come to her senses and give him another chance."

"How long has it been now? A year?" When her sister had died, Ida had been reticent about her grief; she wasn't a woman given to histrionics. I'd made sure, though, that the kids and I spent a lot of time at her house, and she'd seemed grateful for the company, always welcoming us in with brownies or a loaf of freshly baked bread.

She bit into a gingersnap and tapped the side of her mouth with a napkin. "Caroline died almost a year ago. Since she was already a widow, she left me all her money. I put it away in a revocable trust fund, in hopes that Oliver would take me up on my offer to come stay with me while he gets his life back in order. I figured that he'd need a good start once they let him out. He's a good boy, Emerald. Once I see that he's really serious about finishing school or that he gets a good job and holds it for a while, then I'll sign over the trust fund to him. I just don't believe his mother should have cut him out of her will."

It didn't seem right to me, either. "What on earth did he do to make her so mad?" I couldn't imagine Ida offering Oliver a place in her home if he'd committed some horrible crime.

She sighed and set down her cup. "Oh, nothing so terrible, but the fact that he got arrested was enough for her.

Oliver was in the middle of his sophomore year at Oregon State University when he got involved in a cannabis club. He was growing marijuana for medical patients—it's supposed to be legal there, you know. But the federal authorities didn't see it that way, and Oliver was sentenced to three years."

"Three years . . . that's a long time out of a person's life," I said.

"Yes, it is, but since the trial took a year and he was in jail during that time, he's actually been locked up a total of four years. Caroline wouldn't post bail for him. I didn't know about any of this until after he'd been sentenced. She didn't want the family to find out what had happened." She folded her napkin and shook her head.

"How did you find out?"

Ida poured herself another cup of tea and returned to the table. "Oliver started writing to me when he was in prison, once he realized his mother had disowned him."

What a nightmare. "I can't imagine turning my back on my children for something like that," I said.

She shrugged. "That's what my sister was like." Flipping through her wallet, she pulled out a grainy picture of a young man, blond with the barest hint of a mustache. "He sent me this a couple of months ago. The quality of the photograph isn't very good, so it's hard to see what he really looks like, but I sincerely doubt that they let the inmates pose for glamour shots." She gave me a rueful smile.

"When's the last time you actually saw him?" I asked.

"Oh, it must have been right before he turned thirteen; that's when Caroline sent him away to boarding school in France. After boarding school, Oliver attended a private university in Switzerland for two years until he quit without telling his parents and showed up one night on their doorstep, suitcase in hand. He hated the pretentious attitudes at the school. My sister was furious. She gave Oliver an ultimatum; he could immediately enroll at OSU or head out on the streets. He went back to school, but it was only a few months before he was arrested."

Ida shook her head. "That boy always did set things atwitter. He's a born crusader against social injustices." She stared into her cup, sobering. "I'm afraid I haven't been much better than Caroline. When I first found out what he'd done, I was so disappointed in him that I didn't have the heart to go visit. And then . . . well, we started writing, but I've just never managed to make the time, what with one thing and another." Her voice trailed off, and I knew she was feeling guilty.

I rested my hand on hers. "Don't beat yourself up, Ida. You're going to help him now when he needs it, and that's what counts." I knew that Ida missed her own son who had moved to Japan a few years back to teach English. She must be looking for a way to make up for that sense of loss. "So he's going back to school? How old is he now?"

"He had almost two years left to go when they raided his apartment, and he's agreed to enroll at Western Washington University this fall. What with waiting for the trial and all, he just turned twenty-six, so it's not too late, by any means. I'll pay his tuition and give him a place to live as long as he keeps his grades up and stays out of trouble. He has to finish his degree within the next two years, and then he can get on with his life. He was an art history major, though I'm not sure whether he'll go back to that or not." She glanced at her watch and gathered up her things. "Why, here I've gone and talked your ear off, and he should be in on the Greyhound in less than twenty minutes. I'd better run!"

I waved her out and, when Cinnamon returned, vacated the counter. "I'm going to finish up some paperwork." I headed into the office, making sure that I had the dragon with me. I could hardly wait until six o'clock rolled around.

KIP POPPED HIS head into the living room as I sat cross-legged on the sofa, trying to repair a hangnail. "Mom, I need to get the tools out of the shed so I can work on my bike chain."

"The key's on the Peg-Board in the kitchen, next to the spare house key. Don't lose it." I waved him off as he nodded and disappeared. I heard him say something to Miranda, who was in the kitchen fixing dinner, then the sound of the back door slamming. I winced. One of these days he was going to shatter the window panes, and then I'd be taking the money out of his allowance for weeks.

I aimed the remote and punched on Channel 7. Oh joy. The news was on, and there was Cathy Sutton, our perpetually perky local reporter who had the aplomb of a self-satisfied cat and the personality of a thorn bush.

"At approximately three o'clock this afternoon, Daniel Barrington, a former resident of Victoria, British Columbia, was struck and killed by a hit-and-run driver while crossing Main Street and Third. Police are looking for a beige van, which witnesses say made an illegal left turn before hitting Mr. Barrington. The van's speed was estimated at forty miles per hour. Paramedics hastened to the scene but were unable to save his life. Mr. Barrington appeared to be transient, with no permanent address and no next of kin. He had just exited the Chintz 'n China Tea Room, where he is thought to have purchased a tarot reading."

Her coanchor, good old Jack Sullivan, raised his eyebrows. "The Chintz 'n China? If I remember right, that's the shop owned by our local heroine, Ms. Emerald O'Brien."

"That's right, Jack." Cathy flashed the camera a smooth grin that was never quite reflected in her eyes. "In fact, witnesses say that Ms. O'Brien was hailing Daniel as he crossed the street. He turned to answer her right when the van sped around the corner and hit him."

Jack frowned. "Too bad Ms. O'Brien couldn't use her fortune-telling powers to warn him about speeding motorists."

Fortune-teller! Jack Sullivan was always making snide cracks that left a sour taste in my mouth, but this was the first time one of them had been aimed at me. I almost choked on my Talking Rain, and the sparkling water spurted out my nose, the carbonated bubbles stinging all the way. Fortune-teller indeed. First thing tomorrow I'd write a letter to the station and complain.

I glanced at the clock as Miranda came dashing into the room, a panic-stricken look on her face. "Mom, what do I do when the soup starts boiling?"

"Turn it down to medium and stir, unless you want to scrub pots until way past your bedtime tonight."

We were in for a *real* treat; Miranda was wading through the spring home economics unit required for all eighth-grade students at her school. This week she'd been assigned the task of preparing a three-course meal. Along with grilled cheese sandwiches and tomato soup, we were also having what appeared to be a pulverized head of iceberg for salad and a selection of Twinkies for dessert. She'd begged me to sign her slip without making her do the work, but I warned her that cheating students didn't get to cash in on their opportunity to go to Space Camp during the summer break. Since July was still several months away, she'd backed off immediately without a whine or the usual martyred-by-mom attitude she'd picked up the past few months.

"Then what?"

"Then when it's hot enough, we eat. Did you leave the sandwiches cooking in that skillet without watching them?" I sniffed. The ominous whiff of charred bread drifted in from the kitchen.

"Yikes!" She clattered through the swinging doors, and I heard what suspiciously sounded like a swear word, but I decided to forgo comment. Cooking was hard enough even if you knew which side of the bread to butter. For Miranda, every cooking class was a lesson in hell. She hated it, and I had the feeling that, unless something changed over the next few years, by the time she was eighteen, both McDonald's and Burger King would have another steady customer.

I peeked through the archway dividing the living room from the huge dining-kitchen area. "How long until dinner?"

She consulted her watch. "Ten minutes. I'll go call Kip."

I shook out my purse on the desk and went through receipts, throwing some away and filing the others in my business ledger. After I finished stashing everything else back in my handbag, I picked up the handkerchief holding the figurine and unwrapped it.

The dragon had made it home in one piece. I took a closer look. No machine marks. Definitely hand-carved, with delicate patterns etched in gold weaving along the surface of the jade. The carving was so intricate that I could see every nuance, every curve was polished and glowing. My bet was that this was an antique. If my guess was correct, this little dragon might just be worth a whole lot of money.

Where had it come from? And what did it have to do with Daniel?

I wasn't a slouch with psychometry; I closed my eyes and tried to focus on the dragon's essence. A medley of changing patterns swirled in my mind, and I was about to lower myself into the flow to see what I could pick up when Miranda poked her head around the door.

"Dinner!"

Reluctantly, I unlocked the étagère, tucked the dragon in alongside the rest of my collection, and locked the cabinet again.

Kip came racing into the room, a pained look on his face. He'd been in the kitchen; he knew what we were having. With a shake of his head, he said, "At least she can't ruin the Twinkies."

"Thank heaven for small favors." I plastered on a smile. "Come on, kiddo. We're going to eat dinner, and we're going to tell Miranda that we enjoyed every bite."

AFTER DINNER, I punched in Murray's work number. One of Chiqetaw's finest as well as one of my best friends, Anna Murray had recently been promoted to detective, and both she and I were still trying to get used to her new status. "Hey, chickie, how goes it?" We hadn't had much time to hang out together since her promotion, and I missed her company.

She exhaled slowly, as if she'd been holding her breath a long time. "It goes, I guess." She paused, and I could almost hear her looking around to make sure nobody was eavesdropping. "Coughlan's on my back again. He's making sure all the kooks are referred to me; I haven't gotten a real case to work on in the month since I started my new job."

I knew she'd been unhappy but didn't realize things were this bad. "Kooks?"

"Em, I take calls from people who think their dogs have been possessed by aliens or the nosy people who are 'just certain' that their next-door neighbor is "that guy they showed on *America's Most Wanted* last night." Of course, the dude always ends up with a whistle-clean record, and then he blames me, not the drunken neighbor who turned him in. I don't know what Coughlan expects. My record's going to look like shit."

Coughlan. I knew precisely what he expected. He expected Murray to get fed up and quit. I'd heard a lot about him over the past month. Head of detectives, he was a member of that elite group of supervisors from hell. A big man with a big ego, he didn't like the fact that Murray was Native American or the fact that she was a woman. And he considered Tad Bonner—the chief of police who had been Murray's previous supervisor—his continual rival. Over a late-night gabfest with plenty of coffee and cake, Murray and I'd come to the conclusion that Coughlan wanted Bonner's job.

"Good ol' boys like to have their fun, don't they?" I let it go at that. Murray was convinced she could win him over, and nothing I'd said over the past month had made an impression. She'd have to figure this one when she was ready.

"So what's up?" she asked. I heard the shuffle of papers, then the sound of a soda being opened.

Of course she knew all about Daniel from the news at the station, but I told the story from my perspective. "It was like an episode of *The Twilight Zone,* Mur." I was still running a lot of guilt over having played a part in his death, but she reassured me that I'd done nothing wrong.

"Even if you hadn't called out at that exact moment, the officers on the scene think that the van would have managed to hit Daniel. It was just a weird coincidence that you were there, Em. Don't let yourself get too upset over it."

"Thanks. I really needed to hear you say that. I've been feeling so guilty over his death."

"Well, don't."

I asked her about the dragon, and she reiterated what Deacon told me. "In fact, it's probably safer with you than in our holding room. I like these guys, but we have our share of bad apples, and sometimes expensive things disappear."

Maybe she was right. I sighed. "Daniel seemed so lonely. Were you able to find out anything about him?"

"He was just one of a thousand loners, Em. We couldn't find a current address, and the one listed on his driver's license is out of date by two years. Landlord said one day Daniel up and sold all his stuff, packed up a suitcase, and took off. We couldn't find any sign of family, anywhere."

Somehow, her news didn't surprise me. When I thought of Daniel and his untimely end, the weight of the world seemed to settle in on my shoulders. His life had obviously been about as dismal as his death. I shifted the subject to a happier topic—the camping trip the kids and I'd been planning—and we chatted for a few more minutes before my doorbell rang. With a hasty good-bye, I hung up and answered the door.

Ida was standing on the porch, her nephew in tow, a worried look on her face. Oliver was a surprisingly short man and didn't look at all like I'd expected him to. He stood only an inch or so taller than his aunt, and his skin had an unhealthy pallor, like clotted cream. His closely cropped hair was beginning to recede, and he *looked* like he'd been locked away for a few years. His eyes were a preternatural gray, darting around as Ida introduced us, as if he were constantly thinking. In a threadbare pair of corduroy trousers and beige shirt at least one size too big for him, Oliver Hoffman looked older than the twenty-six he was supposed to be.

I took Ida's arm and walked her into the kitchen, while Oliver wandered over to the étagère. "Oliver seems a little . . . spooked?" I offered, not saying what I really wanted to say which was that Oliver had immediately struck me as being a little squirrelly.

"Yes, I noticed that, too." Ida peeked into the living room to make sure we couldn't be heard. "He seems a lot more depressed than he did last week when we talked on the phone. And he didn't quite grow into the man I thought he would; his father was a tall, hefty man. Caroline was short, but stout. Oliver seems awfully thin, but then again, he always was a scrawny lad when he was young. It's more his attitude that worries me, though. A month ago, he couldn't wait to get out of prison. Now ... I'm not so sure."

"Do you think he needs counseling to help him cope with the change?" I asked, not knowing what else to say.

She shook her head. "I don't know. Its nothing I can even put my finger on. The boy just seems strained. Maybe the stress of getting out has affected him more than he wants to admit. He says he's fine, and I suppose he knows best. But, Emerald, I've got another problem I need your help with."

"What's wrong?" I asked.

"My friend Desdemona, the one who lives in Sandpoint, Idaho, was in a serious accident. She was driving back from Coeur d'Alene when a logging truck came barreling around the curve in the road and veered into her lane. She swerved to miss it and hit a tree. She survived, but she's going home from the hospital tomorrow, and she'll be bedridden for a while and needs help. Since she doesn't have any children or the money for home health care, I've decided to drive over to help out for a few days until her niece can fly up from Florida. I'm just a little worried about leaving Oliver alone."

I glanced back into the living room at him; he was staring at my collection of crystal and figurines. "I'm sure things will be okay. Would you like me to keep an eye on him for you?"

A look of relief swept across her face. "I'd be so grateful. It's not that I don't trust him or that I want to check up on him . . . I'm just . . ."

"You're just worried," I finished for her, resting my hand on her shoulder. "You go help Desdemona, and I'll keep watch after Oliver and try to make him feel welcome." Reassured, she let out a sigh of relief, and we returned to the living room.

Oliver jerked his head up and gave me a polite smile. "You have some lovely pieces," he said. "I take it you love art?"

"Crystal and china, actually. They're two of my greatest passions." I gave him a radiant smile, hoping to cajole him out of his reticence. "Tea would be a third."

"You're lucky to have turned your passion into your work," he said and flashed me a grin with just enough warmth behind it to make me think that maybe it was just the stress of having to face readjusting to the outside world that made him seem so strange. Maybe prison hadn't killed his spirit after all.

While I served tea and cookies, Ida pored over the dragon. I filled Oliver in on what had happened with Daniel so he wouldn't feel left out of the conversation. "It was quite the shock; one I'd rather not go through again. I think it's going to take a while for me to cope with his death."

"And they still have no idea who killed him?" Ida asked.

"Apparently not. It was a hit-and-run, no doubt about that, but I don't think anybody there could see the driver, and nobody managed to get the license plate. It happened so fast."

She sighed. "People are so careless, they drive like they own the road. Look at poor Desdemona. So, what are you going to do with the dragon?" Ida turned it over in her palm. "This doesn't look like any ordinary mass-market sculpture."

Oliver peered over her shoulder. "Aunt Ida's right. I think it might be valuable."

What *was* I going to do with it? I could keep it locked up here with the rest of my collection, but it was so beautiful that I wanted others to have the chance to see it, too. "I think I'll take it to the shop with me. I can display it in the Not-For-Sale cabinet. When I find Daniel's next of kin, I'll return it to them. I wouldn't feel right about keeping it."

"Good girl. You keep that cabinet locked, don't you?"

I nodded. I had to. There were items in the NFS cabinet that I'd be devastated to lose, and yet I enjoyed giving others the chance to see them.

"Well, I'm glad about that," Ida said. "I still think you should really get a security system. You're far too trusting." She sounded just like the schoolteacher she'd once been, prim and stern, no-nonsense.

I flashed her a sheepish grin. "Yes, Mrs. Trask," I said, mimicking the hundreds of children that had passed through her classrooms and day care. Truth was, though, I didn't think of myself as trusting. I had a good solid dead bolt on the shop door and sturdy locks on all of the cabinets that held the most expensive pieces. "We live in Chiqetaw, Ida. People here are honest."

"Don't kid yourself. The world intrudes everywhere. You of all people should know that we have our share of nuts and psychos."

I didn't want to think about psychos. I'd had my fill of them near Christmas when I'd almost been killed by one. I tucked the dragon back in the cabinet and offered them more cookies. The conversation turned toward school and art history and whether or not Oliver would find it difficult to get full credit for all the work he did before he was arrested. After about an hour, they stood up to leave. "Ida, be careful on your trip. Send my best wishes to your friend, and call me when you get the chance." I gave the older woman a hug, holding her tight as if I could protect her with my embrace.

She kissed me on the cheek. "My dear, I promise to be careful. Look after my nephew for me, would you?" I promised, offering Oliver my hand. He accepted with a genteel nod that didn't fit his grungy attire, and they took off for home. I watched them walk past the lot of blackberries that bordered the side of my own house. With Ida Trask up the street to my left and Horvald Ledbetter directly across from me, I had lucked out in neighbors, that was for sure. Horvald might be an odd duck, but he always had a smile and wave for us.

I shook my head as I looked at the berry vines creeping over my fence. I should really hound the city to do something about them. The brambles had engulfed whatever might be hiding on the lot next door. They were so thick that they could hide a house under that pile of vines and thorns and nobody would ever know. I'd taken to hiring a man to prune them back twice a year, halting their attempt to breach my fence.

As I watched Ida's retreating back, I found myself restless, unsettled. Maybe I should do a reading, make sure she'd be okay, considering what had happened today. I went so far as to pull out the deck from my rolltop desk, then replaced the cards in their well-worn spot. There was nothing I could say that would make her stay home and, if danger was in the offing, I couldn't do anything to prevent it. And frankly, I didn't have the heart to peek.

I WAS JUST about to peel the loincloth off the gorgeous Polynesian man when a shriek cut through my dream and rudely dragged me away from the tropical island get-away my subconscious had so graciously created for me. Miranda! I tumbled out of bed and pounded down the hall-way. Her door was open, the light was on, and my daughter was cursing a blue streak as she slipped out the window onto the roof.

"What's going on in here? Are you okay? Where did you learn that kind of language?" When I saw that she wasn't hurt, irritation took over. I glanced at her clock. Two A.M.? I never allowed her to stay up that late unless there was supposed to be some incredible astronomical display. I followed her out onto the roof. A lovely flat area right outside her window made the perfect viewing perch for her to watch the stars, and I'd paid a carpenter to come in mid-March and reinforce the guardrail that protected her from falling over the edge. "What's wrong?"

She pointed to the railing. "My telescope. A big crash woke me up, and I looked out . . . it's gone."

We both cautiously leaned over the rail, but it was too dark to see anything. I looked around. Nobody could have been out on this roof. The wind was calm, and everything seemed undisturbed. Maybe a sudden gust? The wind often picked up around here without much of a warning. "Well, get your bathrobe and slippers on and let's go downstairs."

I pulled on my sweats and slipped into my huaraches. While I was waiting for Miranda, I peeked into Kip's room. He was breathing deeply, sound asleep. Good, he didn't need to be up during the middle of the night. Randa and I padded downstairs and out the front door. I switched on the floodlight, and we peered over the low wall of the porch into the front yard. There, glittering under the light, was Miranda's new telescope. She let out a groan and raced down the side steps and around into the lawn. A large cedar bough lay near it, the end freshly broken. I picked up the branch and examined it as Randa knelt near the main tube of the telescope, her expression heartsick.

"My new telescope! You gave it to me for Christmas!" She gathered it up in her arms; the tube was dented, the tripod legs broken. Without asking, I knew that the lens hadn't survived the free fall. My heart sank. The telescope was now six hundred dollars' worth of scrap metal and broken glass. Worse yet was Miranda's disappointment. Ever since she'd opened the box, she'd been treating the telescope with as much love as she once treated her stuffed bears.

I dropped the tree limb on the ground and rested a hand on her shoulder. "The wind must have come up suddenly and ripped the branch off the tree; when it fell, it caught your telescope and took it over the railing." I wasn't sure whether or not I believed my explanation, but it was the only thing I could think of. The squirrels were still hibernating, or at least they hadn't put in a strong show lately. Besides, they weren't big enough to do this kind of damage. They would have had to physically pick it up and heave it over the railing. Nor did we have any birds that could cause such havoc.

I glanced back at the roof, wondering if anybody could have climbed up, but nope, not without a ladder, and we would have seen evidence of anything like that when we were on the roof. No, nobody had been up there tonight except when we crawled through Miranda's window. I was sure of it.

"It'll be okay, honey, this is just a stroke of bad luck. Come on, dry your eyes. Tomorrow is Saturday. Sunday, we'll go buy you another. Don't cry, sweetheart." Comforted with the promise that we would replace her beloved telescope, Miranda let me lead her back inside. While I was at work she could call around and find out if the store had another in stock.

With a last glance at the glittering shards of metal, glass, and plastic now decorating the lawn, I locked the door. Still shaken, we stopped in the kitchen for milk and a cookie before we went back upstairs to our beds. The rest of the night passed without incident.

Three

⸎

DESPERATE FOR A caffeine fix, I stopped at Starbucks before we hit the Chintz 'n China. I snagged a triple shot grandé iced mocha for myself, and the kids ordered apple cider and croissant sandwiches. As the cold chill of the chocolate-enhanced espresso ran down my throat, I went over what we had to do today.

For a Saturday, my errand list was pretty light. First and foremost: the weekly cleanup of the Chintz 'n China. The kids always helped; I'd made it a part of their regular chores. Lana would also be there; she came in on weekends now that Cinnamon was working full-time during the week. At some point, I wanted to run the dragon over to Mr. Hodges, who operated a jewelry and estate store across the street from my shop. He specialized in appraising rare goods and maybe, if I was lucky, he could help me identify and valuate the dragon.

Which reminded me: I opened my Day-Timer and penned a note to start hunting for Daniel Barrington's

family. Murray had called me before I left home to tell me
that the Chiqetaw police ran his information through several
national databases, but nothing came up, and they simply
didn't have the manpower to mount an in-depth search to
continue looking unless some new leads came in.

I tied a bandanna around my head and grabbed a dust
rag. "Kids, take the tearoom. Dust, sweep, scrub tables,
and mop. And *then*," I said, feeling like Cinderella's step-
mother, "you can go." While they polished the tables and
counter, Lana and I attacked the dust bunnies that hid out
on the shelves in the store proper. Within an hour the shop
was gleaming, not a speck of dust in sight. I gave the kids
the go-ahead to take off. "Out of here, before I find something else for you to do."

Kip shot out the door before I could say another word.
Miranda watched him race away, then grinned at me as
she strolled after him. I knew she was headed home to call
the astronomer's hangout in Bellingham—a store called the
Skies & Scopes—to ask if they had another Swift Dobson-
ian telescope in stock.

I grimaced as I made a quick call to my bank branch
and, using the automated service, transferred seven hundred dollars from my savings account into checking. The
price of the telescope had caused me more than a little finan-
cial grief at Christmas. Having to shell out the same amount
just four months later was like a kick in the teeth, but
Miranda hadn't tossed her telescope over the railing, and I
wasn't about to penalize her for a freak accident. I would,
however, insist she start bringing it inside at night instead
of leaving it set up on the roof.

As Lana flipped the sign from Closed to Open and
unlocked the door, a little throng of customers pushed in.
Weird. Saturdays were usually slow until midafternoon.
The mystery cleared up when they crowded around me,
asking about Daniel and the hit-and-run. Like vultures

attracted to the feeding grounds, they flocked in, hoping for scraps of gossip. Lana intervened, bless her heart, encouraging them to "Come have a cup of tea," while I retreated behind the counter. Farrah Warnoff and Lydia Johnson followed me, but they actually needed help.

"I'd like to schedule Monday readings for Mother and myself." Farrah had become one of my most loyal and most annoying tarot clients. At times, I dreaded seeing her come in the door. She usually didn't really *need* a reading, she just liked to tell her friends about her "psychic," which irritated the hell out of me.

I stared at my Day-Timer, packed with a flurry of scribbled names and times, longing to take a giant eraser to the whole list. The money was good, but I just didn't want to handle the cards for a while so soon after Daniel's untimely end. Well, somebody had said honesty was the best policy. I'd find out if they were right. "You know what, Farrah? I'm taking the rest of the month off. I'm just plum worn out."

She patted my arm. "It must be quite a drain on your power. I can't imagine what it's like to have people dying on you right and left. I can see how you need some time to recuperate. How about May first? I believe that's a Tuesday?"

Yeah. Drain on my powers. Oh yep. My powers of patience, I thought, penciling her in for May Day. While I was thinking about it, I leaned around the corner and motioned to Lana. "After the rush dies down, I want you to notify my tarot clients for the rest of April that I'm canceling all my appointments through the end of the month. Don't schedule anybody until May, okay?"

She nodded. I handed her the appointment book and escorted Lydia to a chair next to my desk, where she sat, tapping her impeccably polished nails on the wooden arm. She just wanted to know if her special order had arrived yet, so I dug through the pile of receipts until I found her invoice and matched it to a teapot in the storeroom. I wrapped the pot and filled out the invoice so she could pay Lana at the counter. She gave me a cheery wink as she headed out the door. "Don't let them get you down, Emerald. Just ride the waves." She swooshed her hand through the air. "Go with the flow."

As the afternoon wore on, I began to feel jittery. The caffeine was wearing off, yet my mind was still racing. The destruction of Miranda's telescope had spooked me. And why had Daniel been so resigned, so depressed? Why couldn't the police find any mention of his family? I opened my purse and withdrew the carefully wrapped package containing the dragon. After telling Lana that I'd be back in a few minutes, I dashed across the road, carefully looking to make sure the way was clear. I wasn't going to set myself up for an encore of yesterday's tragedy.

Mr. Hodges had perused the Chintz 'n China a number of times, now and then buying a gift for his wife. He greeted me when I slipped into the hushed foyer of Hodges & Sons. I handed him the dragon. "I'd like to find out an approximate age and value on this, if you can come up with anything."

His eyes twinkled. "A welcome challenge, Ms. O'Brien. Can you come back Monday? I should be able to have an estimate for you then."

"Sure thing." I took my receipt and darted back across the street. As I hit the door, I almost ran into Kip, who came barreling down the sidewalk. He grumbled a hello, and I gave him a sidelong look. Something was up.

"You okay?" He nodded, but I wasn't buying it. I knelt beside him, looking him over for any blood, broken bones, or chipped teeth. Nope, nada, but I knew he didn't get that storm-brewing look unless he was upset. "C'mon kiddo, what's going on?"

"Why can't you just leave me alone?"

I gave him a pointed stare. "Excuse me, mister? What did you say?"

He lost it then, shouting in my face. "Sly and Tony said I couldn't play with them, okay? Sly said Tony's his new best friend, and they laughed at me and called me a wimp and told me to run home to my *mama!* Are you happy now?" With an abrupt stop, he burped. I led him into my office where I handed him a tissue and gently smoothed back his hair. He blew his nose.

"I assume you know better than to shout at me like that?"

Kip swallowed, then nodded.

"All right, we'll consider it a temporary lapse of judgment. So Sly and Tony are best friends now, huh?" I sat down and tried to pull him onto my lap, but he pushed me away. My little boy was growing up. With a bittersweet pang, I let him go, and he slumped in the chair beside me.

"I bet you really feel awful."

"Nope, I don't care." He scuffed the floor with the toe of his shoe. "They said that I wasn't any fun anymore 'cause I said I couldn't go play in the old Winyard house." He lowered his voice and looked up at me, his expression grave and drawn.

The Winyard house! Heaven help us. The Winyard house was a death trap. "Kip, I'm very proud of you. Remember Tommy?"

He nodded. "Yeah, his leg's still busted." Several months before, a group of Kip's friends had gone over there to play, pulling off some rotten slats to crawl inside. Tommy Parker had fallen through the flooring to the basement.

"He was lucky he wasn't killed. I'm glad you have sense enough to say no, though I'm sorry about what happened with Sly and Tony." It occurred to me that he should be rewarded for finally using his common sense. "Tell you what. Tomorrow we're going to Bellingham. How would you like it if I dropped you at the skateboard park there? You can practice while Miranda and I shop."

A smile broke through his gloom. "That'd be great. You mean you'd let me practice by myself while you're in the store?"

Skies & Scopes, which carried most of the astronomy equipment that Miranda coveted, was right across the street from the skateboard park. "As long as you wear your safety gear at all times, right?" He nodded. "You know the drill: keep in plain sight at all times, no talking to strangers or going anywhere with them. In other words—"

"Use my head," he finished for me and threw his arm around me, giving me a quick peck on the cheek. "Thanks Mom. I'm gonna go home and play Nintendo." With that, he slipped out the door.

I eyed the pile of invoices yet to be paid. Time to plow through paperwork again. I'd just started in on the first batch of bills when Lana tapped on the door and peeked in. "Emerald? Someone named Oliver is asking for you."

I brushed my bangs away from my eyes. So much for getting any business done today. I pushed myself out of the chair and followed her to the front counter. Oliver was poking around the shelves. He'd cleaned up pretty good, wearing a rust-colored polo shirt and khaki pants, though he still reminded me of a squirrel.

"I dropped by to let you know that Aunt Ida took off about an hour ago."

I motioned to Lana. "Take your break now; I'll watch the front for a while." I turned back to Oliver. "I'm glad to hear that. So, have you been prowling around Chiqetaw today?"

He shook his head. "Not yet. I spent the morning going over the house with Aunt Ida so I'd know what to do while she's gone, then decided to take a walk. I noticed your daughter outside picking up some sort of metal scrap off your lawn."

Nobody could keep secrets in Chiqetaw, that was for sure. "Last night we had a freak accident; her telescope fell off the roof." I explained about Miranda's peculiar habit of sitting out on the roof at night to watch the stars.

He leaned against the wall, arms loosely crossed. "She sounds like a bright girl. That looked like an expensive telescope. A real loss. You buying her a new one?" he asked, giving me the once-over; the kind of look that makes a woman feel that she's been eyed a little too closely.

I pulled back. I'd been dating a writer named Andrew since December. We butted heads more often than a pair of mountain goats, and I had the feeling that neither one of us was sure just what direction, if any, the relationship was heading. We enjoyed each other's company, though, and the sex was good, but sometimes I got the feeling Andrew wanted to be the "smart one" in the relationship, which kind of bothered me. Then, a week ago, he'd dropped the bomb. He never wanted to get married, he said, and now I wasn't sure what I was going to do.

As if things weren't complicated enough, add in one Joe Files, captain of the medic rescue unit, who was bent on usurping Andrew's place in my life. Joe was easygoing, and we had a lot of fun together, laughing and joking around. We were probably better suited, but the fact that he was ten years younger than me made me hesitate.

At any rate, I wasn't about to encourage Ida's nephew. I decided to stick to lighthearted banter. "Expensive telescope? You'd better believe it. It would be so much easier if she preferred sports; or maybe something artsy." I pointed toward the tearoom. "Why don't you have some tea or cider? I'll see if I can come up with a list of Chiqetaw's highlights while you eat; then you can take them in at your leisure. It won't take long, believe me."

He poured himself a cup of hot cider. "You have no idea how good it feels to be here instead of locked up." He glanced at me warily, and I knew he was gauging my reaction to his mention of prison.

"I bet. How did you manage to stay sane there?" I wanted to get back to work but didn't have the heart to be rude. This was probably the first time in a long while that he'd talked to anybody except other inmates. The lack of culture had to be difficult for someone with an artist's soul.

"You learn to adjust. Prison requires quite a different mind-set, a shift in perception," he said, leaning against the counter as he sipped his apple cider. "Ida was my one saving grace while I was on the inside. Knowing she believed in me made all the difference."

I paused. "If you don't mind me asking, what happened with your mother? What you did doesn't seem so bad to me."

I wasn't prepared for Oliver's swift reaction to my comment. His eyes flashed, and his words came out as sharp enough to slice a brick like butter. "My mother was too busy with her damn friends to care whether I was alive or dead—" He stopped abruptly, inhaling deeply. I could hear the air whistle through his teeth. When he continued, his voice was level again. "My mother threw tantrums when she didn't get her way, and if anybody so much as threatened to damage the family name, she cut them out of her life. My arrest was an embarrassment she couldn't live down."

I detected an edge of bitterness in his tone. "I take it you're the black sheep of the family?"

He snorted. "Are you kidding? I quit the pretentious Kjeldsen Akademi, I majored in art history, I came back to the U.S. without a degree or a prestigious marriage. Those alone were criminal acts in my mother's eyes. When I got busted, it was the final straw."

As he spoke, I tried to catch a glimpse of his aura, but

when I tuned in, a blast of static smacked me upside the head, stabbing me with a piercing ache between my eyes.

"Jeez!"

He scowled. "What's wrong?"

I couldn't tell him what I was thinking. Oliver's energy was a whirl of static; no doubt prison had skewed his aura. Whatever the case, he could stand for a good psychic cleansing, but I was keeping my mouth shut on that little matter. No way was I going to volunteer for the job.

"I just got nailed by a sudden headache."

As I searched for another subject to fill the rapidly growing lull, Oliver raised an eyebrow and cleared his throat. "So, Aunt Ida tells me you're psychic. Tell me about my future, Gypsy woman. That is, if you can."

Demanding bugger, wasn't he? It was clear he was goading me, seeing if he could push my buttons. Irritated, I shook my head. "I'm German and Irish, not Gypsy. My name isn't Madame Zelda, I don't play parlor games, and I don't run a carnival sideshow. Now, if you'll excuse me, I need to get back to work."

A glower passed over his face, then he gave me a sheepish grin. "I apologize. I didn't mean to offend you. I was just curious what kind of show you put on for the locals to get them so hooked. Aunt Ida said people here in town love you."

Love me? Considering the community's response to my solving Susan Mitchell's murder, maybe Ida was right. People did flock to my shop now, but I had a feeling it wouldn't last. I'd be yesterday's news before the spring was out. Before I could respond, he changed the subject, effectively ending the conversation by ordering a chicken salad sandwich and Earl Grey tea. I decided to drop the issue and offered him the morning newspaper. While he ate, I jotted down a quick list of sights for him to see and then dove back into my work.

If I'd been afraid he would continue to talk my ear off, I needn't have worried. He drank his tea in silence while reading the paper. After eating his sandwich, he handed me a five and I counted out his change, then gave him the list of town sights and waved as he headed out the door. Yep, Oliver was definitely an odd duck, no doubt about it, and I wasn't sure just what I thought of him. But he was Ida's nephew, and after three years in prison, I'd probably seem strange, too.

I turned back to my inventory sheets, but within five minutes the phone rang and, exasperated, I grabbed the receiver. The way things were shaping up, I wasn't going to get a thing done today.

"Em, I'm bored!" Harlow's oh-so-familiar refrain rang in my ear.

I put down my pencil and smiled. I always made time for my other best friend. "How long till you're out of the wheelchair, Cap'n?"

"You're getting into a rut. That's the first question you ask me every time you talk to me. The doctor said I'll be on my feet again within the week. At least I'll be able to see them for another month or two before they disappear when my baby balloon swells up." Harlow was nearly five months pregnant and starting to show.

"What did the doctor say about your ribs and legs?" I asked. Her accident last December seemed to have left some lingering damage.

"He said the bones should be healed by now, but apparently I've been low on calcium for a long time, so they're a little bit brittle. My physical therapist thinks that I'm making progress, though I'll be using a walker for a few weeks after I'm out of the chair." I muttered something about buying her some calcium supplements but she brushed me off. "Hey! I saw you mentioned on TV again. You planning on becoming a Kato Kaolin?"

I snorted. "Hope not. I'm not that photogenic. Anyway, I'm glad you called. Want to go out to dinner tomorrow night? I've had a very strange week and could use some company."

"Uh-oh. What's up? I can hear that 'something's not right' tone in your voice."

What was up? What indeed? "I don't know, to be honest. But tomorrow's Sunday, and since I hired Lana, I don't have to work. Maybe if we meet for dinner, I can shake off this mood." She put me on hold to ask her mother-in-law if she could cadge a ride to the restaurant. When she came back, it was all set.

"I'll meet you at five o'clock at the Brown Bear Bar & Grill. I'm so glad my mother-in-law's around. Hannah's incredible; it would be a nightmare to have to go through all this without anybody here. I sure miss James." Her husband was off in Africa on a photo safari shoot.

I said good-bye and hung up, wondering why I felt so uneasy.

GRATEFUL THAT IT was Saturday night, I picked up a bucket of chicken for dinner, setting it on the kitchen counter as I came through the door. The kids could nuke it when they were hungry. Miranda had left me a note saying she was at the library and would be home by seven. Kip was in the backyard, playing some sort of army game.

I traded my shoes for a pair of fuzzy slippers and settled back in the recliner. Andrew was coming over; we were planning on kicking back to watch TV or listen to music. While I waited for him to arrive, I mulled over who I could ask to keep an eye on the kids Sunday evening. I supposed I could just leave Miranda in charge; she was old enough to watch her brother, except that Ida was out of town and I didn't like leaving them alone without a safety net. Randa was a good girl, but I knew very well that she lost touch with reality when she buried her nose in a book.

When Andrew arrived, he ruffled my hair and nuzzled the top of my head. "Why so glum, sweetheart?" he asked, settling in on the arm of my chair.

"It's been a strange week, and I want to go out to dinner with Harlow tomorrow, but I don't have anyone to stay with the kids, and since Ida's out of town, I'm not comfortable leaving them alone."

He shrugged. "I'll come over and stay with them. You go out with Harlow and have a good time."

"You'd do that for me?" I squeezed his hand. He stood up, looking as if he had something more to say. "Yes?" I said, waiting expectantly.

"I've got good news, honey." Beaming, he held up a copy of his novel, *The Mistress of Peachtree Manor.* "Maxis Studio optioned my newest romance, and they may agree to let me write the screenplay. By tomorrow night, my agent will know if I'm supposed to fly down to Hollywood to discuss a screenwriting deal!"

"Really? Oh Andrew, I'm so proud of you!" I jumped up and gave him a resounding kiss.

He ducked his head, suddenly shy. "Thanks, but it's not a done deal just yet. I have to be honest though; I've been waiting for this break a long time. Anyway, I can transfer my calls to my cell and hang out with the kids while I wait for George to call."

He pressed me into his arms as he slid one hand behind my neck and hungrily met my lips. Enjoying the fire, once again I was torn about the relationship. Here was a gorgeous, sexy, brilliant man who wanted *me*. But—and it was a big but—we were so different that, when I was honest with myself, I didn't hold out much hope for the long haul. Frustrated, I pushed away my thoughts and slipped out from under his embrace.

"C'mon babe, let's go to my place for an hour or so." He winked at me, but I was too frazzled to respond.

I brushed his cheek with my fingers. "Sorry, sweetie, but I'm too tired to go out again tonight."

"I could stay here," he ventured, but I nixed the idea. He knew what the score was, and that didn't include overnights at my house just yet.

The front door slammed, and Miranda came in. "I called the Skies & Scopes store; they have one telescope left, and I asked them to hold it until tomorrow."

"That's great, honey."

She gave me a smile, grabbed an apple out of the fruit bowl, and took off upstairs.

I glanced at Andrew; he was scowling at the television. "I know you aren't happy with the way things are. Neither am I, but for now, this is the way it is."

He snorted. "Uh-huh. Let's just skip it, huh? What's on *Nova* tonight?"

I let it drop, and the evening passed with an uneasy truce, but there was no way I could avoid facing the fact that we were on a collision course, headed for "the talk."

AFTER WE RETURNED from a successful trip to the astronomy shop on Sunday, I left Andrew to listen to Randa bubble over about her new—and even better—telescope, and Kip brag about skating with the big kids.

The Sunday crowd was light at the Brown Bear Bar & Grill, supposedly a family diner. The lounge saw more action than the grill, I thought, as I skirted the bar, avoiding the leers from the guys lined up at the counter. There was a baseball game on TV, and it looked like half of the male population of Chiqetaw had shown up to drink beer and shout at the umpire. As I slipped into the dining room, I felt overexposed. I was sporting the new skirt and top I'd bought over a month ago but hadn't yet had the guts to wear. When I woke up feeling like I needed a pick-me-up, I decided that new clothes might do the trick. Now, I wasn't so sure about my decision.

The skirt was a gauzy plum broomstick design, the top a snug ivory camisole made out of cotton eyelet lace that tied up the front. Even though I'd worn an ivory bra, I felt bare-naked underneath. What had gotten into me? I never bought frilly clothes, but when Joe pointed at a catalog sitting on my coffee table and said, "You'd look great in that," vanity won. I'd ordered the duo. As I looked at myself in the mirror, the whole effect was definitely more froufrou than I usually liked. However, the ensemble did accentuate my curves in a positive light, and I felt like I should be out in a meadow, running barefoot through wildflowers with a wide-brimmed straw hat in hand.

I looked around, searching for Harlow. As usual, she was perpetually early. She'd edged her wheelchair up to the table and had already ordered lemonade for us. I gave her a quick hug and slid into the opposite seat. "You are so gorgeous," I said. And she was: rounded and healthy, with no sign of the anorexia that plagued her for so long. Her long, crimped golden hair had been woven into cornrows—much easier for her to take care of. "You look like a pregnant Bo Derek in her younger days. Only your hair is shinier."

She chuckled. "Thanks, chickie." Her eyes flickered over my skirt and top. "Speaking of looks, that's certainly a different style for you. Trying something new?"

I shrugged. "I've been feeling all topsy-turvy lately. Thought maybe this would give my spirits a lift, but I'm not so sure. I think I just look goofy."

She ran her eyes over me, appraising my outfit. If I looked silly, I could count on her to be brutally honest. "Actually, you look ravishing. The ivory sets off the highlights in your hair; it makes the chocolate deeper and the silver sparkle. And the skirt is gorgeous." I beamed. Harlow always knew what to say. She lifted her glass and toasted me. "To the new Emerald. I'd love to see you look like this more often. I bet Andrew loves it."

I reluctantly lifted my glass and took a sip. "Andrew . . ." I sighed. "Now there's a touchy subject." If I smoked, I'd be toying with a cigarette by now, but my vice was a little less dangerous; I tore open a packet of sugar and poured it on my tongue.

Harlow winced as she leaned back in her seat and shook her head. "Stop that. It's not good for you."

"Yeah it is. Sugar gives you energy, so why not go one hundred percent pure?"

She clucked and reached across the table to grab the packet out of my hand. "You still haven't told me what's wrong, and don't lie and say 'Nothing,' because I know perfectly well that you're upset."

"I know you think I'm making a mistake; that I should just forget about Joe and dive into the relationship with Andrew."

"So why don't you?" Her voice was soft. She'd been responsible for my meeting Andrew, and he was her husband's best friend. I could understand why she felt torn.

I tried to explain. "I adore him, but let's face it, no way is he mature enough to handle two kids and a wife who talks to ghosts. In fact, last week we were talking about our hopes for the future—not for us as a couple, mind you, just individual goals. He came out and told me he doesn't believe in marriage. I can't see myself in a long-term relationship without marriage, Harl. And when the sparks aren't flying, we don't have a lot in common. We talk a little, and then we argue."

The waitress interrupted to take our order. "My name's Alicia, ladies, and I'll be your waitress tonight. My, don't y'all look pretty." She gave Harl a wink and me a smile and jotted down my request for fish and chips and Harlow's order for soup, then stuck her pencil behind her ear and took off toward the kitchen.

"Can we talk about something else?" I pleaded. "How's it going for James?"

"He's in the Shewa area. Local rebels have shut down the one runway they call an airport, and he and the crew are stuck until the plane can get through to them. Ethiopia's a powder keg, with all the deaths from famine and the problems with the government." She leaned toward me, and I could see the fear in her eyes. "James heard shots outside the compound; he thinks that there may have been executions. I'm hoping to hell he's okay. It doesn't take much to spark off a war over there."

I decided she didn't need me reinforcing her worries over something she couldn't control, so I brought the conversation back around to me. Harl loved gossip, and I gave her the full treatment. I told her everything about Daniel's visit and subsequent death, about Miranda's telescope, and Kip losing his best friend. "The last thing I need is a string of bad luck. But it'll pass. Nanna taught me that everything comes in cycles, and life's been so good lately that I'm not surprised the universe is throwing a few curves my way. I just hope the curves don't explode into crises." I shifted in my seat, vaguely aware of a growing sensation that I was being watched. I leaned forward and whispered. "Is there somebody staring at me?"

Harlow glanced over my shoulder, then gave me a gentle nod. "Yep, big guy. Uh-oh, red alert, he's coming your way, and either he's drunk or has an ear infection that's throwing him off balance, because he's bouncing off the walls." She busied herself, poking in her handbag for her compact.

I steeled myself as a shadow fell across the table.

Slowly, I raised my eyes. He was big, all right. Actually, this dude had it all over Paul Bunyan. Dark, flashing eyes, long beard, graying ponytail, black leather chaps and jacket. Oh yeah, we were talking Mr. Bad Biker in the flesh.

"Yes?" Leaving all traces of warmth out of my voice, I forced myself to stare him down. Never show fear in the presence of wild beasts, children, or lumberjacks.

He leaned over, trying to look down my shirt. "Guy at the end of the bar bet me five bucks that I wouldn't have the guts to come over and ask you to dance."

Oh, joy. Besides the fact that the jukebox was belting out some country schlock about "my man done did me wrong" that was about as danceable as quicksand, there was no dance floor in this joint. I wondered if he'd figured that out yet. "Uh, no. Thank you for asking."

"C'mon, shake a leg with ol' Jimbo. I don't bite." He leered at me, and I leaned back to avoid the alcohol that exuded from his breath. I could have lit a match and watched the whole place go up in flames. "Leastways, not unless you want me to." He flicked the ribbons on my top and made a move toward the bow.

That did it. I slapped his hand. "Go away. *Now.*"

Harlow stifled a snort. "I've got your back, babe," was all she said.

At that moment, good ol' Jimbo made an error in judgment. He reached out and clapped his meaty paw on my wrist. Big mistake.

"Take your hand off me while it's still attached to your arm," I said, my voice a low growl.

Jimbo yanked my chair around so I was facing him. "C'mon, woman. I want to dance."

The waitress was running in our direction with the manager in tow, but I was quicker. Jimbo hauled me out of the chair, and I let myself go limp. When he struggled for a better grip, I snapped my arm out of his grasp and belted him in the nose, then leaned over and head-butted him right in the gut. Like tall timber being felled, he teetered for a moment, then crashed into a tray rack, sending the rack and its contents every which way. I blinked, realizing what I'd just done. Wow! I'd never been in a bar brawl before.

Jimbo rubbed his head, struggling to right himself through the patchwork of trays and napkins that covered the floor like a crazy quilt. "You bitch!"

"What the hell are you doing, Jimbo?" the manager bellowed. "Get your butt out of here. I told you before, leave the ladies alone." He yanked the big man to his feet while the waitress asked me if I was okay.

Jimbo managed to escape the man's grasp. His words slurred out of the side of his mouth. "Don't think you can get away with this! Throw me out, will you? You better watch yourself, Roberts. I know where you live!" He tripped over one of the chairs at the next table and fell again. After he righted himself, he turned to me. "This is all your fault, you witch!"

Incredulous, still in shock from what had just transpired, I started to hiccup and the next moment found myself howling like a moon-crazed wolf. I managed to get hold of myself and gave him a wide grin. "Kind of stupid to make a witch mad, now, isn't it? Maybe I should turn you into a toad? Oh wait, you already *are* one!"

"Don't laugh at me! I mean it! I'll show you who's stupid—"

The manager and his waiters managed to toss Jimbo out the door as we watched from our table. Harl shook her head. "Too bad, what a waste. All that gorgeous black leather, too."

I stared at her. "You've got to be kidding. You talking about Jimbo?"

"Don't knock it," she said, grinning. "A lot of women go for the dangerous type, and he is kind of cute in a mean teddy bear way, but he's got the manners of a pig."

"Well, I'll agree with you there," I said as the manager returned. He practically groveled at my feet, begging me to believe that his diner was really a safe place to bring the family. I reassured him I wasn't going to sue. He promised that not only would our dinner be on the house, dessert included, but that I'd get a coupon for a free family dinner whenever I wanted to bring my kids in.

After he left, Alicia brought our order, along with an extra plate of breadsticks and complimentary refills of lemonade. She lowered her voice. "You be careful. That Jimbo's a strange one. Some of the waitresses have had trouble with him before; once he gets an idea in his brain, he can't seem to shake it loose."

"Which brain? The one in his head or the one in his pants?" I asked. Harl snorted a spoonful of broth through her nose, but Alicia shook her head.

"It might seem funny now," she said, "but I am telling you, the man is dangerous. He hasn't been right since . . . oh, since his teen years. I'll have one of the waiters walk you to your car when you're ready to go."

"But it's still light out—"

"No matter. Better safe than sorry."

Great. Had I managed to make an enemy rather than just adventure into the land of surreal? "Who is he?"

She began arranging the trays on the rack again. "Some good ol' boy, lives in the woods out near Miner's Lake. I'm not sure who he works for, but he's not with any logging company that I know of. I think he does a bit of trapping and keeps bees; I seen him selling honey at the farmers' market. Things like that. Rumor has it that he hangs out with a group of bikers over in the Klickavail Valley."

Klickavail Valley. Nestled against the foothills of the

Cascades, the forested valley was reported to be the home base for a group of bikers, modern mountain men that had set up shanties on a wide expanse of land that one of their relatives owned. Every now and then, the paper noted some skirmish going on over there, but it was never major enough for the cops to go in and force everybody out.

Alicia finished picking up the napkins and tossed them in the garbage. "Anyway, Jimbo makes a lot of my girls here nervous. He's in all hours. We're a twenty-four-hour joint, ya know; the truckers need to eat all times of the day or night. Jimbo'll come in late, two or three in the morning, to hustle pool in the back room." She made sure we had everything we needed and then left.

Harlow and I ate a subdued dinner and left early. We were both tired.

ANDREW WAS WAITING for me, an exuberant look lighting up his face. His eyes shone as I wearily pushed my way through the front door. I gave him a halfhearted kiss and sank into the recliner, leaning back as I lifted my feet onto the footrest. Ah, luxury.

"I've got some great news, honey."

That's right; his agent was supposed to have called. "What's up? Did you get the phone call you were waiting for?" I was too tired to show much enthusiasm at this point, but I didn't want to hurt his feelings. I forced myself to perk up.

"I'm off to Hollywood tomorrow afternoon! They want me to go down to discuss the screenplay. My agent says he thinks they'll go for my ideas on how to adapt it, and if so, I'm home free." He leapt up and gave me his best impression of Gene Kelly, singin' in the rain.

I scrambled out of the recliner and gave him a big hug. "How thrilling! I'm so proud of you."

He stopped suddenly, grabbed me by the shoulders, and said, "Come with me! We could have so much fun. It will only be for a week."

"Go with you?" The thought of a trip to Hollywood made my skin crawl. I didn't like big cities, and the last thing I wanted to do was to go romping along Rodeo Drive on a Value Village budget. Besides, more practical matters intruded. "Andrew, I can't leave the shop and the kids on such short notice. I simply can't dump all of my responsibilities and go."

His face fell. "You don't want to come with me?"

"I *can't* go with you." Couldn't he understand that being a mother meant I couldn't just take off every time I wanted to? We'd already been through this a couple of times since December.

Andrew petulantly dropped to the sofa, glaring at me. *"Can't, can't, can't,"* he said, a sneer forming on his face. "Every time I've suggested we go somewhere, you *can't* leave the kids, you *can't* leave the shop. They make convenient excuses whenever you don't want to do something. Well, I've got news, Em. Your children aren't babies anymore, and you have plenty of help in your store." His voice turned bitter. "I thought you wanted us to be more of a couple—"

The kids were upstairs, and I was pretty sure they could hear what was going on. "Lower your voice or leave." I inhaled slowly and let my breath out in a thin stream. "Andrew, last week you made it clear that you don't believe in marriage. I'm not asking you to propose to me, so don't start in on that again, but I warned you that I can't let myself get deeply involved with a man who won't even consider the possibility of a long-term commitment. Kip and Miranda are already too attached to you. Are you going to stick it out when things get rough? Being a father figure is a lot different than playing uncle the way you do."

We stared at one another. Was this it? Was this the end? Then, without another word, Andrew pulled me to him, his tongue lightly playing over my lips, his arms holding me like they would never let go. It was so incredibly sweet I wanted to cry, but I gently broke away.

He stared at me, his dark eyes flashing, whether with anger or passion, I didn't know. "No, I don't believe in marriage, at least not for myself. And I don't think I ever want to have any children of my own. But that doesn't mean I'm going to abandon you and the kids. Can't we just take things one day at a time?"

Torn, wanting him so bad my stomach ached, I ground my teeth together and pushed out of his arms, hugging myself as I paced back and forth. "I'm not twenty years old anymore. I have children. I can't take things one day at a time. They need stability, and so I have to plan ahead. They come first, Andrew, and they will always come first until they walk out that door to start their own adult lives."

He let out a big sigh. "What do you want, then? A written guarantee that I won't leave you? I wouldn't be able to give you that even if we did get married."

Defeated, I held out my hands. "No, and it would be ridiculous to even think of asking you for something like that. If I thought there was a good chance you might want to be with us for the long haul, I'd risk it because you're a wonderful man. But I just can't live in the moment without giving any thought to the future. I can't hope to change you any more than you can hope to change me." I gave him a pleading look. It would be so much easier if we weren't so attracted to each other, but the passion between us couldn't be denied.

After a pause, he sat on the sofa and pulled me down beside him, taking my hand in his. "I'm not going to lie; marriage scares the hell out of me. I've seen a lot of relationships sour when they hit the altar, but I don't want to lose you. And you know that I think the kids are great." He glanced at the clock. "I've got to go. I still have to pack. Tomorrow, I drive down to SeaTac to catch the plane. Don't do anything rash while I'm gone. Please?" He gave me another kiss and then grabbed his coat.

I stared at the door as it closed behind him. Did I really want Andrew to give me a ring? It was early in our relationship to be talking marriage, but I wanted some sense that I mattered to him, that I was more than just a girlfriend. If he really cared, he'd say no instead of sheepishly breaking our dinner dates when his buddies called him over for the big game. He'd take me out to enjoy the evening, not just to cajole me into his bed since I wouldn't let him sleep over here. Maybe the subject of marriage was just the tip of the iceberg.

I stared out the bay window into the night. Like a lot of my friends who didn't have children, Andrew owned his own life. He didn't have to answer to anybody but himself, and that was absolutely fine. But I had Kip and Miranda; they came first, and what would it say to them if I let Andrew come and go as he pleased while trampling my feelings?

No, if Andrew really loved me, then he'd understand why I couldn't run off and leave the kids. He'd have said, "I love you. Do what you have to for your family." No, marriage itself wasn't the issue. I just wasn't sure I was ready to face the real problem.

Four

❖

M Y DREAMS WERE scattered by the time I woke up, and I couldn't remember what they'd been. A vague, unsettled feeling hovered over me like a shadow. I peeked out my window. Overcast, with a hint of rain. I loved that wonderful tang that happened right before a rainstorm; it was as if the cedars and moss spritzed the air with their fragrance to warn us to remember our umbrellas. It was barely mid-April, yet I was ready for autumn again, for the red and gold leaves, crisp underfoot, and the mist that rose off the ground to shroud the town in a ghostly fog. Yep, autumn was my season, and I was born on All Hallows Eve, just as my Nanna had been.

After showering, I slipped on a flowing mint-green skirt and coral V-necked tee, then slid a blazer over the top. I buckled my new strappy sandals I'd got at Value-Shooz and stretched out my foot to admire the brilliant heels that color-coordinated so well with my shirt. *Summer colors,* I thought. *Mood brighteners. Feminine and yet professional.*

I brushed my hair and was parting it for a French braid when the kids' alarm clocks went off. Within a few minutes, the inevitable squabble erupted at the bathroom door. Not in the mood for temper tantrums, I yanked open my door. "This is *not* the wide, wide world of wrestling! Miranda, use the shower up here. Kip, use the downstairs shower. Both of you hurry up. Breakfast will be on the table in twenty minutes, and you will both be there, clean, dressed, and with hair brushed."

As I clattered down the stairs, Kip muttered under his breath, but he followed me and disappeared into the bathroom next to the den turned guest room. I faced the kitchen, grumbling under my own breath. Usually I let the kids get their own breakfasts, but the past few days I'd noticed a run on the Pop-Tarts, as well as the plundering of the pastry basket. Time for some decent food. A loud meow startled me. Samantha leapt up on the counter and purred her way over to me. She was immediately followed by her kittens, Nebula, Noël, and Nigel.

"Hey sweetie." I crooned to the calico as I scratched her under the chin. The kittens rubbed up against their mama, and I buried my face in their fur, burrowing my nose against one particularly fat little tummy. I loved the cats, probably as much as the kids did, and they had become an integral part of our household.

It was obvious they weren't going to let me get anything done until they'd been fed, so I dug out the cat food and filled their bowls. As soon as the feline brigade was taken care of, I hunted through the cupboards until I found the instant oatmeal, then filled the teakettle and put the water on to boil. Rather than fry bacon, I lined the strips in the microwave tray, making sure that the drip pan was securely fastened below. As I waited for the microwave to nuke the bacon, I poured juice and milk and made myself a quad-shot espresso, liberally dosing it with cocoa and Coffee-mate.

Just a *little* jolt to wake me up. By the time the kids trudged in, my caffeine headache was fading, and breakfast was on the table.

Kip started for the pantry, but I shook my head. "Fed them already. You and Miranda can clean the litter boxes after school. No complaining." Forestalling a barrage of "ah Mom's!" I went back to my own bowl of cereal, liberally sprinkling on cinnamon and brown sugar, then swamping the whole thing with evaporated milk. At least it was hot, I thought. And oats were good for cholesterol levels.

As they ate, the kids filled me in on their plans for the day. Miranda had made a new friend at school. *Hallelujah!* I thought, but kept my mouth shut except for an appreciative murmur. My daughter wasn't going to turn out to be a sociopath after all.

"Lori isn't as serious about astronomy as me, but she's pretty smart. She wants to be a teacher. We'll drop by the shop after school, then can we go to the library to study?"

"That's fine. Make sure to take your jacket; it's supposed to rain all day." Kip, sans best friend, moped about having nothing to do after school. Maybe I could prevent any stupid stunts designed to win Sly back into the fold. "If you weed the flower beds and dig up dandelions before they start going to seed, I'll pay you two bucks an hour, providing I see signs you've actually been working." Ever on the lookout for spare change, he jumped at the chance. They took off for school, and I glanced at the clock. I stacked the dishes and took a swipe at wiping down the counters. The crumbs stubbornly clung to the tile, and I shrugged. Another chore to finish after work.

Promptly at nine, I tossed my purse in the Cherokee and headed out for the store. I had inventory sheets to go over, we needed to plan our summer window displays, and I probably should send Cinnamon out for soup cups and plastic spoons. My shop was doing so well I could barely keep up with it. Three years ago I'd never have dreamed that my life would turn around the way it had. But now the kids and I were actually happy. We had a home, friends, and if I could clear up the problems with Andrew, I'd have a pretty decent relationship. How could I ask for anything more?

Mentally organizing my day, I pulled into the parking space in front of the Chintz 'n China and cut the engine. *Holy crap! What the hell?* I slowly climbed out of the Cherokee. My display window had been smashed, a thousand shards of glass scattered across the sidewalk. Had some kids gone on a vandalism rampage? I glanced at the neighboring businesses to see if they had been hit, too, but didn't see any other damage. Damn it, that window was going to be costly to repair. I carefully approached the shop, picking my way through the slivers of glass, and reached out with my key, then stopped cold. The door was ajar. Cautious now, I carefully pushed the door open and flipped on the lights. My heart went crashing to the floor as I froze, deer in the headlights.

Teapots, plates, cups, and saucers all rested in a dusty pile of smashed porcelain. Scarves that had covered tables had been yanked off, taking with them baskets of jams, crackers, and cookies. Crumbs scattered willy-nilly across the floor; some of the bottles had broken, and the sweet smell of black currant mingled with that of pungent Earl Grey.

The tables in the alcove housing the tearoom had been toppled, the seat cushions on the chairs ripped open to allow the stuffing to mingle with the chaos that had descended upon my shop. Hesitant, terrified to look and yet needing to know, I turned to look at the NFS cabinet where I stored all of my favorites that weren't for sale. The lock had been broken, as had the glass doors. Almost every shelf stood bare.

Working on autopilot, I picked my way carefully through the ruins, my heels crunching on bits of broken china. One figurine in the cabinet had escaped my intruder's notice. A tiny porcelain cat wearing a tea hat with a rose and a polka dot scarf. Miss Kitty. I couldn't remember where I'd found her, but she'd won a place in my heart. I picked up the delicate trinket and gave it a gentle kiss. As the cool glassine body touched my lips, I tasted salt. Tears, one by one, working their way down to my tongue.

"Oh my gawd! What happened? Ms. O'Brien, are you all right?" Cinnamon stood at the door, gawking at the mess.

Startled out of my painful reverie, I shrugged helplessly. "I'm . . . fine. Somebody decided to trash the shop."

"Have you called the police yet?"

I shook my head, still in shock. Carrying Miss Kitty, I gingerly picked my way through the broken glass and shards until I was back outside, taking care that I didn't touch anything else. I tucked the porcelain cat in the glove compartment of my Cherokee. I'd be damned if the cops took her for evidence. She was going home with me. I warned Cinnamon to stay out of the shop and to keep everybody else out, then flipped open my cell phone and punched in Murray's work number. I wanted somebody over here who was going to care, not some aloof pencil-pushing cop. She picked up on the first ring.

"Murray, it's me." Then, no longer able to hold back the pain, I spilled my story into her waiting ears. "My shop . . . somebody broke in and tore it apart." She reassured me that they'd be right over and told me not to touch anything. I put the phone away and turned back to Cinnamon. "I guess all we can do now is wait."

As we stood there, saying little more than a few scattered

words, thunder rolled, and the clouds broke as rain poured down in sheets.

BY THE TIME Murray arrived, we were soaked and trying to huddle under the awning. She showed up with two policemen, Greg Douglas, whom I knew, and another man that I hadn't met before. Greg carried a fingerprint kit.

"Boy, someone pulled a number on your shop, didn't they?" She peeked in the door, looked around, then returned to the awning where we stood. Shock registered on her face. "Are you okay? Do you need to sit down?"

I nodded, sniffling and blowing my nose again. Cinnamon had found a box of tissues in the back of her car. "I'm cold. I can't stand looking at this anymore. Can we go to Starbucks and I'll answer your questions there?"

Murray patted my arm. "Sure. Just let me tell Sandy and Greg where we'll be." She poked her head back inside the shop where they were working and then escorted Cinnamon and me to her car, where we drove two blocks to the nearest Starbucks. Still in shock, I ordered a quad-shot venti iced mocha with extra chocolate.

Cinnamon stared at me. "That's going to send your blood pressure sky high."

Like I cared. "How much difference can it make, considering how I already feel? I wonder how long will it take them to finish so I can see just how much I lost? I'll need to call the insurance agent, figure out what was stolen and what was destroyed, though that won't make any difference to them. The shop is totaled." As I ticked off a list of things to do and Cinnamon jotted them down, Murray settled in on the other side of the table. She pulled out her own notebook, a sleek, leather-covered affair.

"We're looking at an hour or so, at least. There's a lot to

sort through. Considering how many customers you have, I don't know what we're going to find as far as prints. Needle in the haystack."

"Only that haystack was worth a lot of money. I had some sentimental pieces there, Murray, and some that were very expensive. I don't even know if the cash register was jimmied. I didn't think about looking." I sighed, suddenly aware of how numb I felt. Shock, I guess. "I didn't think things like this happened in Chiqetaw." I sipped my drink and leaned back in my chair.

Cinnamon sniffled. "I'm so sorry, Emerald. This is terrible."

I leaned over to give her a hug and kiss on the cheek. "It'll be okay, sugar. We'll bounce back from this." The shop had come to mean a great deal to the young woman and somehow, over the past year, I'd managed to take on the role of big sister for her. Her mother did what she could, but just the act of taking care of Cinnamon's children had to be a strain for the older woman, who had already brought up her own family.

Murray cleared her throat. "Em, it's no secret that over the past few months you've made quite a name for yourself in Chiqetaw. Is there anybody who has been openly critical of you or who's come into your shop causing trouble?"

I thought about it. My notoriety had been unexpected and, to some degree, unwelcome. I valued my privacy. When the news broke that I'd figured out who killed Susan Mitchell and her daughter, I'd been overwhelmed by requests for psychic help, local interviews, and tarot readings. I turned down the majority of the former two and put the third to good use in my shop. But nobody had said anything bad about me other than a few fundamentalists who decided that my gifts, while useful, were probably spawned by some dude in red tights carrying a pitchfork. After I managed to stop laughing, I thanked them for their concern, then told them to go home and please take their religious pamphlets with them. But altercations? I hadn't really run afoul of anybody since I fought off Susan's killer.

I shook my head. "Nope, none that I can think of." Then, I stopped. There was one person who might begrudge my little bit of good fortune, but I didn't really believe even *he* would stoop so low as to trash my shop. "You know, now that I think of it, Roy called me when the story broke on the news. He wanted to get together and chat. Chances are, he wanted to see if I'd stumbled onto any reward money."

"Did you go see him?" Murray raised one eyebrow. She knew Roy all too well.

I took a long sip of the chilled mocha. "Nope. Told him to go treasure hunting somewhere else, that he wasn't getting out of his child support payments and that he had a duty to call his children once in a while, if only to lie and say he loves them. So I'm not in his good graces, but even Roy has more class than whoever did this."

"When did this conversation take place?" She was jotting notes as quickly as I could feed them to her.

I shrugged. "A few days after Christmas, because I lit into him for not getting presents for the kids. It was one hell of a scream fest. Remember, I told you about it? It's been over three months, though." It had been a doozy of a fight. I'd finally blown up and told him just what a lousy father he was and how he didn't deserve to have children. He'd called me a variety of choice names.

"So he's angry with you?"

"Yeah. I guess." As I polished off my mocha, Sandy, the other officer, showed up at our table. Towheaded and boy-faced, he barely looked old enough to vote. He leaned over and whispered in Murray's ear.

Murray winced. "Okay, nobody on Main Street was

around last night to see anything. And it looks like your cash register is empty. Do you remember how much money you had in there Saturday night?"

I'd been planning on making the deposit this morning and had prepared the envelope Saturday, before I left. Why the hell hadn't I taken the time to run over to the bank when I left on Friday? Daniel's death had shaken me up but now, in retrospect, leaving all that money in the shop seemed pretty damn stupid.

I sighed, feeling sorry for myself. "At least four hundred . . . maybe five hundred dollars in cash, along with several checks. I think the total on the deposit slip was around nine hundred. I didn't pay much attention, just filled it out and stuck it under the till. I also had an emergency reserve in the drawer underneath the register, five one hundred-dollar bills. Oh, there was also the shop credit card in there. Do you know if everything is gone?"

Sandy nodded. "Yes ma'am, the drawer's empty. I'd advise you to call your credit card company right away to report the stolen card. We've dusted for fingerprints on the cash register, doors, windows, counters, anyplace we might actually find something. Give us another half hour to clear out, and you can go back to your shop." He gave me a shy smile. "I'm sorry, Ms. O'Brien. You had some pretty stuff in there. It's a shame to see this happen." Pausing on his way out the door, he added, "I've been in your shop before; the rubble that the vandals left doesn't seem like nearly enough to account for all your pieces. I think whoever did this stole a lot of your inventory. You might want to see if you can figure out anything obvious that's missing."

As he left, Murray leaned back and straightened her jacket. She still looked odd in civvies during the day, but I was getting used to it. Everybody and everything was changing, which would be fine except that I didn't like the way my life was shaping up all of a sudden.

"Sandy's right," Murray said. "It may seem like there are a lot of broken pieces, but I'll lay odds that the expensive items are still intact and in the thief's possession now. You had some Waterford crystal there, and what—Dresden china?"

I shrugged. "Yeah, that's true. I just got in a shipment that included a hazel-patterned Royal Winton teapot and teacup set. The teapot alone was worth close to seven hundred dollars. Next week, the ladies' china club from Abbotsford, British Columbia, is due to come through town. They always buy expensive antiques when they're here, so I stock up a week or two before they get here."

Murray jotted something down. "Get me a list of your more expensive items. You never know what we're going to find when we're poking around. It's a long shot but worth a try. Now, has anybody else been giving you any trouble?"

"Well, Daniel Barrington died after coming to see me the other day, but trouble? He wasn't any trouble to me." The fact was, nobody had bothered me lately except . . . I cleared my throat. "There is one thing—"

"Spill it, girl." Murray drained the last of her latte and wiped her mouth with a napkin.

"I don't know how relevant this is, but Harlow and I went out to dinner last night, and some redneck tried to put the make on me. I got a little mad and sent him reeling into a stack of trays when he wouldn't leave me alone and started to get grabby. He kind of threatened me, but I thought he was just drunk. It couldn't be him, though, could it?"

Murray rolled her eyes, giving me the same look I gave my kids when they were playing space cadet. "I wish you'd tell me these things right off the bat instead of as an afterthought. Okay, let's hear it. All of it." She took more notes while I sketched out the events at the Brown Bear

Bar & Grill and then she folded her notebook again and tucked it in her pocket. "Okay. Call your insurance company. Call your credit card company. Greg will run the prints we gathered through our computer and see if anything comes up. Sandy will interview the neighboring shops, see if anybody noticed anything out of the ordinary. I'll find this Jimbo and see if he has a rap sheet and an alibi. Meanwhile, please consider installing an alarm system before you get all that china from Walter. If I were you, I'd also consider putting in a video surveillance camera."

I hated the thought. I'd moved to Chiqetaw to feel safer, not to get thrust right back into big-city hassles, but it looked like that was quickly becoming a pipe dream. Resigned, I nodded. "You're probably right. This sucks. I lost some pieces that I'll never be able to replace; personal favorites." I took out my cell phone and punched in Lana's number, tersely running through what had happened. "I need you to come in early if possible, as in right now. Dress for cleaning. Bring sturdy leather gloves, I don't want anybody getting cut on broken glass." She said she'd be right over. "Murray, can one of your guys watch the shop until I get back? I'd hate to find that some looter came through while I was home changing."

She assured me they'd keep an eye open until I returned, and we all headed out. The day was shaping up to be prime headache material.

THE INSURANCE AGENT arrived shortly after I returned from changing clothes. He photographed the damage so we could begin the daunting task of matching inventory lists to missing china. While it was impossible to tell which pieces had been stolen and which had been trashed, from the debris I began to see what Sandy had been talking about. The bags of broken china and pottery weren't full enough to account for even two-thirds of my stock. I should have been able to recognize the remains of the Waterford crystal, but there weren't any in sight that even vaguely matched the delicate lead glass. Whoever had vandalized my shop had also stolen a good deal of merchandise. Maybe they'd trashed the rest to make it hard to tell what was gone.

By early afternoon, we'd cleaned up the worst of the mess and I took a break, putting in a call to Safety-Tech, the town's premiere security monitoring company. They promised to have someone come over the next day to install a system. Then I called Marvin Eyrland, who owned a glass company down the street. He came right over and measured the windows. To tide us over until he could replace them, he kindly brought back a huge plywood board and affixed it across the broken front panes.

"I can't thank you enough," I told him.

"No problem," he said. "This is sick. Whoever did this ought to be throttled. I should be able to get the pane cut by tomorrow afternoon and installed before closing. You wanted safety glass?"

I nodded as he flipped his order book closed and waved good-bye. After he was gone, I wandered around the shop, unable to speak. So many bare shelves. Every time I looked over at the NFS cabinet, a lump formed in my chest. So many lovely pieces, including a few passed down to me by my nanna, were either stolen or ground to dust and rubble. One way or another, most of my inventory was gone.

The girls and I'd been working for a couple of hours when Randa came through the door, towing her friend Lori behind her. She gaped at the empty shelves and the bags of trash that littered the floor. "What happened?"

"We were robbed last night. Whoever did it, tore the

shop apart." I leaned on my broom and wiped a trail of dust off my forehead. There was still so much to do; vacuuming was high on the priority list, and hauling the bags out to the Dumpster in back.

Randa's gaze flickered up to mine. She threw her arms around me and gave me a long hug, then turned to Lori and whispered for a moment. Lori waved briefly and took off, and Miranda waded into the mess, looking for some way to help out.

I put in a call to home and managed to catch Kip while he was having an afternoon snack. "We need you right away, please. Take your bike so you can get here quicker, and don't dawdle." He showed up in twenty minutes.

The kids pitched in without complaint. Kip, after his initial spate of questions, grabbed a dust cloth and started wiping down the shelves. Miranda carefully ferried what stock remained unbroken into the bathroom, where Cinnamon washed the dust away. Lana dried the pieces and brought them out to me where I took over, arranging them on the newly cleaned shelves. Promptly at five-thirty, I placed the last plate on the shelves and dusted off my hands on my jeans.

"We're done." I stood back. The sparse dappling of china against the lemon chiffon walls sent my confidence spiraling in a nosedive, and I dropped into a nearby chair, trying to ignore the gash that tore through its upholstery. None of the tearoom furniture had made it through intact. "Look at that. Barely enough stock to make a decent window display."

Miranda patted me on the shoulder. "It'll be okay, Mom. It'll be okay. Aren't you supposed to get some plates or something as a little gift from Mr. Mitchell's mother?"

The "little gift" was actually going to be quite an infusion of expensive china and crystal; but right now everything seemed pale in comparison to the damage the vandals had caused to my shop. I wanted to wring their scrawny necks. I'd worked so hard over the past two years, building the Chintz 'n China piece by piece, managing to garner enough reputation to keep us going. Now that the shop was taking off, some son of a bitch had come along and shredded everything I'd accomplished.

I looked up at Randa. Her dark eyes were filled with worry, and I realized that she could see through my bravado. I gave her a painful smile. "That's right, hon. Everything will be okay. It just hurts to think that someone could come along and destroy so many beautiful things— everything I've worked for—in one night."

Kip's lower lip jutted out. "I wish I could find 'em! I'd give 'em a whopping."

I kissed my son on the head. "You would, would you? Well, thank you, sir. I appreciate the sentiment. Okay, we've done everything we can for now. I just hope they don't come back before the security system can be installed tomorrow."

"We could sleep here at the shop," Kip suggested. Miranda nodded, but I overruled them. We weren't about to take a chance on being here should the thieves make a return trip. I escorted everybody out the door, making sure it was firmly locked. With a little luck, tomorrow morning we wouldn't be facing the same thing that had awaited us this morning. But then again, what was there left to steal?

MURRAY JOINED US for dinner, bringing over three pizzas and a salad. She always knew when I needed her. My best friend, Mur looked like a cross between an Indian princess and a warrior woman. Tall, muscled, and stocky, her personality matched her regal beauty. I gave her a grateful smile as she slid dinner onto the counter.

The kids set the table, and we dug in, nobody saying

very much. Miranda and Kip had never expressed much interest in my shop before, but seeing it destroyed had left quite an impression. After we finished eating, we sat around the dining room table, unwilling to leave the comfort of the kitchen.

"I hate to tell you this, but if this Jimbo character didn't do it, we're probably going to have a hard time finding out who did." She'd stopped to change into her familiar jeans and T-shirt and looked much more comfortable than she had that morning. "I checked out his rap sheet. He could be dangerous, Em. He's got some pretty harsh charges against him."

"Dangerous?" I'd thought he was just a drunken slob.

"Apparently, when he was fifteen, Jimbo lost his little brother to some drifter. The transient, I think his name was Gats, killed the kid—real nasty stuff. Well, Jimbo went a little weird in the head after that, and before the police could track down Gats, Jimbo found him and worked him over real good. Almost killed him, and probably would have if somebody hadn't called the cops. Jimbo didn't do any time; the cops looked the other way, considering what the circumstances were. But after that, he was in and out of trouble. Over the years he's racked up charges for burglary, a lot of assault and battery charges for bar brawls. We suspect he's running guns or drugs, but we don't have any proof. He's never done jail time, though. Always gets off due to one technicality or another. I tried to get hold of him today, but he wasn't at any of his usual haunts. I'll go out looking for him again tomorrow."

I shook my head. We picked up our coffee cups and went into the living room. I asked the kids to give us some privacy, and they took off, Miranda to the kitchen and Kip, upstairs.

When we were alone, I leaned back, resting my head against the sofa. "Everything seems out of kilter." I spilled out my problems with Andrew. "By the time he left, the tension was so thick I could barely breathe. I dunno, I'm not sure what to do."

"Do you love him?" Murray's voice was calming, the voice of reason.

I shrugged. "I honestly don't know."

"If you don't know, then you don't love him. There's no shame in that. He just isn't the right person. I think you're making the right choice by waiting, and if he can't handle it, then that's his problem."

"How about you?" I asked. "How's your love life?" Murray didn't have many affairs, seldom hooking up with anybody, but when she did, the relationships were always torrid and brief, burning out before they could really begin.

She stared down at her coffee cup. "Love life? What love life? I go home and what do I do? I work on a project or call my aunt or read. I don't have much of a social life other than you. At work, I'm the token minority and the token woman. Oh, the guys are nice to me, except for Coughlan, but they never ask me out when they go out for drinks in the evening. Not dates, but you know, to unwind from the day? Greg and Deacon used to, but now that I'm a detective, they've backed away."

"Maybe you and Andrew—" I was joking, but she still gave me a dirty look.

"He's not my type. I'm not even sure what my type is. I thought I knew, but now I think maybe I never did. Anyway, I'm too busy with the problems at work to worry about my nonexistent sex life." She set her cup down. "Want to read the cards?"

The cards. I hadn't touched the cards since Daniel's death. "Maybe in a week or so, when things calm down. They're so topsy-turvy all of a sudden that I don't know whether I'm coming or going. Damn it, everything was settled, and now this—"

The phone rang, and I grabbed it, hoping it was the station with some news about the vandals. No such luck. It was Roy. My ex. My absolutely horrendous, abusive, cheating, cheapskate of an ex-husband who would rot in hell if there was justice in the universe. "What do *you* want?" I didn't feel like being polite.

His voice grated on my nerves. "The check is going to be late this month. I'm in Aruba, so don't sic your goddamn lawyers on me just because I'm a couple days late. This trip is Tyra's birthday present, and I'm not going to let your whining ruin it." I heard a high-pitched squeal next to him and then a flurry of breathless words. His little trophy wife, no doubt, berating him for even calling me.

"How nice she gets a trip to Aruba when you forget to send your children Christmas presents or even a card for their birthdays." I grimaced; I hadn't meant that to slip out, but it was too late now. Oh well, might as well plunge into what really mattered. "How late are you talking?"

"Crap, you've really turned into a bitch, haven't you? Are you so hard up that you can't wait a few days? I don't know how late. I'll be as late as I goddamn well please." Once again, Mr. Father of the Year was showing his true colors.

I cleared my throat. He wanted hardball? He'd get it. "If I don't have your check by the fifteenth, then my lawyers will be in touch with your employer, and we'll garnishee your wages. Do you understand me, Roy? I don't need your money, but your children are entitled to it, and I'll be damned if I let you squirm out of your obligation. Unless . . ." I paused, considering the trump card I'd been waiting to play.

"Unless what?" I could hear interest in his voice, but he obviously wasn't going to make this easy.

"Unless you sign over sole custody to me and give up any rights you have as their father." *Please, oh please, for my children's sake say no, but for my sake, say yes.* Torn, knowing either way we would lose because with Roy, there was no way *not* to lose, I waited for his response.

His voice was softer when he finally spoke. "I'll call my lawyer and have him wire you the money tomorrow. I'm going to send you the cash for the rest of the year, so don't bother me again until January."

"Don't you even want to see your children this year? Don't you even care?" My heart sank. He wasn't going to give in. He had to hang on to the illusion that he was a good father, even though he never even bothered to call the kids or wanted to see them.

Roy let out a huge sigh. "I don't know what you expect out of me." He paused, then continued, patronizing me as if I were a little slow. "Look, I know I forgot Christmas and Kip's birthday. I'm so busy making all this money to send to you for the kids that I don't have time to do things like pick out presents and take them out to the zoo on the weekends. Tell you what, I'll enclose an extra check, and you can get them something and tell them it's from me." And then, he hung up.

I stared at Murray, who had been listening to the whole interaction. "He's never going to admit that he doesn't give a damn about his kids," I whispered. "He's going to go on being a shadow presence in their lives, keeping them hoping. Damn him, I hope his boat sinks while he scubas in Aruba."

She reached out and squeezed my hand. "Well, if he's down in Aruba, then he didn't trash your shop." We chatted for a while longer, then she said, "Okay, I've got to take off. Wish I could stay, but I need to get to bed. I've been going in early every morning since I got this job."

I walked her to the door and then turned off the downstairs lights, checked on the kids, and finally dropped to the edge of my bed. I slowly undressed and got into my bathrobe, debating the merits of a long, hot bath. The day had left me tense and so tired I could barely move, and tomorrow—tomorrow I would have to go down to the Chintz 'n China and face the reality of what still seemed like a nightmare.

My shop. My beautiful shop. I started to cough. I'd managed to repress my tears all day, but now they grew thick in my throat. Leaning forward, I fought against the growing lump in my chest. I wouldn't cry, damn it! I wouldn't give in to the bastards who'd trashed my shop.

Then I remembered. Miss Kitty! I still had Miss Kitty. I belted my robe and made my way downstairs. Picking my way over the chilly ground, I rescued her from the Jeep, then trudged back to my room and set her on the night-stand. Whimsical, I thought. Nothing in her world ever went wrong. She would live in a Winnie-the-Pooh world, where misplaced honey pots were the worst that could happen.

My lower lip began to tremble. Oh, for the days when I could run to Nanna, crying over a skinned knee or an imagined slight from a playmate; when all bad experiences could be remedied by a cuddle on her large, comfortable lap. She would take me in her arms and listen to my story, then tell me to buck up as she kissed me and handed me a cookie. Nanna . . . how I missed her. If only she was here now; maybe she could help me understand what was going on.

I picked up Miss Kitty and gave the statue a gentle kiss. "Oh Nanna, where are you? I need you so much. I don't know what to do. Nanna? Please, help me."

The curtains rustled as a delicate hand rested on my shoulder. As had happened several times over the past years, a golden glow enveloped me, and I knew that Nanna had heard me. I peeked over my shoulder, and there she stood, outlined in the gentle glow of the lamp, apron stretching across the Bavarian print dress she'd worn on her last day in this world. She leaned down, and I sensed more than felt her kiss the top of my head. "Cry, my beautiful Emerald. Go ahead and cry." Her voice lilted along on a sudden and unexpected draft that rushed through the room.

"I'm trying to be strong. I'm really trying—" My voice caught, and I pressed my knuckles to my lips. I could try all I wanted, but it wouldn't change the fact that someone had wantonly destroyed everything beautiful I'd worked to build in an orgy of theft and vandalism. The shields I'd built through the frustrating, bewildering day came crashing down, and I hiccupped once before the floodgates opened. All the while, Nanna remained, hand on my shoulder, watching over me as I gave in to the anger and fear.

Five

✥

I DIDN'T WANT to call Walter Mitchell and admit that I was having problems, but after a battle with myself that raged through breakfast, I broke down and picked up the phone. If they were on schedule, he and his mother should be nearly finished with the assessment of the property they'd recently inherited, and I'd be able to pick up the china they promised to give me after I was almost killed in their old house last winter. Maybe I wouldn't have to close the shop until I could reorder stock.

Walter was pleasant enough when I reached him. He'd better be, I thought. I'd saved his ass. But as surprisingly benign as he seemed, he wasn't the bearer of good news. "I'm sorry I haven't been in touch with you lately," he said. "There's been a snag. We have to go through the appraisal again with a new firm." He coughed, sounding embarrassed. "It seems that our appraiser was recently arrested for tax evasion, and now all of his records are suspect. It's going to take at least two or three more weeks before things are sorted out. You don't need the plate right away, do you?"

I could actually hear a spark of regret in his voice. Damn! I let out a low sigh. "I understand. I'm grateful for the gift, and I'm not going to complain about a little delay." I paused, feeling like I had to give him some explanation for calling, and even though I hadn't planned on it, found myself spilling out the news about my shop.

Walter was a cold, ruthless man. Not only had he cheated on his late wife, but rumor had it that he beat her up regularly. I shouldn't like him, and I didn't, at least not on principle. But he had a certain charm that was hard to ignore. He murmured a sympathetic response. "Do you need a loan to tide you over?"

Hasty backpedal! Under no circumstances would I allow myself to become indebted to good old Walt. The china was my reward for saving his butt; anything more would be far too intimate. I thanked him and extricated myself from the conversation.

I pulled out my calendar and glanced through the upcoming events, ticking off notes as I went. I'd have to cancel the tour from Abbottsford, BC, due to arrive Saturday. They expected a full shop, and if I wasted their time, I'd chance losing them as customers. We wouldn't be making much money for the next couple of weeks, not until the insurance check showed up. I could restock the shelves on my own credit, but what if Applewood Insurance didn't come through? Nope, restocking would have to wait for a few days. A glance at the clock told me it was time to head out to work and try to make the best of a bad situation.

Before I opened the shop, I crossed the street and tapped on the window of Hodges & Sons. Mr. Hodges let me in, even though it was fifteen minutes earlier than his store opened. He handed me back my dragon, wrapped in a layer of bubble wrap. "Well, I don't know who made it, but it's an exquisite piece. Emerald, do you have any idea how old this is?" There was a queer tone in his voice.

I shook my head. "Fifty or sixty years? That's why I brought it to you. What did you find out?"

"Not much, but enough for a start." He cleared his throat. "The only thing I can tell you for sure is that this statue is close to five hundred years old, from the latter part of the Ming dynasty and, I'd say, worth over five thousand dollars. You'll need an expert on art from that period to pinpoint more accurate information."

I gaped at the little jade figurine in my hand. "Five hundred years old? Five thousand dollars?"

With a nod, Mr. Hodges handed me a paper on which he'd written a few names. "You might consult one of these people. They're all experts in Chinese porcelain and art, and one lives in Glacier. That's not too far away. Emerald, whoever sculpted this was still somewhat inexperienced, I think, but must have developed into a master craftsman. I'd bet the statue either comes from a private collection or wasn't discovered until recently. I couldn't find any records for it, but that doesn't mean much, considering this isn't my area of expertise. I certainly don't advise that you leave it lying around."

In shock, I thanked Mr. Hodges, paid him his fee, and returned to my shop. So the dragon was old, very old, and valuable. Daniel Barrington had been carrying an antique worth far more than any piece I'd ever owned. Why had he kept it wrapped in a handkerchief in his pocket? And why hadn't it been in a safe-deposit box? If it was a family heirloom, where had it come from and how had the resigned and desperate man who'd been in my shop come across it? Had his family been wealthy at one time? And just who were they? So many questions!

With a sigh, I unlocked the door and locked the dragon in my desk drawer. My questions would have to wait until later. Repairing the Chintz 'n China was going to take every bit of my energy today.

CINNAMON CROOKED HER head around the corner. "There's a television reporter and a cameraman out here. They want to talk to you."

A reporter? Cameraman? Puzzled, I smoothed my hair and made sure my skirt was smooth, then strode out to meet them. The minute I saw who it was, I knew we were in for trouble. Cathy Sutton. Her watchdog had a camera around his neck instead of a leash. "May I help you find something?" I asked, extending my hand as I spoke.

She pumped my hand like she was trying to jack up a car. "Pleased to meet you. Cathy Sutton. I heard that your shop got vandalized and wanted to interview you for our six o'clock news."

I gave Cinnamon a surreptitious glance and she rolled her eyes. "Since when do vandals robbing a shop warrant a television interview, Ms. Sutton?"

She looked confused; I supposed people usually clamored to be on television. "Well, it's news. You're news. You *did* solve the Mitchell women's murders."

Oh goodie! Now I rated right up there with other B-list celebrities who managed to hit television for one odd reason or another. "Yes, but that has nothing to do with my shop being vandalized."

She flashed me a breezy smile. "Emerald—may I call you Emerald? Emerald, isn't it possible that whoever ran down Mr. Barrington thinks that you saw him do it and is sending you a warning, trying to convince you to keep quiet?"

I glanced at the cameraman, who was moving around, eyeing me with his camera. "Uh, don't point that thing at me."

Cathy broke in. "This is Royal, our cameraman. Don't be shy; he'll always shoot your good side if you ask him nicely."

"Just testing film speed, babe . . . just testing my film speed." His voice was too smooth; it sounded like he'd been weaned on Scotch whiskey.

I glared at him, and he backed off. I turned back to Cathy. "Listen, I have a long day ahead of me, and I'd rather pass on the interview. Thanks anyway."

She shifted her weight to her other foot and scrunched up her face in one of those, "yes-but" expressions. "You know, we really don't bite. Maybe if you talked to us, we could help find whoever did this to your shop?" Cathy was doing her best to put me at ease, but she was trying too hard, and it set me on edge.

I leaned against the counter. "I'm not the only person who saw the van that hit him. It sped away so fast there was no chance to catch the license plate or anything. We were all too busy trying to help Daniel."

Cathy flashed me her award-seeking smile, then nodded. "I can see your point, but surely you have some ideas about who killed Mr. Barrington? Did he say anything to you during your conversation that might point to the identity of the killer?"

That's right, just hold on and don't let go, I thought. Cathy had the instinct of a pit bull, I'd give her that much. "I'm sorry, but my readings with clients are confidential. Did you ever consider that this might have been a random hit-and-run, with no premeditation? That some jerk might have been out for a joyride and took the corner too fast, which happens all too often, and Daniel happened to be in the wrong place at the wrong time?"

"I suppose that might be the case," she said, conceding my point. She dropped the microphone and motioned to the cameraman. "You might be right, Emerald. Crime in

Chiqetaw seems to have skyrocketed, though. I'm wondering if we don't need a stronger police force? Tad Bonner is a good man, but he doesn't seem to be doing much to lower the rising crime rates. Maybe it's time for a change at the helm." Her eyes flashed with a triumphant gleam, like a cat who was on the verge of catching her mouse. I knew she was up to something but couldn't pinpoint what.

Tired of the head games, I began herding her toward the door. "I really don't know. Maybe . . . but I'm not the person you should be asking. You'd be better off asking the police themselves what they think." I shrugged.

She murmured some noncommittal answer and cleared her throat. "Thank you for your time. Maybe next time we can have a longer chat. Meanwhile, are you going to take any new measures to protect your shop? Do you think the vandals will be back?"

Overwhelmed, too tired to fend her off, I told her about my plans for security monitoring and how I wished it wasn't necessary but that under the circumstances, it was the safest thing to do. "As to whether they'll be back, I don't know. I hope not."

Cathy studied me for a moment, then motioned to Royal, turning off the charm like she had a light switch hidden in her pocket. "Okay. Let's go."

I couldn't help myself. My mouth shot into overdrive before my brain could catch up. As she headed for the door, I said, "A piece of advice, Cathy. Don't try too hard. This isn't New York, and you're not Diane Sawyer."

Cathy turned around, her face a blank slate. "Excuse me?"

I gulped. Had I really just said that? "I mean, there's nothing here to use as a stepping-stone to fame." I stopped, suddenly aware that I'd insulted the woman a second time. Month after month of listening to her drone on must have fried a few brain cells.

"You can say that again," she said through a forced smile and clenched teeth. "So, do you have any other advice for me?"

I mentally kicked myself in the shins. Never anger people who can make you look stupid on air. "Noooo," I said, then added, "Have a good day, and come again."

She raised one eyebrow and set her lips in a firm, almost prim, line. "Oh, I'm *sure* we'll meet again, Ms. O'Brien. You seem destined to land in the news." Her heels clicked against the tile as she quick-stepped out of the shop. Royal broke into a crinkled smile and gave me a thumbs-up and a wink as he followed her.

"I dunno, Emerald," Cinnamon cleared her throat. "There's something about that woman that I don't like. You probably should have stopped while you were ahead."

"You're probably right, but you know what? I don't give a damn. Life seems to be going to hell in a handbasket this week; I might as well pile on the carnage."

Before long, I was running ragged, stock or no stock. All my regulars who had heard about the damage flocked to the shop. I knew full well that Drew didn't need another Limoges box, and that Perky Tremont had all the tea she needed for a good three months, but they filled their little shopping baskets with all the trinkets and tea and packages of English biscuits that had remained intact.

The tearoom was filled, and nobody complained about sitting on folding chairs at the card tables we'd borrowed until I could have the chairs reupholstered. Amanda Weddle slapped a stack of paper plates and some Styrofoam cups on the counter for me—a good thing because I'd forgotten to pick any up. I gave her a grateful smile.

As customer after customer traipsed in and found something to buy or to eat, my heart swelled. Each tinkle of the shop bells meant yet another person who'd accepted me into the heart of Chiqetaw. On occasion, I had wondered whether the people here truly liked me. I was a different breed than most of the matrons of this small town. By the end of the day, I had no doubt that they considered me one of their own.

What little stock I'd had left was gone. The cash register was jammed with bills and checks, and Safety-Tech had come and gone, installing our security system. The shop was now monitored constantly. I sighed and asked Cinnamon to run over to the bank with the deposit. After she left, I walked through the shop, staring at the empty shelves. If I'd ever wanted to make changes as to what I sold, now would be the time. But I loved the chintzware and the china, the tradition of teatime, and the delicate porcelain. No, we would restock. The Chintz 'n China would live.

I PUT THE dragon back in the étagère when I got home. Too afraid to leave it at work, even though we now had a security system, I tucked it into the back of my cabinet, hoping it would be safe. What the hell was I going to do with it? Finding Daniel's next of kin seemed the logical place to start, and the police were going to be of no help, so that was one more task I had to tackle.

A message had come in from Andrew. I punched in his hotel number and was surprised when he picked up on the first ring. Our first few moments were awkward—they always were after one of our disagreements—but soon he was telling me all about Hollywood and how tomorrow was the first meeting on the script and his agent thought he had a good chance of landing the contract to write the screenplay.

I murmured at the appropriate times, excited for him and yet feeling distant. Hollywood was a world apart from Chiqetaw, and big deals and producers and stars didn't play any part in my life except when I went to the movies.

After he ran down, I told him my own news, that the shop had been trashed.

"Then come down for the week. There's nothing stopping you now!"

I took a deep breath and slowly exhaled. "Did you hear what I said? My shop was destroyed. I lost everything, Andrew, including a sizable amount of cash."

There was a sudden pause, and I could hear the wheels turning in his head. "I'm so sorry, Em. I don't know what I was thinking. What did the cops say? What are you going to do?" He had quieted down, and I could hear the remorse in his voice.

"The cops haven't got a clue; and it isn't for lack of trying. Murray's heading up the investigation. I'm waiting for the insurance check, and Safety-Tech came today to install an alarm system; I ended up handing over a check that is going to really bite into my budget, but I don't have a choice. Andrew, we were doing so well, the kids and I, and now this. We'll be okay, but I'm kind of scared." It took a lot for me to admit my fear, but I needed his support, his encouragement.

He cleared his throat. "I'm sure the insurance will cover your losses."

"Losses, yes, but I lose money when there's nothing to sell. I lose time. I have to cancel shopping excursions from my little old ladies' fan club up there in British Columbia. It adds up, and these things aren't refundable."

An edge of impatience sliced through his voice. "I'm sure your shop will be fine, Em. Now, want to hear about my week so far? You'll never believe who I met!"

Unable to muster up any enthusiasm, I looked up as Randa skipped into the room and waved to catch my attention. "Andrew, I have to go. Miranda needs to talk to me. Have a great meeting tomorrow and all the luck in the world to you. I hope everything goes just the way you want." He stammered out a quick good-bye as I replaced the receiver and turned to Randa. "What's up?"

She curled up on the sofa next to me. "Was that Andrew?"

I nodded. "Yep."

"Did you guys make up? Who won?"

So she had heard us fighting the other night. I shrugged. "Let's just say we've settled on a truce. Some arguments are too complicated for anybody to win." She seemed to accept this, pondering it for a moment, and then filing it away. I reached over to run my finger along her cheek. "You are such a pretty girl, and so smart. I'm proud of you, know that?"

A winsome grin flitted across her face. She arched an eyebrow at me. "Ah, very good, Mama-san." She straightened up, serious again after the all-too-brief moment of play. "Mom, I need your permission for something."

My heart dropped. What now? A trip to NASA? A first-class ticket on the next *space shuttle?* "What do you want?"

She held up a notepad. "I've made a list of reasons why this is a good idea. Don't say no till you hear me out, okay?"

Uh-oh. The *list*. Probably something unreasonable. Too bad. Since I'd almost been killed, we'd been developing a rapport that we'd never had before, and now I'd be forced to destroy the bridge we'd made. I nodded for her to go ahead.

"I've been thinking about how much time and money I could save if I skipped into high school this fall. Or maybe even college. I doubt I could manage that far but—"

The look on my face must have stopped her, because she slammed the list down on the sofa and jumped up. "You promised you'd listen before you decided!"

Taken aback at her sudden fury, I held up my hands.

"Have I said a word? You'd better think twice about using that tone of voice with me. Now slow down and give me the specifics."

With a sigh, she began again, her enthusiasm growing as she spoke. "I found a program that offers what they call accelerated learning. I'd take a bunch of tests and, if both you and the school administration agreed, I could skip a few grades and that way I could get into college faster."

I stared at her. So this is what all those extra books were about; she'd been lugging stacks of them home from the library over the past few months. "Give me a clue here, hon. What makes this so important? Why do you want to skip ahead? Are you having trouble with the kids or teachers?"

She bit her lip and stared at the sofa. "I'm bored. I make straight A's and I'm bored. The kids are all a bunch of idiots. Well, most of them. Not Lori, but otherwise, I feel like I'm in kindergarten." She looked up at me with a ghost of a smile on her face. "Mom, I don't want an ordinary life. I know what I want, and I just want to go after it."

I don't want an ordinary life. My brilliant Miranda. So driven, with her head in the stars. If I could only hand her the resources, I knew she could manage to achieve anything she wanted to. She was two when she looked into the night sky and made her first wish on a twinkling star. Now her head was filled with visions of galaxies and star clusters and black holes. Going on fourteen, but still my little girl. Skip a grade, or more? I knew it could be done, I had friends who had managed it, and they did just fine. But there was a price to pay, and a check wouldn't cover the costs. Could Miranda handle that price? Could she leave her peer group behind without regret?

I glanced out the window. Horvald Ledbetter, our neighbor from across the street, was inspecting his tulips. Obsessive-compulsive as far as I could tell, he could be found out in his yard at all hours of the day or night if he thought something was wrong with his garden. I stared at him for a moment while I thought.

Finally, I turned back to Randa, who was waiting quietly. I knew she expected me to say no outright. "Here's the deal. I don't know. I really don't know what to say about this one. Why don't you get me the names of whoever I'm supposed to talk to at the school, give me a copy of your notes—and I don't just want to see the positive spin on things—and let me think about it for a while."

Her eyes widened. "You mean you really will think about it?" I nodded, and she jumped up and gave me a peck on the cheek. "Thanks, Mom. I wish you'd just say yes, but at least you didn't say no yet." By this time tomorrow, I'd be loaded down with more research than I ever wanted to see.

I flipped on the television and found myself staring directly into my own eyes. Oh no, Cathy Sutton was airing that damn tape. I couldn't believe the gall of that woman! Miranda leaned over my shoulder as Kip pounded down the stairs. He skidded to a half by my chair. "Mom, you're on TV! Sly just called to tell me."

I shushed them and turned up the sound. Cathy's nasal twang came over the airwaves loud and all too clear. "Ms. O'Brien denied knowledge of any connection between Daniel Barrington's murder and the destruction of her shop but had this to say when questioned further."

My face suddenly splashed across the screen. Thank god I'd been wearing makeup, but I still looked irritated and unpleasant. Again, Cathy's voice-over startled me. "Emerald, isn't it possible that whoever ran down Mr. Barrington thinks that you saw him do it and is sending you a warning, trying to convince you to keep quiet?"

The film cut to a shot of the outside of my shop as my voice rang out loud and clear. "I really don't know . . . maybe . . ."

"Damn it, I told her I didn't want to be interviewed." I jumped up, shaking my finger at the television. "They said they were just testing film speeds! That wasn't even the question that I was answering! They pieced together clips of what I said."

Cathy wound up her story. "Whatever the case may be, as unhappy as she is about the fact, Emerald O'Brien seems destined to be a fixture in our local news. I'm sure we all look forward to more of her adventures that add such *local* color to our area."

Infuriated, I zapped the TV with my remote. "How dare she! I'm calling the station and lodging a protest right now." But even as I grabbed the telephone, I knew it was a lost cause. My shop was a public place. The media had a right to be in a public place. If they could televise their attempted interviews with politicians and suspected criminals and alleged victims who didn't want to be taped and kept saying "No comment," Cathy Sutton could air her tape of me and make snide comments and I didn't have a leg to stand on. Even if I could win a retraction, it'd be aired on some last-moment late-night broadcast when everybody was turning off the television to get ready for bed.

I dropped back into my chair and stared numbly at the kids. "Damn."

Kip giggled. "You're mad."

"Damn right I'm mad. That woman should be taken off the air as a danger to herself and others."

Miranda leaned on the arm of the sofa. "You didn't see the driver, did you?"

I shook my head. "No, I was too busy watching Daniel. If anybody caught the license plate, the police would know by now."

"What happens if the person who did hit Mr. Barrington sees it and thinks you know who they are?"

Now that idiot had my kids scared. That was the last time I'd ever talk to her. However, I might just punch her out next time we met. "I don't really think that's going to happen," I said. "People know Sutton always exaggerates her reports."

Settling into the chair at the computer, Kip turned to me. "I'm sure glad you're mad at her and not me right now."

I flashed him a smile. Sometimes my son had a way of making the irritations of life seem brighter. "Funny boy. Funny."

He hesitated, then cleared his throat.

"What is it, honey?"

"Uh, I know you're really busy lately, but are we still going camping this weekend?"

Camping! Oh God, with all that had gone on the past couple of days, I'd forgotten about our reservation at the resort. I winced. Now was not the best time to go, but I'd promised the kids, and Kip had been so good during the time I'd grounded him; I hated to let him down. I took a deep breath and held it, thinking. The deposit was nonrefundable, I'd lose a hundred dollars if we didn't go. Kip stared up at me, his eyes earnest and hopeful.

"Okay," I finally said. "I'm still not convinced this is the best idea right now, but I did promise, so we'll go."

Kip's eyes lit up. "Yay! I was hoping to look around for rocks for my science project." They were studying geology, and he was currently in the crystal phase all kids go through when they discovered quartz and fool's gold.

"Cool. What about you, Randa? You still up for it?"

I didn't think she'd be that interested, but she surprised me. "I could take my old telescope—the one I had before you bought me my new one for Christmas. The viewing will be a lot better out there, as long as there aren't any clouds. I know you're worried, Mom, but I think you need a break."

Well, she was right about that. "Then it's settled. I think I'll ask Murray to tag along. She's been having a rough time adjusting to her new job, and I think she could use a break, too." If she went along, not only would I feel safer, but it would also give us a chance to discuss some of the strange things that had been going on lately.

"May I invite Lori?" Randa asked. "She likes astronomy, too, though she doesn't want to be an astronaut. She wants to teach." I was so relieved that Miranda actually had made a friend her own age that I would have agreed to her dragging a dozen kids along on the trip.

I took over the computer, and we typed up a list of things to be done before the weekend. I delegated the chores to the kids since I had to work.

Miranda cleared her throat. I waited. "Um . . . Mom, can I . . . I know this isn't the best time to ask, but is there any way I might be able to buy a few new clothes?"

New clothes? My no-nonsense daughter who owned four pairs of black slacks, three pairs of jeans, two skirts—one black, one gray—and a dozen shirts of various neutral shades, was asking for new clothes? She never expressed an interest in shopping except when something grew raggedy or too small. I had despaired of ever getting her into anything remotely feminine. She liked the severe look, but it didn't seem natural for someone her age to be imitating Donna Karan.

Wondering what brought this on, I considered our bank account. "Well, a few things, sure. Of course, sweetheart. Do you want me to go with you, or do you want to go with Lori?" I wasn't going to interfere; if she expressed the remotest interest in going out with her new friend, I was all for it.

Randa blushed again. "If you don't mind, I'd like to go with Lori. Can I get my hair done, too?"

Too shocked to comment, I simply said, "You aren't

going to get it cut much, are you? It's so pretty when it's long." I ran my fingers through the long, raven locks that hung past her shoulder blades.

She shook her head. "I want a shag—long and layered. It would be easier to keep up." Her words fell over one another, and I realized she wasn't trying to rationalize her desires to me, but to herself.

Adolescence was hard enough without having your mother psychoanalyze you. "Tell you what, next week I'll give you the charge card, *if* you promise to stick within the budget I set."

With a hasty nod, she slipped off the sofa. "I need to make some notes in my journal for tonight's star watch." She tripped off up the stairs, and I heard the ka-thunk of her door.

Kip looked at me, a glint in his eye. "She's turning into a girl, isn't she?"

I grinned at him. "Yeah, I think so . . . but somehow, I don't think Miranda's going to be like one of the girls on *Who Wants to Be a Pop Star.*"

He shook his head. "Nope . . . more like *Dexter* meets *Tank Girl.*"

Yep, I thought, my son was pretty observant. I motioned for him to join me in the kitchen, where we decided on chef's salad for dinner. After setting Kip to tearing lettuce, I gave Murray a call. She was still at the office.

"Don't you ever go home anymore?"

Her voice told me I'd picked the wrong evening to tease her. "Coughlan left for the rest of the week, which would be just dandy except he dumped a stack of reports on my desk and told me to get them typed up. Em, this is work the clerks should be doing! I'm a detective, not his secretary, but he said if they aren't done by Monday, he'll write a warning in my file that I'm not keeping up with the work."

"Can't you go to Tad Bonner? Tell him what's going on."

Why was she letting this jerk walk all over her? Murray never let anybody take advantage of her, but it was like she was paralyzed when it came to this guy.

She hemmed and hawed and finally blurted out the truth. "I can't. Tad didn't want me to take this job. He said that he didn't think I had what it takes to be a detective. He didn't mean anything bad by it; he said I'm one hell of a cop, but that I just didn't have the personality to fit the job. I can't go to him now and tell him he was right. I'd be humiliated."

Incredulous, I stared at the receiver for a moment, wondering if I'd heard right. "Murray, you wouldn't be admitting he was right. You have some legitimate concerns with the way Coughlan is treating you. If Bonner can't figure out the difference between harassment and ineptitude, then he's a poor chief of police."

She stammered a bit more, then sighed. "Em, when I took this job, I swore I was going to make it work. I can't give up now, and I can't let anybody else fight my battles for me. I'll have the damn reports done by Friday. I know Coughlan doesn't think I can do it, but I'm going to prove him wrong. He'll be speechless."

She was going about this all wrong, I thought. No matter what she did, she'd never impress the man. I kept my mouth shut, though. She probably wouldn't listen to me on this anyway. "Hey, do you want to go camping with us this weekend? We've been planning on this trip for several weeks; I've got a nonrefundable reservation for one of the cabins at Tyler's Resort."

She perked up. "That sounds like fun. When are you leaving?"

"Friday night. We'll drive back on Sunday morning. Come with?"

After a brief pause, Murray said she'd love to come. "By the way, I saw you on television tonight . . . again."

I groaned. "I hate that bitch. So what's the scoop? Can I sue her?"

Murray snorted. "Sue her? You'd be lucky if the courts let you write her a fan letter. I'm fed up with the government. Before you know it, we won't have any right to privacy left at all." And then, before she could really get started, she cut herself short. "Soap box issue. I'd better stop before I lose track of time. I'll call you at the shop on Friday morning."

As I returned to my cutting board, I thought about Murray and her promotion. She was making a mistake if she thought Coughlan would break down and offer her the respect she craved. Men like that never did. If they couldn't fault you for one thing, they'd find something else wrong with you. Roy had taught me that lesson.

Kip and I were putting the finishing touches on the salad when the crash of splintering glass filled the air. I raced into the living room, yelling over my shoulder for Kip to wait in the kitchen. The huge bay window that overlooked our porch and front lawn lay shattered into a thousand pieces. A brick rested in the middle of the jagged fragments covering the living room floor. There was something painted on it, but I was barefoot and couldn't get to it without slice-and-dicing my feet.

"Holy hell! Kip, get back in the kitchen," I said as he peeked through the swinging doors. I could hear Miranda's footsteps as she raced downstairs, and I yelled to warn her. "Don't go in the living room! Go through the hall into the kitchen, and stay there with Kip. Grab a pair of my shoes from the hall closet and take them with you before you do."

I gingerly backtracked into the kitchen. Kip stared at me, wide-eyed and frightened. "What's going on, Mom? Who's doing this?"

"I don't know, honey." I held him close for a moment, then brushed his hair with my fingers and picked up the phone, hitting Redial. For the third time in two days, some force had intruded into my life and destroyed my property. First, Randa's telescope, then the shop, now my house. Why were they targeting me? And what . . . or who . . . would it try to destroy next?

Six

❖

"WHAT IN THE world is going on, Em?" Murray surveyed the damage to my living room window while a couple of uniformed officers poked around outside, hunting for footprints or other clues that might lead to whoever just destroyed my window. She held the brick in a latex-gloved hand; the writing along the side of it was in white paint and spelled out a nasty four-letter word that started with a *c*.

I motioned for her to wait a minute and went back into the kitchen. "Randa, you and Kip round up the cats and put them in the downstairs guest room with a litter box and water. We don't want the kittens getting into the broken glass. Use the hall if you can, instead of walking through the living room. Then, go ahead and make sandwiches to go with the salad, and eat. And both of you make sure you've got good shoes on."

Kip started to protest, but Miranda, sensing I wanted them out from underfoot, promised him the last piece of apple pie. I flashed her a grateful look as they got to work. I returned to the front porch, my stomach a tangle of knots.

"What's going on? I wish I knew. First Miranda's telescope takes a dive, then my shop gets trashed, then my home. I feel under attack."

I couldn't escape the thought that if either the kids or I had been in the living room when this happened, we could have been seriously injured by the flying glass. Murray was talking to one of the cops who had responded to her request for a uniformed team. While she was occupied, I took the opportunity to call Joe. I needed a strong shoulder to lean on, a masculine shoulder, and I needed it right now. He offered to come right over.

Murray and I sat on the newel posts by the porch steps. The other officers joined us. They hadn't found any indicators pointing to who might have done this. "The only evidence we have is that brick; we're dusting it for prints. There aren't any footprints in your front lawn that we can find. Truth is, unless we lift a print, your vandal could be anybody." She glanced at the driveway. "Who's that?"

Horvald Ledbetter was coming up the stairs, a concerned expression on his face. "What happened? I saw the police cars and came over to see if you were okay." He looked worried, and I realized that maybe my neighborhood wasn't so aloof after all. I started to introduce him to Murray, then stopped. Great. Oliver, Ida's nephew, was right behind him. He startled Horvald as he pushed past the older man and craned his neck, trying to get a glimpse of the broken window.

"I saw the police from my aunt's house," Oliver said.

"Somebody decided I needed to redecorate." I motioned for them to find a seat. "Did either of you notice anybody strange around the neighborhood this evening?"

Oliver shrugged. "I'm afraid that I wouldn't know

who's a stranger and who isn't, at least not yet. I'm sorry about your window, though. That looks pretty nasty."

Horvald plopped himself down on the porch swing. "Strangers? Let me think."

I rubbed my temples, my headache threatening to explode into a migraine. Horvald pulled out a roll of Menty-Mints and offered me one. I gratefully accepted the mint-chocolate cream. Chocolate made everything better.

Oliver pushed past Murray, toward the door. "I'll be glad to give you a hand cleaning up." Ida would have made the same offer, but truth was, I just didn't want strangers mucking about in my house.

I shook my head. "No thanks, I'll take care of it."

He blew off my concerns. "Don't worry about it. My aunt told me to give you a hand whenever I had the chance, and I'm not going to let her down."

"Listen, Oliver—" As the weariness of yet another disaster descended on my shoulders, I realized I didn't have the strength to argue. "That's very kind of you."

He reached out and for a moment I thought he was going to pat my hand, but then he simply removed the whisk broom and dustpan I'd carried out from the kitchen in my state of dazed confusion, and set to work out on the porch. A few minutes later, he asked me where I kept my garbage can. I told him that it was near the back of the house, next to the kitchen door, and he disappeared down the steps and around the house.

Murray frowned. "Who's that?"

"Ida's nephew, Oliver. I told you about him, remember? He seems nice enough, in an odd sort of way. So, what should I do? Get a security system for my home, too? I don't want to live in a locked box. I don't even know why this is happening." I couldn't imagine turning my house into an armed fortress.

"The telescope was probably just an accident. Maybe

the same person who trashed your shop is also responsible for breaking your window." She leaned against one of the columns.

I thought about it for a moment. "I don't know. I suppose it could be two different people. Stranger things have happened, but I think you're right. I think the incidents are related in some way. I just don't know how or why."

"Given the writing on the brick, we just might be looking at Jimbo. This stunt would be right up his alley."

I glanced over at Horvald. He looked so deep in thought that he probably couldn't even hear us. "Did you catch up to him yet?" I'd almost managed to forget my altercation with redneck-boy.

She grinned. "Yeah. He insisted he had no idea who you were and said he'd never heard of your shop. We got a half-assed alibi out of him for Sunday night, but it hasn't checked out yet. I'll have another talk with him after I leave here. He's probably over at Reuben's or the Brown Bear. I gather he spends most of his spare time there. No girlfriend. No ex-wife—apparently nobody was ever stupid enough to marry him. No kids around that I can tell. He's a loner and keeps to himself except when he's drunk."

Horvald snapped his fingers. He'd been concentrating so hard that I'd been worried he might blow a circuit. "I remember something! Last night I was out working in the zinnia garden. I was getting cold and was about to go inside when I saw a chopper drive by, real slow. I think it was black with red detailing along the sides. The man riding it was wearing black chaps, a black helmet, and dark glasses. I remember thinking that he didn't belong in this neighborhood, or I would have noticed him before."

Murray jotted the info down. "Anything else? License plate, maybe?"

Horvald went back to concentrating but shook his head

after a moment. "I'm sorry. I was worried about my flowers. The aphids are going to be thick this year, and I wanted to make sure they didn't set up house on the zinnias. Only noticed the biker because, when I was young, I used to ride, and detailed bikes always catch my eye."

I could tell Murray was suppressing a smile. The thought of this grandfatherly man on a Harley seemed almost comical, but then again, there were a lot of old bikers around, and they were still in good shape. "That's fine. Do you think you'd recognize it again if you saw it?"

Horvald gave us a self-satisfied smile and dipped his head. "Yep. It was a beauty, hard to miss." He mumbled good-bye and hurried across the street to his yard, settling back into weeding the patch of phlox spreading parallel to the path that led from the sidewalk to his house. He was trying to train the floral groundcover, but it still looked like a giant pink jumble to me.

Sandy Whitmeyer popped out, holding a paper bag. "Detective Murray? Surprise of surprises, we managed to lift a couple of prints off the brick. Everything's ready to go."

"Excellent," Murray said, her eyes lighting up. "Okay, if everything's bagged, then head back to the station with the evidence. I'll be along in a few." The sound of tires crunching on gravel heralded Joe's arrival. Murray flipped her notebook shut. "Em, it looks like we've got everything we're going to get here."

I wanted to hug her but refrained. I wasn't about to show her anything but professional respect when other officers were present. There was no way of knowing who might be one of Coughlan's snitches. They headed over to the prowl car.

Joe shouted a quick hello to them as he bounded up the stairs. He gave me a hug and a kiss on the cheek, then stood gaping at what had, until recently, been my living room window. After a few minutes, Miranda and Kip joined us on the porch.

Randa perched on the wide railing that overlooked the front yard. "Mom, Mrs. Trask called, but you were busy with the cops, so I took a message."

"What did she say?"

"She said she won't be back for about a week; her friend was really banged up and needs her. She left her number for you to call her."

"Thanks, sugar. You're a good girl."

"No problem. Kip and I did the dishes and made a sandwich for you," she added. My two miracle workers. They could be such little buttheads, but when I needed them, they came through. "What are we going to do about the window tonight? The living room's still full of glass."

I shrugged. "I don't know. I really don't want to leave the house alone, but I'm not letting you two stay here until we get it fixed. I'm going to call Harlow and see if she'll keep you overnight. I'll sleep here and keep watch."

Miranda squirmed, obviously uncomfortable. "Mom, you could get hurt." Kip chimed in, echoing her sentiments. I tried to reassure them, but they were both adamant about me not staying alone. Defeated, I slumped back onto the swing and gave Joe a pleading look. If he took my side, they might back off.

Straddling the porch wall, he rested his head against one of the columns. Jeez, the guy was gorgeous. Viking blood, for sure. I took a deep breath and brought my focus back to where it belonged as he offered a compromise. "What if you kids stay over at Harlow's and I stay here with your mother and make sure she comes to no harm? That way everybody will be happy. We can rig up a tarp across the window until tomorrow."

Everybody happy indeed! His eyes danced with a light that no amount of scolding was going to vanquish. Miranda and Kip agreed and raced down the foyer hall, into the kitchen to phone Harlow. I gave Joe a scathing look, but he just grinned. "You're staying here with me? My dear, you know how Andrew would feel about that. Regardless of who sleeps where, he's going to be pissed."

"I also know that you'd be in danger here by yourself, and I don't see Andrew anywhere around to help out. So no protests, Ms. O'Brien. I'm younger than you and stronger than you and I can run a whole lot faster."

He winked at me and, infuriated but laughing, I accepted his offer. The kids would feel better, I'd be safer, and at least I wouldn't sit up all night imaging noises and intruders in the house. I repressed a snort. Actually, I probably would be imagining things. Just not scary monsters and drunken rednecks. Maybe my cabana boy could pop back in my dreams and give me a rubdown to take the knots out of my shoulders, only I had the feeling that if he did, Pedro would be wearing a uniform and fire helmet this time instead of a loincloth.

"I emptied the glass into a box that I found near your back door, then set it near the garbage can. I didn't think you'd want it loose in the can." Oliver edged his way around the house and back up on the porch, looking from Joe to me, back to Joe again.

I jumped; I'd almost forgotten he was around. "Thanks, Oliver. I owe you one. You take after your aunt, all right." He was staring pointedly at Joe and, still blushing, I tripped over my words as I introduced them.

Oliver eyed Joe. "You're the playwright, correct?"

Embarrassed, I shook my head. Ida must have filled him in on local news. "Joe's captain of the medic rescue unit. You're thinking of Andrew. He's out of town; hopefully striking a deal in Hollywood right now."

Joe shook Oliver's hand, while speculating on how hard it would be to replace the window. "If you can buy the glass, I can probably do the work. I'm not too shabby with a hammer and nails," he said, understating his talent. I'd seen the results of his handiwork.

"I can help if you like," Oliver offered. I protested that he was doing too much, but he laughed me off. "Please, let me help. I've spent the past three years sitting around doing nothing; I like being active."

We measured the window; tomorrow Joe would order the new pane. I would turn the reins of the shop over to Cinnamon and wait at home for the glass to be delivered. I pressed some cookies on Oliver before he left. As I retreated to the kitchen to make tea and eat my sandwich something seemed out of place. I looked around, but everything looked in order. Probably just nerves. After all, somebody had tossed a brick through my window; that was bound to shake me up.

Joe drove the kids over to Harlow's while I cleaned the glass up off the living room floor, managing to inflict several nasty cuts on my fingers as I picked up the bigger shards, then vacuumed sliver after sliver off the back of the sofa and the floor. Thank heavens I hadn't chosen a shag carpet, or I'd never have gotten the mess up. As it was, we were going to have to watch our step for a while.

After Joe returned, we fitted a tarp across the window and sat around in the growing darkness, playing games and watching low-budget horror flicks on the Sci-Fi Channel. As the evening wore on, our conversation took a detour.

Joe fiddled with the Scrabble tiles as we cleared up from our game. "So tell me about your ex-husband, Em. What did he do to make you run?"

"You don't beat around the bush, do you?" I settled in with my popcorn.

"Life's too short. If I want to know something, I ask."

Why did I take the kids and run? "Too many reasons to count, the last being that my daughter arrived home from school early one day just in time to catch Roy screwing his mistress in *her* bed. Poor kid is still traumatized over it."

He whistled and leaned back on the sofa, stretching out his legs. "Too bad you don't have a big brother who could have whipped his ass for you. Sounds like that boy needs a lesson in manners."

"Yeah, well, he seemed to think that since he paid for the house, he had free license. He pushed me around a lot; beat me up once or twice. Nothing that would show, he was careful to keep up appearances. He never hit the kids, though. I would have killed him if he did."

Joe let out a loud sigh. "Too much of that going around. Well, it looks like you managed to make your way just fine."

I gave him a satisfied smile. "Yeah. We do fine; well, until recently, that is. The kids are happy, I'm happy, we have a home and pets and my shop is popular. I'm not complaining, even with the way this last week's gone. Cycles come and go; everybody has their off times."

"Emerald, do you realize how pretty you are when you smile like that?" He leaned toward me, and goose bumps raced up my arms.

I stared at him, breathless. "Joe—I . . ."

He reached out and ran his fingers along my cheek. "Don't say it. I know what you're going to say, and I don't want to hear it. I just want you to know how I feel. I want you to remember that I'm here, because my guess is one day you're going to turn around, and Andrew's going to have flown the coop."

I couldn't breathe, couldn't think. His fingers didn't produce the sharp sparks I was used to with Andrew, but a gentle rolling wave of desire that went on and on. I fought for self-control, reminding myself that Andrew was my boyfriend and, regardless of our difficulties, I wasn't about to hurt him. A thin layer of perspiration beaded up on my lip. "Joe—" I warned as I slid out of the way when he leaned in for a kiss. "I can't. You wouldn't respect me if I cheated on Andrew. I know you too well. And I've got too much self-respect to do to him what my ex-husband did to me."

He pulled back. After a moment, he sighed. "Sometimes I hate it that you're so damned wonderful. I won't pressure you, but I won't promise to stop thinking about you, either." With a grin, he arched his eyebrows then wiggled them in a playful leer.

Relieved that we'd passed the test but confused because everything between us felt so right, I decided that activity was my best defense against getting sucked into the feeling again. "Twerp. I've got to feed the cats. I'll get your blankets in a few minutes."

"Need help?" He followed me into the kitchen.

I scowled. "Man, you are askin' for it! Now, if you *really* want to help, you can empty the garbage for me."

He snorted, then hoisted the bag out of the trash can. "As I said, I'm hanging around. It's only a matter of time until you change your mind and realize that I'm the right guy for you." With a final wink, he took off out to the driveway.

In the safety of my kitchen, I leaned against the counter and fought back the desire to rip off my clothes and play doctor with Joe the Medic. My pulse was racing, and if he took my temperature now, I'd have a fever so hot you could light matches on it.

I forced myself to focus and grabbed the cat food, filling four dishes and carrying them to the guest room on a tray. They could stay in there all night; otherwise they'd raise havoc trying to play with the tarp because they were cats, and that's what cats do. On the way back into the living room, I made a quick detour to the linen closet to collect a quilt, sheets, and another pillow, then tossed them on the sofa.

"There you go, you can make up your bed. Night, Joe. Sweet dreams."

He rested his hand on my arm. "Wait up. I didn't get my good night kiss."

Laughing, I tried to break away. "And did I say you were getting one? Sleep well, fireman. The tarp should protect you from bugs and beasties and things that go bump in the night."

With a gentle hand, he lifted my chin so that I was staring into his eyes. "Good night, Emerald. Please don't fret, I'll keep watch down here." He slowly reached down and placed a gentle kiss on my forehead. My knees melted, and I wanted nothing more than to slide into his arms. His eyes were sparkling. "Pleasant dreams."

Pleasant dreams? I doubted that my dreams would be restful, and I wasn't surprised when sleep ran me a merry chase until the late hours of the night.

THE PHONE WOKE me up; probably a good thing since my dream was starting to take an unsavory turn toward the nightmarish side of town. I blinked twice, then grabbed the receiver. "Huh?"

"Good morning to you, too." Murray's voice shook me fully out of the dream. "Got some news for you. The print paid off. Jimbo was holding on to that brick. I went hunting for him this morning, but no can find. He got smashed at the Brown Bear last night, got in another argument with the manager, then wandered off. When we checked out his . . . I guess you could call it a house—the man lives in a shack out near Miner's Lake—he wasn't there. I saw some loose bricks in the yard, though, and I think they match the one that came through your window last night."

I took a deep breath. "And he's still on the street?"

"Yeah. I also checked on his alibi for where he was

Sunday night, and it didn't jibe. We suspect he might be the one who vandalized your shop, Em. We don't have any proof, but we do know he holds grudges."

Grateful that we had at least one answer, I said, "Okay. So, what are you going to do about him? He's obviously mad at me. I don't think the kids and I are safe while he's still wandering around free."

"We're trying to find him, Em. When we do, he'll be charged with destruction of property. I've asked for a search warrant to go through his house; I've got probable cause now, and I'm thinking that maybe we can find evidence regarding your shop." She was brisk, almost brusque, but I could hear the underlying weariness in her voice.

"Job's getting to you, isn't it? I can hear it in your voice." I wanted to help, to be able to reach out with a magic wand, tap her on the forehead, and make everything all better. "Murray, have you thought about what I said before? About talking to Tad Bonner?"

She cleared her throat. "Yes, and I'm not going to go whining to him, no matter how nice he is. You just don't get it, Em. Anyway, did you sleep okay?"

Oops, touchy. I backed off. "Uh, yeah. Joe was here. He slept downstairs." She snorted. "Nothing happened," I protested.

"Too bad. He's a nice guy. I like him." I could hear papers rustle, and then she was back to being all business. "I'll call you if we have any new information. Meanwhile, stay alert. I checked on the vehicles Jimbo has registered at the DMV, and sure enough, one of them just happens to be a black chopper with red detail."

I signed off and crawled out of bed, ducking into the shower for a brief rinse before I clambered into a pair of culottes and a gauze top. As I slipped on my huaraches, I thought about Jimbo. So he'd decided to make good on his threat. Well, at least I knew who to look out for. When I jogged down the stairs, Joe was talking on his cell phone. He flipped it shut after a moment and eyed me with a speculative gaze. "Headed south of the border, señorita?"

I flicked his head with two fingers and pointed him toward the kitchen. "Haul ass in there, and I'll make us something to eat."

As I broke eggs into a bowl and beat them lightly for an omelet, he told me that he'd called Eyrland's Glass Works. "Apparently you're such a good customer now that you rate a ten percent discount. Keep smashing windows, and pretty soon, you'll get one free."

"Gee, thanks for the suggestion. Brilliant, dearheart, brilliant."

"Thank you. I'm glad you agree; I am brilliant."

He looked so smug that I threw a dish towel at him. "Since you're so smart, figure out how to wash and set the table while I make breakfast."

Laughing, he wiped off the oak tabletop and set it with place mats and napkins. "They're delivering the glass sometime this morning, so after breakfast, I'll hit Home Depot for the installation hardware. Want to come?"

"Nah. I've got to pick up the kids and drop them off at school. And somebody has to be here for the delivery truck." I handed him a plate of toast and eggs. As we ate, I filled him in on what Murray had told me about Jimbo.

He wiped up the last of his egg and licked his fingers. "Sounds like a troublemaker to me. If they can catch him, they'll probably offer him a plea bargain if he cops to vandalizing your store, too." He tossed on his jacket and hit the road.

As I was washing the dishes, the phone rang again. The kids were up and ready for school. Since Harlow was still wheelchair-bound, she couldn't drive. As I told them I'd be out to pick them up as soon as I could, I realized that I couldn't leave the house alone. I hated to impose on my neighbors, but I raced across the street to Horvald's. He was out. I wondered briefly if there might be a Mrs. Ledbetter, but nobody answered the door.

Who else could I get to look after the house while I was over at Harlow's? Normally, I'd ask Ida. I glanced down at the comfortable house on the corner. Oliver? I didn't like the thought, but I had no other choice. I darted down the street and rang the doorbell. Nobody answered, but the car Ida had rented for Oliver before she left was in the driveway, so I assumed that he was home. Maybe he was working in the basement. I hesitantly tried the door; it was unlocked. Music streamed in waves from the kitchen. Something classical, but I didn't recognize it. The house smelled of Lysol and Lemon Pledge.

"Oliver?" I called out, tentative, not wanting to interrupt, but nobody answered. I was about to leave when the state of the living room caught my attention. Spotless. Completely spotless. No dust, no clutter, no jumble anywhere; the plants were shining, and every leaf was clean. The pictures were level-straight, and all the windows were polished and gleaming. Ida was a champion housekeeper, but even she'd be impressed.

Ida! I'd forgotten to call her back. Oh well, I thought, it would have to wait until later. I bit my lip as I looked around. Maybe he was in the kitchen? If I peeked, it wouldn't really be snooping since I needed to ask him a favor. I cautiously pushed open the swinging doors and poked my head through. "Oliver?" No answer. I took another step forward, then another. Nobody here, either, but once again, the room was a marvel. The counters were clean, everything in its place with no dirty dishes in sight. I ran my finger along the porcelain sink. No grease, no mess. Nope. Downright unnatural.

"Looking for something?"

"Oh!" I whirled around to find myself staring into Oliver's curiously cool eyes. His expression was unreadable; he was wearing work gloves and carrying a hammer. "I rang the bell, and you didn't answer. I came over to ask a favor." So maybe it hadn't been such a bright idea to come in uninvited. Ida and I had the typical knock-and-enter arrangement common to small towns, but this was Oliver, and while she was gone, this was his house.

"I was in the basement. What can I do for you?"

The room suddenly felt too small, the door too far away. I edged toward it, wondering what the hell was wrong with me. Stress, I thought, as I tugged on my collar. I was just feeling the effects of all the stress I'd been under lately. "I need to pick up the kids and drop them off at school, but Joe is out, and the glass company will be delivering the new pane sometime today. Would you mind staying at my place until I get back? To keep away any intruders and maybe sign for the glass if it arrives early?"

He nodded; the eager beaver look was back. "No problem; I can help Joe install it. Can you wait ten minutes? I should finish up the last of this one project." As he headed back to the basement, I took off for home.

While I waited for him to arrive, I stood in front of the étagère, looking at the dragon. It occurred to me that not only was Harl a patron of the arts, but in her new research position, she probably had access to some obscure sources for historical information that I couldn't access. I tucked the statue in my purse, hoping that she might be able to give me some ideas on how to go about tracking down Daniel's relatives. I shrugged on a light jacket as Oliver knocked on the door.

"I'll be back in about an hour. Thanks so much," I said as I clambered into the Cherokee and pulled out of the drive.

The drive out to Harlow's was long and winding, and I

seldom took the shortcut since she'd been forced off the road a few days before Christmas, but today I was in a hurry. Yep, the ravine was filled with brambles and bad memories. Of course, one good memory, too. I'd met Joe that night.

Joe. What to do about him? I couldn't ignore the fact that I got along much better with him than with Andrew. As much as I cared about Andrew, I always felt like we were one step away from a disagreement. Joe . . . Joe was easy. Comfortable. But would the age difference create problems?

Irritated, I shook thoughts of both men from my mind. Scrap it. After all, it wasn't like I was planning on marrying either one of them. Andrew had made it clear he didn't believe in marriage. Joe was far too young to become a surrogate father.

The road wound through the ravine, hugging it like a snake. During winter, the ice and snow obscured the shoulder, and the lack of leaves gave a stark, black-and-white look to the area. Now that spring was here, leaf buds studded the bramble vines and trees, and the promise of summer to come hovered in the fresh smell of damp moss. Through my open window, the rush of the creek kept up a steady rhythm, the current swift and dangerous. Whitewater season, we called it. As the snow melted off the Cascades glaciers, the runoff channeled into the streams, bringing with it rapids and whitecaps that spewed mist high into the air. A sudden longing swept over me; if I could only stop and meander along the creek's side, to sit by the water and let my stress roll away with the waves. The weekend camping trip sounded more and more appealing, the longer I thought about it.

I turned onto the driveway that led to Harlow and James's home. As I slipped out of the car and headed toward the sidewalk, there was a shout as Kip and Miranda tumbled out of the house. Harlow followed, easing her wheelchair onto the ramp that James had built for her. Her tummy was expanding, all right; her baby girl was going to be a whopper. Though Harl had managed to avoid a recurrence of anorexia, I had a sneaking suspicion that labor was going to be hard on her. She had such a narrow frame and no hips to speak of. What weight she'd gained during pregnancy so far had all gone to her tummy and boobs.

I kissed the kids and leaned over to give Harl a hug. "Hey babe, how are you?" The kids gave me quick pecks on the cheek before racing off to chase frogs. I dropped onto the bench near the front door.

"Miserable. I want out of this chair as soon as possible. It's driving me nuts to have to sit so still, and my back hurts!" Harl groaned and adjusted her position. I swung around behind her and began rubbing her shoulders. She took a deep breath and let it out slowly. "Oh God, what I wouldn't give for a cigarette." Harlow had quit smoking in December when she decided to have the baby. She wasn't handling it very well but surprised all of us by her determination.

"You can do it, sweetie. Just think, by the end of next week you should be out of that chair, right? And your little girl will be so much healthier if you stay away from the cigs. You're going to make it just fine."

"Yeah." She sniffed and hiccupped. "Thanks, Em. I don't know how I'd have made it through the past few months without you cheering me on. If only James hadn't had to make this trip, but I know he needed to go." She lowered her voice. "I have a problem. Hannah has to leave."

"What's up?" I rested on the bench next to her. Hannah, her mother-in-law, was a wonderful if overpowering woman.

"Last night Hannah got a call from Helena, Montana.

Her father died. She doesn't want to tell James yet. If he comes back to the States now, he'll blow this photo shoot, and once you screw up something this big, you don't get a second chance. There's nothing he could do anyway; the funeral will be long over by the time he could get back. But with Hannah gone, that means I'll be alone for a few days."

"So she's heading out today?"

Harl glanced back at the house. "She's pretty broken up; she and her father were really close because her mother died young. I feel so sorry for her. No matter how old you are, when a parent dies, it still hits you hard. I've called for a nurse attendant to help me, but she won't be able to get here for a couple of days."

I didn't like the thought of Harl being out here alone. "You could stay with me. I've got the guest room downstairs, and we still have the ramp Joe and Andrew built for me when I was on crutches a few months ago."

She considered the idea then shook her head. "I've got too much work to finish. Professor Abrams is a wuss, fretting all the time, but he's really a dear." She laughed. I knew she liked her new employer and he, in turn, adored her. It was hard for anybody to meet Harlow and not go gaga. She was one of those people that made every person she talked to feel special. "The Professor's asked me to stay on after the baby's born. I told him that I'll have to slow down a bit, but he says he's never had such an organized assistant before."

I snorted. "Sounds like you've got him wrapped around your little finger, like you do every man. I'm glad you like the job, though."

She bobbed her head. "Oh, I do. In fact, James is bringing back a few artifacts that he found for the Professor to look at. They're from some obscure tribe in northwestern Ethiopia. They may actually turn out to be ancient Egyptian."

"While we're talking antiques, take a look at this." I pulled out the dragon and showed it to her.

She held the dragon gingerly. "So this is the little guy. Gorgeous."

"Hodges gave me a list of experts on art in the Ming dynasty." I showed her the paper he'd written the names on. "Do you know any of these people?"

She eyed them carefully, tapping her long fuchsia nails on the arm of her chair, then pointed to the last name on the list. "I know Mary Sanders. She's smart, and she's friendly. Why don't you give her a call?"

I took the paper back and folded it, putting it in my pocket. "Do you know where she lives? Obviously somewhere in Washington by the area code but—"

Harl grinned. "Lucky you! She lives in Glacier. Didn't you say you were headed out that way to go camping this weekend?"

"Yeah. Glacier, huh? I could drive back to the town and talk to her on Saturday while Murray watches the kids at the cabin. I could take the dragon with me."

"I'll give her a heads up to expect your call. She owes me a couple favors."

As interesting as the conversation was getting, I needed to skedaddle. "Okay, I'm taking off. The kids are late for school. Murray's on Jimbo's trail. Did I tell you his prints were on the brick that slammed through my window, and we think he might have been the one who trashed my shop? That'll teach me to head-butt drunken rednecks."

Harlow shuddered. "I dunno, Em. You be careful. Something doesn't feel right, and you're the one who taught me to pay attention to my intuition."

I called the kids and we piled in the Cherokee. I dropped them off at their schools, making sure their teachers knew why they were late. Making it home just in time to greet the deliverymen with the new window, I tucked the dragon safely away, then joined Joe, who had just arrived, hardware in hand. He and Oliver got to work on the installation while I planned out the camping trip. After a little while, I made lemonade and sandwiches.

Oliver and Joe were discussing various ways of caulking drafts. I cleared my throat. "Lunch is ready."

"Great!" Joe said. "We're ready for a break." They trooped into the house and washed their hands in the sink. I set the plate of sandwiches on the table.

"Ladies first," Oliver said. "So, any idea who broke the window?"

"Some guy was bothering me the other night while I was out with a friend. They aren't sure if he was the one who vandalized my shop, though."

He shrugged. "Most likely. If he went to the trouble of throwing a brick through your window, he's probably also the one who robbed your store."

"Well, they aren't sure, but no doubt you're right. So, how are you getting on in Chiqetaw? Have you signed up for classes yet at WWU?"

He swallowed his bite of sandwich and washed it down with a big swig of lemonade. "I called the registrar's office and talked to them. The earliest I can get in is winter quarter, so I'll get a job until then. I don't want to live off Aunt Ida any more than necessary."

The back door opened, and Kip raced in, breathless. "I forgot my homework!" He eyed the sandwiches on the table. "Can I eat lunch here? Otherwise I won't have time when I get back to school."

I told him to wash his hands and got him a plate and poured him a glass of milk. He slid onto the chair next to Oliver. "Hey, Mr. Hoffman! Hi Joe!" After he'd chomped into his sandwich and washed it down with the milk, he cleared his throat. "Mr. Hoffman, Sly says his mom called you a con. Were you really in prison?"

My darling Kip silenced us all with his question, and I immediately turned as red as a lobster begging for melted butter. I hadn't told the kids about Oliver yet, nor had I informed Joe. Oliver had a right to his privacy, and it wasn't like he'd been locked up for anything violent. Joe shot me a questioning look.

"Kip, that's none of your business. I want you to apologize immediately." I hushed Oliver as he started to speak.

Kip's lip quivered a little as he said, "I'm sorry. I didn't mean to be rude."

"Okay, grab an apple, and get back to school before you're late. When you get home this afternoon, go out to the shed and haul out the camping gear so it can air out. We don't need the tent since we'll be sleeping in a cabin, but we'll bring it along just in case."

Joe cleared his throat noisily, but when I looked at him, he just stared blankly at his plate. I gave Kip a hug and, clutching his folder of homework, he took off out the door and grabbed his bike, pedaling as fast as he could.

I glanced at Oliver, hoping he wasn't too mad. "I'm so sorry. Kip didn't intend to be rude; he's at that age where his mouth works before his brain, and if he wants to know something, he's used to asking. I encourage their curiosity, even though they don't always get the answers they're hoping for."

Oliver shrugged. "I figured it would come out. If this Sly kid knows, then I'd better expect that the rest of the town will know. Ida probably talked about me to people during the time I was locked up."

"Where are you from?" Joe asked. "Is Ida your only living family?"

"Portland, Oregon, and yeah, my parents are both dead. Why do you want to know?" Oliver polished off the last of his sandwich and chips, then chugged his milk.

Joe persisted. "Where were you incarcerated, and why?"

He seemed determined to pick at the subject.

I blushed. I might not be a gourmet chef, but I was, at least, a gracious hostess. "Back off, Joe. My kitchen isn't an interrogation room."

Joe glared at me; I knew he wanted to pursue the subject, but I shook my head, and he just shrugged. "Sorry. Sometimes I guess I'm nosy, too."

Oliver shrugged. "Whatever. Aunt Ida offered me a place to stay so I can get my head together and get back on track." He gathered up his dishes and carried them to the sink. "If we want to finish that window, we'd better get moving."

Joe gave him a nod and said, "I'll be out in a minute." After Oliver had excused himself to the porch, Joe thoughtfully rubbed his chin. "Something's off there."

"Jealous?" I meant to tease him, but he scowled.

"If I *am* jealous, it's not of your new neighbor. No, Ida's nephew is hiding something. When will she be back?"

I glanced at the phone. "According to her message, another week or so. Desdemona is in a really bad way. Joe, she loves Oliver, so go easy. I think you just don't like the idea of an ex-con living next door, but some people who are in prison don't belong there, and not everybody with a criminal record is dangerous."

He relaxed a little and gave me a faint smile. "I guess you're right. Maybe I'm just worried because of everything that's happened to you over the past few days. Too many upsets in a short period of time."

I patted him on the arm. "Murray's on top of the investigation. The insurance check is coming next week, and I'll be able to replace the stock at my store. Safety-Tech installed the security system there. And as far as my window, well, the cops know who did it and are after him right now. Murray won't let anybody hurt me. Now how about getting busy?"

I followed Joe into the living room as he headed back outside. A flicker of light from the étagère caught my eye. The dragon had changed positions. It had been facing the kitchen wall. Now it faced the front of the house, looking straight at the broken window, and I could swear the eyes were glowing.

What the hell? Not again. Maybe I hadn't been imagining things at the shop when I first thought the statue was staring at me. I checked the door handle. Yep, the door was locked. Fumbling with the key, I reached in to flip the dragon back around. As I did, my bracelet caught on the crystal unicorn that the kids had bought me for my birthday two years ago and, startled, I jerked. Tangled in the gold chain, the figurine tipped over, and the horn broke. Swearing, I cautiously removed the unicorn and the broken horn, hoping I could fix it before the kids found out.

Seven

✤

I MANAGED TO glue the unicorn back together before the kids got home from school. After I replaced the horned horse in the étagère, I reached for the dragon. Could I have been mistaken? Had it really moved, or was my memory off? The more I thought about it, the more uncertain I was. But no, I knew that I'd placed it in there facing the door to the kitchen. Of course, with everything that had happened the past week, I wouldn't be surprised to find my concentration skewed. I hesitated, staring at the figurine. There *was* a strange aura around this piece, though I couldn't pinpoint why it unsettled me. And the eyes really *had* been glowing.

If the dragon had moved, what could have caused it? Poltergeists were volatile spirits that tossed objects around and moved furniture, but I didn't think that was what I was dealing with. And a spirit directly attached to the dragon would manifest in other ways. I carried it into the kitchen, away from the noise of Joe's handwork, and tried to tune in to the energy again.

At first, all I got was static, not even the rainbow swirl of colors and energies. Great. *We're sorry, but your astral radar appears to be experiencing technical difficulties.* I inhaled deeply and slowly let out my breath, once again lowering myself into the depths of trance. The static washed over me and set my nerves tingling with pinpricks of fire. I was about to give up when I caught the faintest glimpse of an image and abruptly found myself thrust into the middle of an astral adventure movie.

A rider was spurring his mount forward. Long strands of blond hair whipped out from beneath a tufted fur hat, and he wore what looked like an aging leather robe and trousers. He raced out of a wide, snow-covered grassland, across the steppes, urging his horse ever faster toward a path that led up into a range of mountains. Behind him, clouds swirled around the mountain peaks; a storm was brewing.

The image shifted, ever so slightly, and the rider was walking now, leading his horse behind him as he forged a path through the knee-deep snow that covered the ground and turned the trees into a picture-postcard Christmas forest. As the visions marched on in silence, snowflakes, as large as my thumbnail, began to fall, heavy and thick. Stopping in front of the entrance to a large cave, the rider led his horse inside, and I followed, as if in a dream, watching as the man hauled a pack off the back of the animal and shook out two heavy blankets. He gathered together a few branches from the floor of the cavern and tried to light a fire, but the spark wouldn't take. Finally, looking exhausted, he huddled under the blankets.

As he sat there in the fading daylight that filtered in from the storm, he took out something and began to play with it. The dragon. The jade dragon, as beautiful as it was when sitting in my hand. The man tucked it back into a pouch on his belt and once again drew the blankets close around him, leaning against the wall of the cave. As he closed his eyes, the image faded from my sight.

I shook myself out of the trance, still feeling the pull of the dreamy half-conscious state that always came with working on the astral realms. Jeez, I hadn't expected a full-scale journey! Though I meditated a lot and had the occasional premonition or psychometric flash, I wasn't used to being dropped right into the middle of the action. What could the vision be telling me? How had the man come to possess the statue? Had he ever escaped from the cave, or did his bones rest there still, high on some mountain, forgotten by time?

"You have so many secrets locked away inside, don't you?" I asked the statue. "What's your history? How did you get here, from so long ago and such a faraway land?" The dragon remained silent, noncommittal, and with a last look into its milky jade eyes, I replaced it in the cabinet and got out my steno book and jotted down both the position I left it in, along with the vision I'd seen. Next time, I would know for certain if it had moved. If there was a next time.

BY THE TIME Oliver and Joe finished up the last touches on the window, the kids were hauling camping gear out of the shed by the armload. They'd discovered an extra sleeping bag and a number of accoutrements that I didn't even know we owned. Though we didn't belong to the Winnebago set, it looked like we'd be roughing it in style.

Roy, on the other hand, had bought an RV for his new wife, but he never asked to take his children along on his camping trips. Come to think of it, I doubted if that RV saw much use at all. His ditz, Tyra, defined "roughing it" to mean staying anywhere except in five-star hotels.

By the time I strolled out front to see what the guys were up to, the window was installed and looked great. All I had to do was give it a good polish. Joe glanced at his watch; he went on duty in an hour and had to get to the firehouse. Oliver had planned to spend the evening exploring Chiqetaw, so I promised to repay them with dinner another night.

As I dug through the cupboards for the Windex and paper towels, it occurred to me that Jimbo had to have been pretty far up in the yard in order to toss the brick over the porch wall. No way could anybody lob a rock from the sidewalk over the fence, across the front yard, into our window. There were simply too many tree branches and hedges and banisters and balusters in the way. No, he had to come in close to get a good shot.

I shivered. The last thing I needed was some psycho near my kids. I finished cleaning the window as the kids came in, covered in dust balls and cobwebs.

"The garage is a mess." Kip had developed a habit for overstating the obvious.

Miranda shuddered. "There were spiders in there. A lot of them. Can we call an exterminator?"

"The poison's bad for the environment and for us," I said automatically, regardless of the fact that I was thinking the same thing the minute I saw the cobwebs. Miranda and I shared a phobia of spiders, and I hoped that this weekend out of doors wouldn't bring too many crises of the eight-legged variety.

Kip let out a snort of disgust. "They're only spiders. I'll clean out the garage if you pay me, Mom."

Pay him? I should pay him for what I could assign as a chore? He was getting more materialistic every day. Nine years old and a budding Bill Gates, or—hopefully only in Bizarro World—D. B. Cooper. "A buck an hour, and you be careful."

Shortly before dinnertime, with no desire to cook, I called ahead and made reservations at the Forest's End Diner. We'd been eating out a lot lately, but I wasn't going to kid myself. I'd never make it into the Apple Pie Queen of the Year set. I pinned my hair up and headed for the shower, advising the kids to do the same. "No going to dinner looking like dust moppets."

Soaking wet, I dashed into my bedroom where I finished toweling dry and then sat down for the one truly feminine ritual I never skipped.

I powdered under my breasts, behind my knees, and in the crook of my elbows with Opium dusting powder, enjoying the silky touch of the puff as I examined my body with a critical eye. My skin was smooth and even, not bad for thirty-six going on thirty-seven. Even my face only showed a few laugh lines. I was a little plump, but I'd grown to love my curves and no longer minded the fact that I didn't have six-pack abs and that my butt was nicely padded, except for when I hung out with Harlow too long. But Harl could even make Cindy Crawford feel self-conscious.

I layered my arms and legs with matching body lotion and then spritzed myself with a quick spray of eau de toilette. Smelling like a spice emporium from the Orient, I dug through my dresser and shimmied into my favorite purple satin bra and matching panties. Pretty but comfortable, I loved this bra, though I'd removed the padding. My boobs were big enough without any need for artificial help.

I pulled a black floral sundress with a flouncy hem over my head, slipped on a pair of fuchsia espadrilles with ties that wound up my leg, and twirled in the mirror. Not bad,

not bad at all. The silver glints that streaked my hair set off
the black of my dress and, once again, I decided I could
live without a dye job. Ceremoniously, I plunked a wide-
brimmed straw hat on my head and went downstairs.

The kids were waiting, and off to dinner we went. By
the time we reached the restaurant, we were all starving.
Kip ordered a deluxe burger and fries, Miranda asked for
chicken parmesan, and I ordered a steak, New York cut,
medium rare, good and thick. As we ate our appetizer of
mozzarella sticks, I brought up the subject of summer
break, which wasn't that far off.

"What do you want to do this summer?" Before Miranda
could chime in, I added, "I know you're going to Space
Camp. I mean other than that." As each of the kids finished
first grade, I encouraged them to set summer goals, and it
had become a tradition at the end of every school year. It
gave them a sense of accomplishment and direction, and
kept them from getting bored during the weeks away from
school.

"Have you made your lists yet?" I toyed with my salad,
briefly thinking of my dwindling bank account. Hopefully,
we wouldn't have too many more unexpected expenses, or
we'd soon be eating spaghetti every night until things
evened out.

Miranda wiped a string of cheese off her chin. "I'm
going to write a paper about the orbits of the planets
around the sun. I'll read it to my astronomy club. Mom,
have you thought about what I asked? I know I didn't get
the information to you about it yet, but the window broke,
and I didn't have time to get everything together yet."

"What's she want now?" Kip's mouth was full of salad,
and he spewed little droplets of dressing all over the table.
I reached over and tapped his chin.

"Don't talk with your mouth full, and it's none of your
business." I turned back to Miranda as Kip took his napkin

and began to wipe up his mess. "Get the info to me as soon as you can if you want me to think it over for this year."

The waitress brought our dinners then, and we dug in, my mind drifting back to the vision I'd seen while holding the dragon. Were the images the product of my imagination? Were they real? Had I tuned in on the death of a man that happened centuries ago as he took refuge from a storm, trapped in a cave by the swirling snows? And if he did die, alone and forgotten, then when did the dragon next surface, and how? So many questions, and no way of knowing the answers.

A PERSISTENT RINGING in my ears woke me up at five in the morning. "Oh cripes, who the heck is that?" I squinted around, looking for the phone. Maybe one of these days I'd win the Lotto. Grand prize: an entire night's sleep.

It was Murray, sounding a little panicky. "Em, are you okay?"

"Yeah, why?" I blinked, forcing my eyes open. Dawn had broken, and the sky was growing lighter in the east, pale rays of light beginning to flicker through the curtains in my bedroom.

"Where were you last night around eight? I tried to call you. Jimbo didn't show up again, did he?"

I pushed myself up on one elbow, then shifted a pillow behind my back and leaned against the headboard. What could have chased Murray into such a panic? "The kids and I went out; we had dinner at the FED," I said, using the town nickname for the Forest's End Diner. "What's going on?"

"There was an incident last night. The manager of the Brown Bear Bar & Grill went home late. . . . He found his wife on the floor. She left choir practice early to go home and interrupted somebody ransacking the house. Whoever it was knocked her out, hit her over the head with a blunt instrument. She's in the hospital now. Doesn't remember a thing except some man was in there, but she couldn't describe him because he was wearing a ski mask."

Hello, this was an eye-opener, all right. I downed the glass of water sitting on my nightstand. Suddenly cold, I pulled the blanket up around my shoulders. "Jimbo? You think Jimbo did it?"

She took a deep breath and let it out slowly. "He's our prime suspect at this point. He was in the restaurant last night, ranting at the manager about getting thrown out the other day. He left earlier than usual, drunk. The minute I heard, I called Greg and got the scoop. I'm heading in to work now."

"Do you really think Jimbo would attack a woman?"

Murray fumbled with the phone, and I could hear a zipper being pulled up. She was still dressing. "Jimbo's a big man, Em. He's a loner, and his rap sheet's filled to the brim with assault charges. Remember, he almost killed that transient who murdered his little brother. I've seen a couple of the men he's beaten to a bloody pulp during bar brawls. They were big men, his size, and they were sporting broken noses and jaws and bruises up the wazoo."

Not good news. "Well, hell. How's the manager taking it? He was really nice."

"As well as you could expect him to. He's on a rampage, wants to go find Jimbo himself. Hold on, another call." Nerve-racked and suddenly wishing I was still safely asleep, I waited until she came back on my line. "Okay, that was Greg again. Jimbo's disappeared. Somebody's probably hiding him; my guess is that he might be up in Klickavail Valley. Be careful, please."

"Thanks," I stammered. "Things are getting out of hand. First there's Daniel, then my shop, then the window, then this. And last night I had one hell of a vision while I was scoping out the dragon."

Murray didn't answer for a moment, then she slowly said, "You're right. Something's up. I don't know what it is, but we should get together and talk. Are you positive you still want to go on the camping trip?"

I thought about it. Was it safe to take off, leave the house and go wandering out in the wilds? Maybe, maybe not. But I'd already promised the kids, and I really didn't want to go back on my word. We were only going to be gone for the weekend, and the resort couldn't be any more dangerous than our own home at this point.

I really needed to get away, to destress, and for me, one of the best places to do so was the mountains. There was nothing like the solitude of the wilderness to calm me down and clear my head, and if Jimbo came back for a second break-in, better the kids and I were out of town. Maybe they'd catch him by the time we returned on Sunday.

"Uh-huh," I said with a sigh. "Yeah, the trip's still on. I promised the kids, and I refuse to knuckle under to fear. Now that I think of it, though, I'm going to drop the cats off at a kennel for the weekend. I'd feel better if I knew for sure that they're safe. Can you still go, or is this case going to keep you here?" I selfishly prayed she'd be able to join us. The thought of heading out into the woods without protection scared me. Murray always brought her gun along on road trips.

She snorted. "You don't think I'll actually get assigned to Norma's case, do you? No such luck. So yes, I can still go. I'll meet you tomorrow night at your place, around four? If we head out by five at the latest, we'll get to the resort in an hour or so. Have everything ready to go, and I'll pile my stuff in the car tonight before bed."

I yawned and promised that I'd keep alert. What I wanted to do was to crawl back under the covers and hide, but that wasn't going to happen. I dragged myself out of bed and hit the shower, wincing as the needlelike spray caught my face. Ever since the spirit I'd dubbed Mr. B & U had attacked me in my bathroom, I'd made a few changes. I now had a clear shower curtain so that I could see anybody or anything that decided to invade the room, and a rack on the wall next to the tub so that I need never be more than a hand's grab away from a robe or towel.

A blush of light hit the rose window and spread through the room, splashing the walls with tangerine, a sight that never failed to make me smile. I slathered a dollop of moisturizer on my face, debated on whether or not to bother with makeup, and finally compromised, dusting a thin layer of powder over my cheeks and nose, and swiping my lips with a sheen of bronze lipstick. On final examination, I stopped for a coat of mascara. Harl would be the ruin of me yet, the way she kept pushing me to nurture my inner sophisticate.

I slipped into the sundress I'd worn the night before and raced down the stairs, checking to make certain that the living room window was still in one piece. When I went outside to get the paper, a light breeze ruffled my hair. Looked like it was going to be warm today. We might even reach sixty degrees.

I waved at Horvald, who was out misting his roses, and he waved back. The paperboy had tossed the newspaper in the middle of the front yard again, no matter how often I asked him to either stick it in the newspaper tube under the mailbox or to bring it up to the front porch. I dashed down and snatched it up from the dew-laden grass. On my way back, I stopped and stared at the porch swing.

There, wrapped in a thin tissue paper, sat a gorgeous bouquet of tulips. I picked them up and looked for a card, but there was nothing there. My throat began to close, but a thought hit me and, before I jumped to conclusions, I ran across the street.

"Horvald, did you put these on my porch this morning?" I asked. "There wasn't a card."

He glanced at the tulips and gave me a wide grin. "Missy, I wanted to brighten your day. You seem to have had a rough time of it lately. Any time you want a bouquet for your table, just ask, and I'll make you up a pretty one of whatever flowers I happen to have in season." He went back to his weeding.

I winked at him. "You're a sweetie, Horvald. I appreciate it!" I asked him if he would keep an eye on the house while we were gone—just take a peek out his window now and then to make sure everything looked intact. He promised he would and, relieved, I made my way back over to my house and put the flowers in water, setting the vase on the coffee table. Samantha came along and leapt up to examine the new addition to the living room. I could tell she was debating whether or not to chow down on the leaves. "Stop that you twit. Shoo!" She gave me a snooty look that said I was bright as a dog's butt and huffed her way into the kitchen, tail and nose twitching in the air, to await her majesty's breakfast.

The kids were up; they made a beeline for the fridge, so I grabbed myself a Danish and ate in front of the television, leaving them to breakfast on cereal in the kitchen. The story about Norma Roberts was all over the news. Cathy Sutton was uncharacteristically sober as she reported their findings.

"Mrs. Roberts told her friends at her church choir practice that she had a stomachache and needed to go home early. She left the church at seven-thirty P.M., and a neighbor spied her car pulling into the driveway at around seven forty-five. When Douglas Roberts arrived home at midnight, he found her unconscious, near the front door. Mrs. Roberts is in serious condition, though expected to make a full recovery. She remembers very little of the incident. Her purse is missing, along with several valuable pieces of jewelry."

The camera cut to Tad Bonner, the chief of police. He

looked tired. "Norma Roberts surprised the burglar and was struck with a heavy brass candlestick. It appears that the assailant entered the Roberts home through a side window. We are urging all citizens of Chiqetaw to lock their doors and windows and to prune back any shrubbery that obscures windows or entrances to their houses."

The camera switched to a picture of Jimbo. I stared at the screen, swallowing the mouthful of pastry that was trying to stick in my throat. Bonner continued. "We're looking for James Warren in connection with this case. Warren goes by the nickname of Jimbo, and has a large tattoo of a bat with a skull's head covering his upper left arm. He's currently wanted on an arrest warrant for property damage, and we're asking anyone with any information about Mr. Warren's whereabouts to contact the Chiqetaw Police Department. Do not approach Mr. Warren directly; he may be dangerous. I want to emphasize that Mr. Warren is simply considered a person of interest, and we are not calling him a suspect in this particular case, *at this time.*"

At this time. I heard the emphasis in Bonner's voice.

James Warren. So that was Jimbo's name. Nerve-racked and more than a little scared, I flipped the channel to the Cartoon Network and joined the kids in the kitchen.

"Hey, I'm thinking we should get that home security system we were talking about at dinner last night." I lightened my voice so they wouldn't hear my fear, but they sniffed it out anyway.

Kip eyed me solemnly, spewing Lucky Charms out of his mouth as he asked, "What happened?"

Miranda gave him a disgusted look. "Quit talking with your mouth full, nozzle face." He stuck his tongue out at her; it was covered in crushed oats and marshmallows. When I cleared my throat, they quieted down, and Miranda turned back to me and asked, "Mom, did something happen? You look really upset."

I debated with myself; how much should I tell them? If Jimbo wasn't satisfied with smashing my window, then he might come back. And if he *was* the one who trashed my shop and who assaulted Norma Roberts, then we might all be in danger. I had no choice; they had to be warned.

"Okay. The manager of the Brown Bear Bar & Grill found his wife unconscious on their floor last night. She was hit over the head when she interrupted a robbery at their home. The police think that the assailant may be a man who has a grudge against me. They think he might be the one who broke our window and that he might also have robbed the shop."

Miranda's terrified deer-mouse look sprang to her face. "You made some guy mad enough that he might want to hurt you?"

"What did you do?" Kip interrupted. As usual, he seemed too enthusiastic over what was supposed to be bad news. "C'mon, tell!"

Briefly, I told them about the Jimbo incident. "He wouldn't leave me alone, so I pushed him into a rack of trays. He was drunk, and furious by the time they managed to throw him out."

Randa sniffed. I could tell her sense of outrage was waging war with her fear. "He deserved it. But now you think he might have hurt the manager's wife?"

"I don't know, honestly, and neither do the police. They're looking into it. Until we know the truth, I want you both to be extra careful. When I'm not home, always keep the doors locked. Check who's outside before you let them in. Under no circumstances, open the door to anybody if I'm gone unless you peek out the peephole and see that it's Joe or Murray or Harlow." I sighed. This is what I'd moved to Chiqetaw to avoid. Now the world was slowly but surely catching up.

"Maybe we should get a dog," Kip suggested.

"What's that got to do with anything?" My son could be the king of non sequiturs when he tried.

"Dogs protect their owners."

Aha! Now I understood. The squirt had been trying to get me to agree to a dog for weeks now. To him, this spelled *golden opportunity*. "Nice try, kiddo," I said, "but I don't think so. Samantha and her brood provide enough animal companionship in our home." I decided to drop them off at school. Jimbo might be hanging around, and I didn't want him anywhere near them. "Get your stuff together." I grabbed my purse and keys. With a quick look at Horvald's bouquet, I thought that at least *someone* had managed to brighten my day.

WHEN I GOT to work, Joe had left a message offering to take the kids and me to a movie Friday night. I played phone tag, leaving a message that we'd be gone for the weekend, then turned my attention to the shop. The insurance check hadn't arrived yet, so I put in a quick call to Applewood to ask what was going on. They said it had been processed and would be on its way to my bank shortly.

Cinnamon poked her head around the corner. "Lana wants to know if you still want her to come in today, since there isn't much to do until we get restocked."

I squinted, thinking. I'd been wanting to re-cover the shelves in a different paper; now would be the perfect time, before the new stock arrived. "Tell her to come in now, dressed for grunge work. We'll spiffy the place up while we're waiting for the check. I'm going shopping for paper to line the shelves."

I grabbed the new credit card that my credit company had FedExed me, and headed for Home Depot.

As I poked through the sale bins, not seeing anything I liked, a familiar voice caught me by surprise. It was Eunice

Addison, Walter Mitchell's mother and the donor of all the expensive china I'd soon be getting. I had to be nice to her, even though she set my teeth on edge every time we met. "Emerald, what are you doing here today? What a cute dress—a little short, but cute. It sets off your figure so much better than some of those baggy dresses I've seen you wear."

Baggy? I didn't wear baggy dresses. And *short* was a relative term. My sundress grazed the top of my knees; it wasn't like I was wearing a minidress. I pressed my lips together and smiled.

"I'm sorry about how long it's going to take to get you the china," she said, then lowered her voice. "We heard about the break-in. Shameful, just shameful. All your pretty china. The Ladies' Auxiliary Society discussed the situation the other night, and we wondered if you might be able to plan a tea for us next Thursday? We number fourteen, and we'd love to hold our meeting in your shop if you could provide a light luncheon for us. Nothing fancy, of course, I realize that you've lost a lot of wares."

My jaw dropped. She was actually doing me another favor. "I think we can accommodate your meeting," I stammered. "I'll reserve the tearoom from one until four. Will that be long enough?"

She bobbed her blue-curled head and adjusted her Chanel suit. At least a size too small, the jacket clung to her at an odd angle, but I supposed with the kind of money she had, none of her society friends were going to mention it. "Perfect. Whatever it costs, just have an invoice waiting for me. We'll see you next Thursday, at one P.M., my dear. And good luck with your shopping!"

She wended her way through the aisles toward the front of the store. I scribbled a note in my portable Day-Timer about the tea. "Frilly sandwiches. Watercress. Lemon cake. Petit fours." People never failed to amaze me—and sometimes, it was via a pleasant surprise. Now, back to my hunt. In the last bin of shelf liners, I saw what I wanted: a pale ivory lace pattern dappled with tiny viridian ribbons and plum chiffon flowers. Perfect for the Chintz 'n China.

I carried the last seven rolls to the counter, along with several of plain ivory and lavender in case we needed extra. I handed my card to the cashier, and she rang up my purchases. As she swiped my plastic, a *beep-beep* rang out. Oh great. Now what? "I'm sorry, ma'am, but this isn't going through. It says your account has been closed."

What? Closed? Ridiculous! "That's not possible. This is a new card; they changed my account number, and it should be open and active. Try again, please." I held my breath as she tried again, but once more the beeping signaled a rejection. After the third try, I handed her my personal credit card, and she rang them up on that, but she insisted on cutting up the shop card thanks to some damfool message from the authentication bureau or wherever they ran the credit card numbers through. I stomped back to my store, thrust the contact paper into Lana's arms, and put through the call to the credit card company.

"I'm so sorry," the customer rep said after checking out my account information. "It looks like our operator entered the wrong code and closed your business account after ordering the new card. We'll be happy to reopen it and FedEx you another new card. You'll receive it within three business days."

I sputtered until they gave me an account number to use until I got the new card. "Yeah, I'm sure you're very sorry." Dropping the receiver into the cradle, I leaned back in my chair. Yet another lovely mishap in my week-from-hell marathon.

At least the call to Larry, my sandwich wizard extraordinaire, went okay. "Hey babe, I need a special order next Thursday, a week from today."

"Whaddaya want, hot stuff?" Larry always flirted with me, but I didn't mind. I knew he was joking, and he knew he was joking. It was just his way of being friendly.

"Oh God, I have fourteen society matrons coming in expecting something in the range of a high tea. Better give me an assortment of finger sandwiches . . . cucumber, watercress, tomato, maybe roast beef—the fancy, frilly stuff. I also need cakes and scones. These women are Anglophiles. Petit fours would be great if you have them. For soup, can you give me a light chicken consommé and a shrimp bisque? I can't serve wine here, but maybe you can come up with a trifle? And a veggie-dip platter? That should fill them up." And it would take a hefty bite out of my budget, too. Eunice would be receiving her invoice, all right.

He whistled. "Pricey, but sounds great. Okay. Can do. What time do you want them delivered?"

"Make it noon, since we have to set up by one." I thanked him and signed off, wandering out of my office into the main store. Lana was making headway with the shelf paper. "That's nice, very nice. A good change," I said. "Subtle but pretty." I looked around for something to do, but they had everything under control. I started back toward my office when the phone rang. Cinnamon motioned me over.

"Emerald? It's Lincoln Elementary."

Kip's school? Oh God, now what? I grabbed the phone. "Hello? What's wrong?"

Vonda, the school nurse, answered. "I don't want you to worry, but I'm at the hospital with your son."

"Hospital!" I yelled so loud I'm sure I broke her eardrum.

"Please don't be upset. Kip sliced his thumb open. The cut needs stitches, but it isn't serious."

"Isn't serious? If he needs stitches, it's serious!" Why

did everyone insist on telling me not to worry when I had every reason to panic? "What happened? How?"

"A freak accident. It was Kip's turn to feed the class hamster, and when he finished and headed back to his seat, he tripped over a backpack that had fallen off one of the kid's chairs. He landed on the craft table and sliced his thumb on the paper cutter. We had your permission slip, so I brought him right to the hospital."

I inhaled deeply and let my breath out in a slow stream. "How many stitches are we talking about?"

"Not many. Fifteen."

"That's the whole side of his thumb! I'll be there as soon as I can. Let me speak to the ER nurse."

Vonda put the nurse on.

"Mrs. O'Brien, don't worry. Your son will be fine. The doctor is getting ready to stitch the injury now. Children get hurt like this every day."

"Don't tell me not to worry." I lost it and started yelling into the phone. "I have two children; I know what trouble they can get into. If the cut needs fifteen stitches, it's not a minor cut!" I stopped short. Why was I wasting my time on the phone? "You're sure he's going to be okay?"

She patiently explained once again that Kip was going to be fine, and I forced myself to calm down. She wasn't an idiot, and this wasn't her fault. She was just following procedure. I stammered out a brief apology and said I'd be there in ten minutes. As I hung up, a wave of dizziness swept over me, and I grabbed the counter. Cinnamon raced around to help me to a chair and brought me some water. After a moment, my sense of equilibrium returned.

"I'm okay," I said. "Just stress. This past week has been hell." I sipped the water and asked her to get me an ibuprofen, then told her that I was taking the rest of the day off, along with Friday and Saturday. Since we had no new inventory as of yet, I'd be back on Monday, and she and Lana were to run the shop as usual, finish repapering the shelves, and make the deposits every night. If there was an emergency, she had my cell number, and I authorized her to do whatever she felt best should I be out of contact.

Cinnamon reassured me everything would be fine, and I gave her a quick hug and took off for the hospital. I drove carefully. So many things had happened that I wasn't about to chance anything more.

Eight

✦

VONDA AND THE ER nurse were telling the truth. Kip was going to be fine, and the cut would heal, though he'd probably have a scar. I, on the other hand, was a nervous wreck. By the time I got there, the doctor was bandaging the cut, but not before I managed to get a peek at the line of sutures holding the edges of the wound together.

"What on earth were you doing, honey? What happened?"

Kip told me the whole story again, embellishing it as only a nine-year-old can who has the full attention of an adult. He ducked his head, pain still etched on his face. "I got dizzy and tripped, I guess. I didn't see the backpack."

Vonda chimed in. "Mrs. Weaver feels terrible. She keeps the paper cutter closed, but somehow, today it was open, and when Kip reached out to catch himself, his hand went sliding along the edge. It was a freak accident."

Freak accident. There had been a lot of freak accidents lately. I thanked Vonda and then gave the school nurse

Roy's insurance information. The court ensured he still paid the premiums for the kids. I gathered Kip up, and we headed out to the parking lot, where I made sure he was comfortably settled in the back of the Cherokee. On the way home, we stopped at QFC to pick up the ingredients for fettuccine Alfredo, one of his favorite dishes. I added a peach pie to the basket, greens for a salad, paper towels, and children's aspirin.

As we pulled into the driveway, he touched my arm. "Mom, I know I'm clumsy, but I'm not blind. Mrs. Weaver closed the paper cutter when we were done with our art projects, and that was right before I went over to feed Skippy." His eyes were round, and he looked confused.

"You're sure about that?" One more log to throw on the fire.

He nodded. "Yeah, I'm sure. I saw her check it. She never forgets. I just . . . I dunno, I'm kinda scared. There was a lot of blood."

I ruffled his hair and gave him a kiss on the forehead. "I know, sweetie. Our heads and hands always bleed more than other parts of our bodies, so it does seem scarier. Come on, let's get the groceries inside and make dinner." Kip started to grab one of the bags, but I stopped him, handing him the package with the paper towels in it. "Here, you can carry this one-handed, it's light enough."

Miranda was sitting at the table, her nose in a book and a glass of milk in her hand. She looked up when we came through. "Mom, you're home early!"

"Kip had an accident at school, and we ended up at the hospital." I handed her a bag and she set it on the counter. As I shrugged out of my jacket, she started unloading the groceries. Kip flopped in a chair and leaned back, pale and drawn.

I foraged through the pantry shelves. There! The bottle of tonic I'd made last year. A mixture of herbs, spices, and liquid vitamins, it tasted like plant food but strengthened the blood. Kip grimaced when he saw it but didn't argue; this was a battle he knew he couldn't win.

"One tablespoon," I told him. "Then you can have an Oreo."

He grumbled under his breath but accepted the dark green liquid, wincing as he slurped it down. I handed him a cookie. Randa blanched when I popped a spoonful in her mouth, too. She grabbed a cookie and bit into the dark chocolate, wincing. "Mom, did we ever tell you how rancid that stuff tastes?"

"Many times, and do you think that's going to make me change my mind? This is good stuff, guys; it'll build up your blood—"

"Curl our hair—"

"Give us the strength of Hercules—"

I glared at them, then cracked a smile and laughed. "I know, I know . . . but seriously, it's good for you, so don't complain, okay?"

Randa clutched her hands to her chest and melodramatically swooned to the floor. "We understand, Mother Dear. You give it to us because you love us."

"Smart-ass," I said, grabbing her hand and pulling her to her feet.

In an all-too-rare gesture now that she was a teenager, she threw her arms around my shoulders and gave me a quick peck on the cheek before turning to Kip. "Lemme see your hand." She examined the bandage. "What happened?" He told her the story and, for once she was sympathetic, even going so far as to pour him a glass of milk.

I glanced at her, a gentle smile playing on my lips. "Thanks, Randa. That was sweet of you."

She shrugged. "No biggie."

As I filled the stockpot with water for the noodles, there was a knock on the kitchen door. Oliver slinked in, wearing blue jeans and a work shirt. His hair was thick with dust. He eyed the bustle in the kitchen. "Sorry to interrupt your dinner preparations, but I wondered if you might know anybody who has a pickup? I've got a lot of old boards and stuff to haul to the dump."

I jotted down the name and number of the guy I called when I needed an all-around handyman. "David's done some hauling for me before; he's reasonable."

Oliver pocketed the paper and sat down near Kip. "Hey bud, what's with the bandages?" Kip proceeded to go through his story again, and I could tell he was getting tired. Oliver snorted. "Fell on a paper cutter? That takes talent. They call you Missy Graceful at school now?"

Kip blushed and stared at the floor. Thoroughly pissed at Oliver's callous tone of voice, I wiped my hands on a dish towel, then guided Kip into the hallway. "You look tired. Why don't you go lie down until dinner? I'll call you when it's ready." I smoothed back his hair and gave him a quick kiss on the forehead. Kip flashed me a grateful smile and took off for his bedroom.

I returned to the kitchen and leaned across the table, staring directly into Oliver's face. "Listen to me; I don't care if you're Ida's nephew or the Pope. Don't ever embarrass one of my kids again. Ida won't put up with that behavior when she gets back, so you'd better knock it off. Got it?"

A subtle shift in energy drifted through the kitchen, as if the temperature had just plunged. Oliver hung his head. "I'm really sorry, Emerald. I didn't mean to offend your son," he said. "I'm sorry; please tell Kip that I meant no harm. I'd better be going." Before I could say a word, he vanished out the door.

Miranda gave me a long look. "Mom, Kip said Oliver was in jail."

I rinsed my hands and went back to preparing dinner.

"He spent three years in prison. It wasn't a violent crime; I'd never let a dangerous criminal in the house, so don't worry about that."

She squinted, thinking. "I don't really like him. He doesn't act very much like Ida," she said, glancing nervously at the back door.

I reached over and locked the dead bolt. "Is there something wrong that you're not telling me, Randa?"

After a pause, she shook her head. "Nah . . . just a funny feeling, I guess. Want me to make the salad?"

Salad, she could handle, especially when the greens were precut and washed. I made certain to thank her. Randa was considerably more helpful than she'd been a year ago. While she pulled out the greens and tomatoes, I set about grating cheese for sauce. While waiting for the water to boil, I checked for phone messages. Joe had called.

"Em, this is Joe. I've got to work this weekend after all, so guess Friday night is a complete rain check for both of us. Miss you. Say hi to the kids. Call me at work if there's any trouble." *Click.*

I stared at the pile of parmesan on the cutting board. Joe was busy, and yet he went out of his way to ask how we were, to let me know I could call him any time I was in trouble. Tears pricked the back of my eyelids. Damn it. Why hadn't Andrew phoned me since that first call? Was he so caught up by all the starlets down there that he'd forgotten about me? He knew how upset I was. Didn't he even care? Or was he just tired of my "whining," as he called it? Well, if that's the way he wanted it—

"Mom? Mom?" Miranda poked me in the side and, startled, I dropped the bag of fettuccine noodles. They spilled all over the counter. "Jeez, you okay?"

"Yeah, I'm fine. I was just daydreaming." I gathered up the noodles and slid them into the boiling water.

"Looked more like you were having a daymare to me," she muttered, raising her brow. She went back to chopping tomatoes and slicing the cucumbers.

I had to get hold of myself. With a long, slow breath, I grated the last of the cheese. Finished with the salad, Miranda set the table while I stirred the noodles and whisked the Alfredo sauce, trying to push the dark thoughts out of my mind long enough to focus on what I was doing. They lingered, though, nagging whispers that wouldn't shut up. When dinner was ready, I called Kip from upstairs.

Within minutes, he groggily stumbled into the room, rubbing his eyes. He stuffed his face with a dinner roll before he even slid into his chair. Miranda and I took our places, and we silently dug into our dinner. Nobody seemed to feel like talking. Not a problem, I thought. It wouldn't hurt us to eat in a companionable silence.

After dinner, we checked out the camping gear and rolled sleeping bags. The kids packed their backpacks, while I hit the cupboards, filling a box with enough food to last us a week. Tomorrow, I'd fill the ice chest, then swing by and pick the kids up right after school.

"Can I run over to Lori's?" Miranda asked.

I glanced out the window. Jimbo was out there some-where, and my name was on the top of his list. That made the kids potential targets. "I don't want you walking or taking your bike, but I'll drive you there in a few minutes. Call her to make sure it's okay if you come over."

Delighted at the prospect of a free ride, she put in a call to Lori and received an invitation to stay the night, so I sent her upstairs to pack up her pajamas and her toothbrush. We drove the ten blocks to Lori's house. Lori's parents, a bland, relatively nice couple, seemed thoroughly blasé to anything but their dual careers as lawyers. They promised to drive the girls to school in the morning.

Kip and I stopped at the station house on the way home.

While Bobby, a friend of Joe's, let Kip clamber around in the driver's seat of the fire engine, Joe and I sat outside on a bench in front of the station. I told him about Norma Roberts.

"So Jimbo's prints were on the brick that came through your window? If I find him before the cops do, he'll never throw another rock at anybody's house." The look on his face was volcanic. "He's probably the one who tore up your shop, the slimeball."

"Don't you go getting yourself in trouble because of me," I said.

"If you're going to worry about anybody, worry about Jimbo." Joe noticed I was shivering. The nights were still chilly, and rain was on the way again. He wrapped his jacket around my shoulders.

Touched, I leaned my head against his shoulder for a moment. He slid his arm around me, and we sat there quietly, staring at the indigo ink that stained the evening sky. Finally, I sighed and gently pulled away. "I wonder if Jimbo really conked Norma Roberts on the head. He sure didn't want to take no for an answer when I rejected him, but I chalked it up to boorish, drunken behavior. Now I'm not sure."

"Have you seen him since then?"

"Nope." I shook my head. "I'm hoping by the time this camping trip is over that he'll be in jail and that the police will have figured out the Roberts case."

Joe took my hand and held it between his own. "Call me day or night when you get scared. I'll always come to help you. Even if you and Andrew get married, even if you decide you want to live the rest of your life in seclusion, I'll be your friend, Em." He lifted my hand to his lips.

Trembling from more than the cold, I grazed his cheek with my fingers. "You are a good man, Joe Files. And I've got to round up Kip and get home."

As we drove away from the station house, Kip casually mentioned that he liked Joe. "Andrew's nice, but Joe understands kids better," he said. And I knew, without a doubt, that he was right.

ONCE WE GOT home, I finished loading the dishwasher while Kip played computer games. I was folding the dish towel when Kip yelled for me. Thinking he'd hurt his hand again, I raced into the living room.

He was standing in front of the étagère, and I joined him. "What's going on, kiddo? You see a ghost?" My question wasn't entirely rhetorical; Kip was exceptionally psychic, and we'd had quite a few experiences with spirits.

He shook his head, but his eyes were trained on the dragon. "Mom, something's weird about that statue. I saw the dragon turning by itself. I was at the computer, and it turned and looked at me."

Hell. Not again. If Kip saw it, too, that meant I wasn't imagining things. Not that our lives were exceptionally normal to begin with, but moving statues brought up images of bad B-grade horror flicks. I leaned in to get a closer look. Yep, it had changed position again. I darted over to the desk and flipped open my steno book. Sure enough, it had moved, and nobody else had access to my key.

"Did I say the eyes were glowing?" Kip's voice trembled.

"No, you didn't. What color did they change to?" I already knew the answer.

"Bright red. I'm kind of afraid," he said. "Statues aren't supposed to do that."

"No, statues aren't supposed to do that, are they?" I laid my hand on his shoulder. "It's okay to be afraid, Kip. I get afraid sometimes, too. Our fear helps us know when it's time to be careful. Now, you step back over by the computer." When he had moved aside, I unlocked the door to the étagère and cautiously reached in to pick up the dragon. The statue felt bone cold as I lifted it out of the case and closed the cabinet.

Settling down on the sofa, I cradled the jade in my hands. "Kip, do me a favor. Run upstairs to my jewelry box and get my crystal pendulum." I had a quartz crystal necklace that doubled as my divining pendulum. Kip raced off; after a moment, he breathlessly galloped down the stairs and handed me the necklace. I set the dragon on the table.

"I want you to feed the cats while I do some work here." He hesitated; I could see the interest sparking in his eyes. "Kip—" I warned. With a nod, he was off to the kitchen, a chorus of meows following him.

Squinting, I tilted my head and examined the dragon. The fact that an inanimate object was doing the cakewalk in my china cabinet was, on its own, enough to worry me, but those glowing red eyes . . . Yep, they were a bad sign all right, be the bearer human, animal, or dragon statue. For some reason, red eyes usually equaled mean beasties in the astral realm, and I'd been there, done that, wasn't thrilled about a replay.

"So you *can* move on your own, huh? Okay, let's see what you're made of." I propped my wrist firmly on the arm of the sofa so that the necklace hung over the edge of the table and set the dragon beneath the crystal. Gingerly, I let the necklace swing from the chain until it slowed and then stopped. "Show time. What've you got, big boy?"

As usual, the pendulum started slow, barely moving, but then the chain jerked in my hand and began to swing from side to side as if some invisible force had taken hold of it and was twisting it in circles. Startled, I tightened my grasp as the pendulum speeded up until it was flying in counterclockwise circles.

Gasping, I found myself catapulted into a secluded courtyard. I could see nothing beyond this small enclosure, but the smell of white ginger filled the air, and jasmine flowers peeked from behind the thick hedgerow of vines that bordered the tiled patio. In the center of the patio rested a marble block. A young man of Chinese descent bent over the pedestal, his hands bound, his neck stretched across the marble. He looked to be about twenty years of age. A tall, lean figure shrouded in a black robe loomed over the youth; he carried a long, narrow sword.

To the left, on a gleaming throne, an emperor watched over the scene in the courtyard. He wore a yellow robe decorated with brilliant Mandarin patches, and embroidered on the patches were gilded celestial dragons. The dragons stretched across the back of the robe and down the sleeves. In one hand, he cupped the statue of the jade dragon. With the other, he motioned to the shrouded figure. The executioner swung his sword high. I cringed as the blade hovered over the young man, who cried out in a shrill voice, words I couldn't understand. His eyes raged and as the sword descended, a swirl of smoke appeared in the courtyard, a bloodred mist that seeped into the jade dragon. The young man smiled as the executioner's blade kissed his neck.

Boom. The vision disappeared, and I was still on the sofa, breathless and disoriented. The pendulum was spinning faster now, burning my hand. I reached for the crystal, hoping to put a halt to the crazy carousel ride it was on, but before I could do so, a *snap* sent the quartz cabochon flying across the room. It landed against the opposing wall with a thud. Shocked, I stared at the limp fourteen-karat gold chain that dangled from my hand. The ends had melted, like wax. It was only then that I became aware of a stinging sensation in my palm; the skin had been rubbed raw by the whipping force exerted by the metal. I set the statue on the table and cautiously retrieved the pendant. The quartz cabochon was fractured in a dozen places.

"Damn it! That was my favorite necklace!" A little light-headed from the sudden rush of energy, I leaned forward to observe the statue. What in hell was going on? And had I really just witnessed an execution? I felt queasy; the vision had ended just as the blade touched the young man's neck, but my imagination filled in the blanks all too easily. What was going on? This was the second vision I'd had in two days. Were they images out of the past, giving me a glimpse of the history of the jade dragon? Or were they products of my overactive mind, created in a desperate attempt to bring some understanding to the situation?

Whatever the case, the dragon was harboring some pretty powerful energy. I picked up the figurine again and ran my fingers over it, checking it thoroughly. No wires, no hidden compartments where a motor might be placed, no breaks, no hinges. Preoccupied, I locked it back in the cabinet as Kip returned to the living room.

He looked at me expectantly. "Did it really move?"

I gave him a wary look. "Yeah, it moved. Kip, did you notice anything in particular right before or right after? Anything out of the ordinary?"

He scrunched up his face and finally shook his head. "I just felt like I was being watched." He looked at my pendant. "What happened? Your necklace got broke."

"Broke is right." I sighed. "I don't know why it snapped. Maybe the chain was just getting old." My explanation seemed to calm him down, but in my heart, I knew that wasn't the truth. Whatever energy made my necklace break was connected to the dragon. Where on earth had Daniel Barrington gotten the thing?

I had to find out what I could about its history, and one of the best ways to do that would be to consult the expert in Glacier. Time to give her a call and hope she'd be home this weekend. I found the list Mr. Hodges had given me and picked up the phone to call Mary Sanders. As I introduced myself, it was clear that Harl had called ahead like she said she would. I asked if I could bring the dragon by on Saturday, and Mary agreed to meet me at two P.M. I took down her address and glanced at the clock.

Murray was still at her desk, as per usual these days. She answered the phone on the first ring. "Hey. I was about to leave. I just got those reports finished, and tomorrow should be an easy day for me." She sounded tired but relieved.

"Coughlan's still gone?"

"Till Monday, then it's crunch time again. What's up?"

"What's new? Let's see, Kip cut his hand on a paper cutter at school. He fell on it, actually, said a backpack suddenly appeared in his way and tripped him. We ended up at the hospital getting fifteen stitches in his hand. And the dragon has decided to start moving around, and now I'm getting visions from it."

"Dragon? What dragon?"

"The one Daniel had. It moves." I felt like an idiot, but Murray had seen stranger things than inanimate objects deciding to hoof it somewhere. She'd believe me.

She coughed. "It's a statue, Em. It can't move."

"Oh, yes it can." I told her about the two times we'd caught it in action. "I was going to wait until we reached the resort to tell you about the visions, but I might as well tell you now." I detailed the two scenarios I'd witnessed while holding the statue.

Murray was silent for a moment and then said, "I think you'd better find out more about that thing. Are you sure it's safe to have in the house?"

"Uh, I dunno. It hasn't done anything, other than turn around in circles, break the chain on my pendulum, and take me on a couple of virtual reality trips. I guess it's okay. I'm carting it along with us tomorrow; there's a woman in Glacier that Harlow hooked me up with. An expert on Ming dynasty art, I understand. Has the police department officially given up looking for Daniel's next of kin? I'm thinking that maybe they know something about it."

Murray put me on hold for a moment while she dug out his file. "Yeah, we've closed it down. We haven't been able to locate any family, and we just don't have the manpower to do a thorough search. Nobody seems to know where he lived. His license was expired, and the address on it is out of date."

"Then I've got some sleuthing to do. I'd like to be prepared for any other surprises the creature might have up its scales."

She laughed. "You're talking about that statue like it's alive. You'd better watch it, Em, before your imagination gets away with you. You know, you manage to get yourself in some interesting predicaments, and you usually drag us all along for the ride."

"Speaking of predicaments, did you find Jimbo yet?"

She reluctantly told me she hadn't and promised to make sure a prowl car passed by the house a couple times a night for the next few nights. We chatted a little more, and then she asked, "Do you mind if I add one more person to our camping trip?"

"Another? Who is it?" This was going to be a real gathering. I just hoped that Kip wouldn't ask to bring Sly. I'd tried to put an end to the friendship earlier in the year but ended up feeling sorry for the little runt and let Kip start playing with him again, but Sly still bugged the hell out of me. I just knew he was going to grow up and turn out to be a con man.

"White Deer's coming into town. I thought she'd enjoy the trip."

White Deer, I liked. "Bring her along, she's more than welcome. But I think that's all that will fit in my car." Three adults, three kids and a passel of camping gear. Yep, it would be a snug trip, even in my monster SUV.

Murray said she'd be here at around four P.M., and I told her we'd be ready to go. Kip looked over at me from the computer as I hung up. "White Deer's coming along?" I nodded, and he cheered. The kids had taken quite a shine to her in December, when she'd been visiting Murray. Murray's aunt was following the path of a native healer, though she tended to do things with an updated twist; I gathered her decisions didn't always fly with some of the elders of her tribe.

I glanced at the clock. "Bedtime, skipper. Tomorrow's going to be a busy day, so you hop upstairs and get into your pjs."

He exited his game and put away the CD. I asked him if he wanted me to come up and tuck him in, but he shook his head. "I'm not a little kid anymore, Mom. I can put myself to bed."

My heartstrings quivered, but I gave him a quick hug and peck on the cheek. "Good night, then. You go right to sleep." After Kip trundled off to bed, I curled up on the sofa, wondering what I should do about all the chaos that had been happening lately. Could there be a common focus? I couldn't get a handle on any out-of-the-ordinary energy hanging around, other than my weird but pretty dragon buddy, but that didn't mean some force wasn't around, cloaking itself from me.

I glanced over at the computer that Kip had vacated. Might as well get started investigating Daniel Barrington's past. Though not a computer whiz by any means, I could handle basic searches on the net. I slid into the chair, brought up a browser, keyed in Daniel's name and hit Enter. A few seconds later, the browser displayed a number of results. I began to click through the web sites; the first few pages were no goes, but on the twenty-fourth web site—pay dirt!

The site was one dedicated to psychotic criminals from England. Oh great, had Daniel been a psycho? But no, when I clicked on the name *Barrington,* I began to understand some of his misery. The entry was scanned from a newspaper clipping, dated October 5, 1975. I skimmed through, until I came to the meat of the article.

Harcourt Barrington, 54, was brutally murdered last night by Cheever Douglas, an inmate from the Rainhill Mental Hospital. Douglas escaped in a laundry bin. Once outside the institution, he fled to the outskirts of London where, caught in a downpour, he sought refuge in a farmer's barn. Ian Landers, the farmer, spotted Douglas and chased him off, but not before the inmate managed to secure an ax. Douglas is then thought to have made his way to the Barrington estate, where he broke in and used the ax to murder Harcourt, striking him twenty times.

Barrington is survived by a daughter, Deirdre, 20, and a son, Daniel, 16, both of whom were staying with friends in the country during the attack. Barrington was preceded in death by his wife, Molly, who died in 1967 when she was struck by lightning.

Douglas was caught in a nearby pub, the murder weapon tucked behind a tree near the establishment. His fingerprints were found on the ax and in the victim's home. He is being held back at Rainhill pending his court date.

There was little more on the story or on Daniel's background, but by now I was thoroughly fascinated. The past held some dark memories for him. His father was axed to death, his mother struck by lightning. I wondered just when Daniel had left England. I glanced at the clock. Almost eleven, but maybe I'd look just a little further. I flipped through several more sites and was about to give up the chase when I stumbled across a death notice from an Alberta, Canada, newspaper. From 1986, it must have been archived after the fact.

> Peace River, Alberta, Canada
> December 22, 1986
>
> Marissa Barrington, 26, and her twin boys Charles and Daniel Jr., eighteen months old, were killed this morning in a freak accident when the car they were in crashed through the West Mirror Bridge and sank in the icy waters of the Peace River. Mrs. Barrington was driving the car, and witnesses say it looked like she hit a spot of black ice and lost control. Rescue attempts were mounted but too late; mother and sons were dead by the time rescuers pulled them from the waters. Funeral arrangements are being made by Harper & Harper's Eternal Rest Funeral Home. Mrs. Barrington is survived by her husband, Daniel Barrington. . . .

I stared at the picture of the family. Daniel was young, smiling for the camera, eyes bright and happy. Marissa Barrington had been a dark redhead with delicate skin. She bore a refined look, with a sparkle in her eye that told me I probably would have liked her. The babies were adorable . . . babies who'd never had the chance to grow up.

I printed out the information from the sites and stuffed the pages in a file folder. No mention of the dragon, no mention of his childhood other than the murder of his father and the bizarre death of his mother. Poor man, losing his wife and twin boys must have hit him hard. Where had he been during the intervening time? Had other horrible things happened to him?

My mind wouldn't shut up as I turned off the computer, yawning so wide my jaw popped. Fascinating or not, it was time for bed. I checked the doors and made sure they were locked, then trudged upstairs and fell into a dreamless, uninterrupted sleep.

THE NEXT AFTERNOON, while I was packing the Cherokee, Oliver showed up. I gave him a cool smile. I wanted to like the man since he was Ida's nephew, but the truth was, I didn't feel comfortable around him and couldn't pinpoint why. "What's up?"

"I was wondering if you have someone to look after your cats while you're gone?"

I shook my head. "Thanks, but I dropped them off at the kennel early in the morning."

"I can save you the money." He leaned against the car.

My patience was beginning to wear thin. "No, I said I've already taken them to the kennel. They'll be taken care of, and I won't have to worry about them."

He backed off. "No problem, just thought I'd offer. So, ready for your trip?"

I bit my lip. The poor guy was really trying; maybe I should give him the benefit of the doubt. I'd promised Ida I'd keep an eye on him, and three years in prison had to have skewed his sense of courtesy. No doubt Ida would whip his manners back in shape once she returned.

"Yeah, and we sure need it," I said. "The past week and a half have been traumatic, to say the least. Maybe by the time I'm back, they'll have caught whoever ripped off my shop." He offered to help me arrange the tent and bags in the car. I accepted, then waved as he took off up the street.

I put in a call to Cinnamon to make sure everything was

running smoothly. She said, "Any smoother, and we'd be out of business. We have no stock, and we're down to the lunch crowd."

"Good point," I said. I made sure she had my cell number and the numbers she would need if she had to call Safety-Tech.

By the time I went to pick up the kids at school, the car was packed except for the ice chest. When we got home, Randa raced upstairs to dig out her old telescope, since I refused to let her take her new one. I told her to double-check her window to make sure it was shut tight and locked. As she burst back into the front yard, Lori's mother stopped her BMW in the middle of the street, just long enough for Lori to scramble out of the car. I waved, but the woman had already squealed off in a cloud of dust. Somehow, I didn't think we'd be getting together with the Thomas family for dinner any time soon.

One last stop at the étagère to tuck the dragon into a padded package, and we were ready. Mary Sanders's address was secure in my purse, though I supposed she wouldn't be hard to find in such a small town. I locked the door and went out to stow Lori's backpack in the SUV just as Murray and White Deer rolled into the driveway, with Joe right behind them. He made us stand back while he transferred Murray's equipment to my car. Murray grimaced when I asked how her day had been.

"One of those 'don't ask' days. I've been getting enough of those to last a lifetime. Hey, Joe's done! Let's roll. It's going to get dark pretty quick in the mountains."

I gave Joe a hug; he pulled me close and tapped me on the nose. "You be careful, witchy woman. I don't want to have to come rescue you again."

"You be careful at work this weekend," I countered. "You've got a dangerous job, and I want you to promise me to watch your step."

He gave me a quick squeeze. "You've got it, woman! I'll be careful. Say hi to Smokey the Bear for me!"

Laughing, I motioned to the others, and we piled in the Cherokee, leaving Murray's car in the driveway, and headed for the highway. Pushing aside worries about Jimbo and conks on the head and dragons that moved by themselves, I made the decision that nothing was going to ruin this weekend. Nothing.

Nine

❖

AS WE WOUND through the road leading to Mount Baker, the sun slowly began to sink into the west. Days in the temperate rain forest always seemed to darken earlier than they did in the city, with thickets of fecund vegetation crowding out the light. Few people realized just how alive these mountains were. The Cascade Range had given birth to a family of volcanoes. Mount Rainier, a pristine, snow-covered peak, was as dangerous as she was beautiful, towering over Seattle as a constant reminder of the destruction forces that had, and would again, overwhelm the coastal region.

As if to prove her sister's claim, Mount St. Helens blew her stack in 1980 and laid waste to a swath of land that now resembled the craters of the moon. I'd been there once, picking through the desolate and eerie landscape. And then there was "our" volcano. Isolated, covered in glaciers and snow, Mount Baker housed some of the most rugged forests in the state. Buttressed against the North Cascades

National Park, the mountain claimed a quiet and isolated throne for itself.

As we hugged the curves on Highway 542, Murray and I quietly discussed what I'd found out about Daniel's past. With Lori and Miranda immersed in a debate about women astronauts, and White Deer and Kip chatting away, I didn't have to worry about being overheard.

By the time we reached Maple Falls, I'd been driving thirty-five minutes, and it was nearing six P.M. We made a quick stop for last-minute supplies, then headed on toward Glacier, some seven and a half miles up the road. The town, barely larger than a postage stamp, was located within a valley inside the Mount Baker National Recreation Area, and acted as a gateway to the Mount Baker Wilderness Area. We rolled on through, anxious to get to the lodge before dark.

"Where's the lodge?" Murray consulted her map.

"Left on Paintbrush Loop, about five miles ahead." I opened my window and took a deep whiff; the air was so clean and crisp here that it pierced my lungs. The vegetation grew thick as the highway curved along; firs heavy with moss crowded both sides of the road, leaving only a narrow runway of sky to filter through. As we pushed farther into the heart of the forest, the light became muted, dappled with shadow, offering dark recesses within the thickets. The racket in the car began to die down as the ever-present trickling of miniature waterfalls alongside the road grew louder.

"There's the turnoff," I said, pointing at the graveled drive to our left. Named for the wide swathes of Indian paintbrush that bordered the roads during summer, Paintbrush Loop led through a thick copse of cedar and fir, out into an open meadow containing the main lodge of Tyler's Resort, along with seven cabins. Patches of snow still dotted the upper reaches of the lea. Since the resort was so popular,

I'd made reservations early, just in case, but the parking lot was nearly empty. We tumbled out of the Cherokee.

I stretched and popped my back. A sudden gust of wind sent me reeling. Nothing like mountain air to wake up the senses. "Come on, let's go check in."

The lodge had been built sometime in the sixties but had been recently remodeled. To the left, the lobby led to a dining room; to the right stood the inevitable gift shop next to the rest rooms. While Kip and Miranda headed to the bathrooms, I gave my name to the registration clerk. She pushed the book across the counter.

"Hello, I'm Marjorie. Please sign in and list all members in your party."

I did as she asked and handed over my credit card. She swiped it through the slot. "Not many people here," I said, glancing around.

Marjorie shook her head. "April's our transition month. Too late for skiers, too early for summer tourists. You can have your choice of cabins. They all have the same layout: two bedrooms, a small kitchenette–living area, full bath, gas heat, and a woodstove. There's a fire pit outside each cabin, along with a picnic table, so you can roast marshmallows if you want. The firewood's in the bin next to each cabin."

She showed me a map, and I chose Meadow Lark, the cabin farthest away from the lodge. It might be too cold to camp outside, but at least we wouldn't have to be next to the main drive.

She typed in our cabin number on the screen. "Newlyweds are staying in Briar Rose, and an elderly couple is staying in Salmon Creek, closest to the lodge. They have a chocolate Lab, but he's well-behaved. Other than that, you've got the entire area to yourselves. The lodge is open twenty-four hours a day; if there's an emergency, just come on in and push that buzzer. Somebody will be out to help you immediately." She pointed out the emergency buzzer. I hoped we wouldn't have to use it.

"There's a pay phone outside the lodge and two in the lobby. The dining room is open from six A.M. to three P.M., and from five P.M. until nine-thirty P.M. Last seating for dinner is at nine o'clock. The hot tub and swimming pool are around back, with an outside entrance. They close at ten P.M. Here's your receipt and your key cards."

She handed me two wafer-thin cards. High tech meets Bambi, I thought. I thanked her, then we drove over to our cabin. I perched myself on the picnic table while the others unpacked, turning slowly to take in the view. The place was as pretty as I'd remembered it. One time, when Roy and I began to realize things weren't going too great in our marriage, we'd hired a baby-sitter and come up here to talk things over. I'd never forgotten the sheer beauty of the trip, even though we'd argued constantly.

Lori and Miranda would take the back bedroom, with Kip sleeping on an air mattress on the floor. Murray, White Deer, and I would share the other bedroom. I asked Randa and Lori to go fetch some wood. They raced off, giggling. It was good to see my daughter happy. Sometimes I worried that she'd *never* find a close friend.

While I put away the food, Murray went outside to set up the fire pit. White Deer and Kip finished carting in the last of the supplies.

"Mom, can we go exploring?" Randa asked after she and Lori brought in several armloads of wood. I excused them on the promise that they wear their whistles at all times and be careful if they meet any strangers.

"I want to go look at the stream! It's right inside the woods over there." Kip pointed to the edge of the woods encroaching on the open meadow.

We walked over toward Salmonberry Creek. Wide and shallow at this point, it tumbled down from the glacier-clad mountain, with narrow forks diverting off into the forest all along its route. Eventually, these forks wore down the soil, forming ravines throughout the woods. Even from ten yards away, I could hear the roar of the whitecaps.

"The glacial runoff is too high. It's white-water season, and the current is rolling along at a pretty good clip. I don't think you'd better go over there alone, you'd drown if you slipped and fell in."

"I'll go with him," White Deer volunteered.

I laughed. "Hey, if you want to go frog hunting with Kip, be my guest." They took off, leaving Murray and me alone. We walked back to our cabin in silence, letting the cool mountain air play over us. I inhaled deeply to flush out the stress of the last few days.

"I'm going to start dinner," I said. Murray followed me, and while I got out the ingredients for mac 'n cheese, she lit a fire in the woodstove. The gas heat would make a nice backup, but there was nothing like the smell of woodsmoke to whet the appetite. We worked in silence, listening to the birdsong echo through the meadow as they winged their way home to their nests for the night.

Murray stretched out in the rocking chair that sat by the bay window overlooking the back of the meadow. "I'm so glad I came," she said.

I poured noodles into the boiling water and began slicing tomatoes for the salad. "It's good, isn't it?" And it was. I sat down at the table and yawned, rolling my neck first to the left, then to the right. I eased into a full stretch. "Oh, yeah, I needed this."

Murray tried to smile but her facade quickly dissolved. "I've been so stressed out the past month that I never sleep anymore, and I haven't had any time to give to Sid and Nancy." Sid, a red-tailed boa, was always overanxious to make friends, and Nancy, a toothy gnarly green tree boa, delighted in climbing onto wall fixtures and leaning out to

flick her tongue at unsuspecting guests. Murray doted on
her reptilian babies and didn't understand why some of her
visitors cautiously sidestepped the constrictors.

"You really hate the new job, don't you?" I opened my
purse and pulled out a Hershey's Krackle bar. I snapped it
in two and tossed her half. "Here." I firmly subscribed to
the idea that chocolate was a wonder drug whose benefits
had been long overlooked by the AMA.

She put the candy in her mouth and sucked on it a
moment. Then she shrugged. "What can I say? There's no
going back. I don't want to sell my house and move away,
so I have to learn to accept it."

Sometimes her fatalism got to me, but usually, I kept
my mouth shut. That primal acceptance of what befell her
was an essential part of Murray. Today, however, I was in
one of my stubborn moods. "I know you like to go with the
flow, but it seems to me that the current's heading directly
for the sewer with you in tow. How can you let Coughlan
get away with the bull he's pulling?"

She tried to explain. "Don't you see? If I complain, I'll
be labeled a snitch, and nobody will ever trust me again.
This isn't a high-powered division in the city where bad
PR will pose a threat to their image. We're talking about
the Chiqetaw police station."

I shook my head. "So, if they came out and said, 'Murray, we don't want you here because you're Indian' or
'because you're a woman,' you'd accept it and go peacefully? Don't ask me to buy that—"

"This is different, Em. I can't explain. It . . . it's just different. If I do my job and prove myself, Coughlan will
eventually have to respect me."

Different my ass, but I could see she didn't want to talk
about it. She was deliberately blinding herself from the
truth, a trait Murray had never before exhibited as long as
I'd known her. Something was going on, but I had enough

to handle with the problems piling up in my own life. I decided to back off. I stood up and dusted my hands on my jeans, then leaned out the door, my voice echoing as I called for everybody to hightail it back to the cabin for dinner.

White Deer and Kip trudged up from the creek; Kip's sneakers and the cuffs of his jeans were soaked. I raised one eyebrow.

"Frog chasing," White Deer said. "It wasn't the creek; he ran through a little rivulet that feeds into the stream. Ankle deep at the highest."

Kip grinned at me. "The whitecaps on the stream were pretty rough. I promised I wouldn't go in, and I didn't."

"Honestly. You'd manage to get wet if the nearest mud puddle were a hundred miles away. Go change and hang those near the stove so they dry out." How boys' clothes always managed to find the quickest route from the closet to the hamper was beyond me, but Kip kept a never-ending stream of laundry flowing my way.

He grinned and raced off to the bathroom. A few minutes later, he handed me the wet jeans, and I draped them over a hanger and hooked it near the stove.

While the girls washed their hands, White Deer set the table. "Oh, that smells heavenly," she said as I dished up dinner for the kids.

Lori wrinkled her nose as she slid into her place and grabbed her fork. "We don't get to eat macaroni and cheese at home. Mom says it's *bur-gee-swa,* but I like it. I always buy my lunch at school when they have spaghetti 'n stuff like that."

Bourgeois, huh? That told me just which rung on society's ladder Lori's parents had me pegged for. I poured her a glass of milk. "So, your parents are both lawyers?"

She nodded, a white ring forming around her lips from the milk. "Yeah, though Mom's on leave on account of she had a nervous breakdown a year ago when she lost a big case and got fired from her firm. Dad was offered a partnership up here by some old college friend of his. We lived in Bellevue." That explained a lot. Bellevue, land of the uber shoppers and high-tech millionaires. I bet anything they lived on Mercer Island, where the water ran brown and the blood ran blue.

"Well, I hope you enjoy the weekend," I said. She gave me a thumbs-up and dug into her food. After dinner was over and the dishes put away, Miranda asked if we could bundle up and go stargazing. We gathered up graham crackers, marshmallows, chocolate bars, blankets, and her telescope, and headed outside where the night sky had deepened into a brilliant indigo, and stars twinkled overhead like icicles on a Christmas tree. We gathered around the stone-ringed pit as Murray and White Deer set a fire to crackling.

After watching the flames for a while, I put myself in charge of the assembly line of graham crackers and chocolate bars. Smores. Yum. White Deer had brought one of those old-fashioned cast-iron popcorn poppers, and she shook it over the fire, waiting for the kernels to explode into white cotton. Twenty minutes later, covered with melted chocolate, strings of marshmallow, graham cracker crumbs, and salt from the popcorn, we looked like we'd just finished looting Wonka-Land. *We're just a gang of rogue Oompa Loompas,* I thought, passing out the Wet-Wipes.

Randa and Lori headed out into the middle of the meadow, telescope in hand. Deciding to brave the chill, the rest of us followed, oohing and aahing over the vista of sky that unfolded over our heads. We took turns with the scope as the girls pointed out constellations and planets until we were all thoroughly chilled and our heads were spinning with visions of stars.

On our way back to camp, Kip froze, pointing out two deer standing silent on the other side of the lea. Randa worked her hand into mine and leaned against me, resting her head on my arm. Lori nudged her way closer to me on the other side, and I reached out to encircle her shoulders with my free arm. She relaxed when she felt my arm, and I could sense her mingled fear and wonder as she watched the hinds. Murray and White Deer knelt near the rocks. Kip followed suit.

The deer were vigilant but unafraid, and they continued their feed until, satiated, they picked their way across the lea and vanished into the forest. As I watched them go, I had a sudden, swift longing, wishing that they would stay, that we could stay and leave everything behind. When the deer were out of sight, White Deer laughed. Her voice tinkled through the night air. "On that note, it's time to douse the fire and go inside."

Kip yawned and slipped into his sleeping bag without any prompting. Lori and Randa followed suit, climbing into bed without a murmur of complaint. I left a night-light burning so they could find their way to the bathroom and opened their door just a crack so we could hear them if something happened during the night.

We turned off the lights so that only the crackling flames from the woodstove lit the cabin. White Deer and I curled up on the sofa. Murray stood at the window, staring out into the night. She squinted, then said, "I see two bats."

White Deer gave her a long look. "You know what that means. Renewal through rebirth. The choice of transformation." Murray tried to shush her, but White Deer brushed her off. "You hate your new job; you're not being treated fairly, yet you refuse to do anything about it."

"I am doing something—my job!" Murray turned away from the window. "I'll be back in a minute," she said abruptly. "I'm going to the bathroom."

After she left the room, I leaned over and said in a low voice, "She's stubborn."

White Deer grinned. "She's always been stubborn. So is

Lila, her mother. Murray could be her twin. That's why they don't get along very well. They lived with me, you know, when Murray was a little girl. I've never seen such a willful child."

She gave me a long look; her eyes reflecting the glow of the flames. My psychic radar jumped. I had long known that White Deer possessed strong medicine; her totem was the lynx, the bearer of secrets. For as little as she spoke, she was an excellent teacher. Now that we were out in the mountains, her strength and power illuminated her like a beacon.

"Yeah, she told me. She said you put them up for several years, including Harvey." An alcoholic, Murray's brother was in jail more often than he was out of it. Harv wasn't a violent man, just lost.

As if reading my mind, White Deer said, "I think she tries so hard because of her brother. He's the black sheep of the family, you know. Lila and Charley were disappointed by the way he turned out, and Murray does her best to make up for his mistakes. The sad thing is, she doesn't have to. She chooses to accept a burden that they never placed on her shoulders. Lila and Charley love her for herself, and they love Harvey, too, even though he's always in trouble."

"What are they up to now?" Every September, we drove over to the Quinault reservation for the Murray family fish fry, where Charley's parents threw a party on the reservation that lasted three days. All their children came home for the annual event, along with everybody they considered part of their extended family. Lila and Charley always included us in their invitation, and we stayed on their ranch, making our camp in the loft in the barn.

White Deer shook her head. "Charley and Lila opened a small store. Souvenirs and stuff, you know—tourist crap, fry bread, a few groceries. They make enough to get by. I help out when I can."

The bathroom door opened, and we changed the subject as Murray returned. I felt a vague sense of guilt, as if we'd been talking behind her back, even though we really hadn't. As the ink-stained night engulfed the wilderness, a brilliant flare streaked by, arcing across the heavens.

"A shooting star! Make a wish." Murray put her arm around my shoulder as we stood side by side at the window, watching.

A wish . . . I closed my eyes tight and wished that things would sort themselves out . . . for me, for Murray . . . for everybody I knew and loved.

THE NEXT MORNING, we awoke to birdsong and the glimmerings of a clear morning. Murray volunteered to make blueberry hotcakes while White Deer commandeered Kip and the girls for an early-morning hike and then a plunge into the hot tub. I glanced at my watch. Eight-thirty.

"Murray, in your opinion—your gut feeling, not your official position as a detective—do you really think Jimbo attacked the Roberts woman?"

She stirred the batter, pouring in a dollop of vanilla and a scoop of blueberries. "I don't know, Em. As I said, he's been in and out of trouble since he was fifteen, but the truth is that Jimbo hasn't ever attacked a woman. For all of his charges, rape or attempted rape never entered into them, and he's never been charged with battery of any kind against a woman. Every man he's been in a brawl with was just as mean as he was."

"If they catch him, can the judge just let him go free?"

She shrugged. "Depends on whether he can make bail. Anyway, the issue is moot if the department can't catch him." She poured batter in the pan and adjusted the flame. "Do I think Jimbo attacked Norma? Honestly, I don't know.

I just wish we could find him. The fact that he's running doesn't look good. Why do you think I made sure I left work on time yesterday? I wasn't about to let you come up here alone."

Grateful, I gave her a quick squeeze around the shoulders. "So, where does that leave me? I've got a security system at the store, but I feel weird getting one for the house. We didn't move to Chiqetaw just to become prisoners in our own home." As the heady aroma of hotcakes filled the room, I arranged the bacon on a square griddle pan and slid it on the back burner. Then I set the table with butter and syrup.

Murray cleared her throat. "Look, I know you don't like it, but your first concern should be the safety of your family. If you get a security system that just ties into the doors and windows, then you won't have to worry about Kip setting it off when he gets up to go to the bathroom."

"Yeah, but won't the kids have to remember the alarm every time they run in and out? And what about Miranda and her star watching on the roof? She comes and goes through her window. Eventually somebody's going to forget."

"There are ways around that; security systems are a lot more flexible than they used to be. The question should be: Do you trust Jimbo enough to think that he won't hurt you or the kids?"

I lowered myself into a chair by the table. "That was hitting below the belt, but you're right. I guess for safety's sake, I'd better call Safety-Tech when we get home."

"I know how much you hate the idea, but honestly, it's going to be a lot safer for you." The bacon sputtered as she slid another pancake onto the warming plate. We heard voices. White Deer and the kids were back. Breakfast time.

At one-thirty P.M., I left the kids with White Deer and Murray and drove into Glacier. Mary Sanders's house wasn't hard to find, and as I pulled into the driveway, I saw her peeking out the window. She must have been waiting for me.

Mary wasn't anything like I'd expected her to be. Harlow's artsy friends were usually polished and honed to a sharp edge. More often than not, they would greet me with a polite murmur, then totally ignore me the rest of the night. Mary Sanders was rounded, apple-cheeked, wearing a dress and apron that would have been a hit back in the fifties with the suburban-mom crowd.

"Come in, please, make yourself at home." She steered me to the kitchen table, where a teapot and two teacups rested. "I thought you might like a cup of tea. Harlow says you own the Chintz 'n China Tea Room, and I thought, *Why, Mary, I think that's where Edward said he got the tea set that he gave you for Christmas,* so I asked him, and sure enough, he bought it at your shop last December."

Her words fluttered around my head like a bevy of birds. When I finally realized she'd stopped talking, I graciously accepted her offer. "Thank you for seeing me today. Harlow said you might be able to figure out a puzzle I've gotten myself into."

She poured our tea and settled herself at the table. "Harlow said you were searching for information on a statue?"

I pulled out the bubble-wrapped package. "A figurine, really. Your specialty is the Ming dynasty?" My preconception of what Mary Sanders would be like ran smack up against the image of the woman sitting across the table from me.

"I have a master's degree in fine art, specializing in Chinese porcelain. I wrote my thesis on the art of the Ming dynasty." She pulled out a pair of glasses from a case in her apron pocket and slipped them on her face.

I set the dragon on the table. Mary's expression shifted, and the bright friendliness changed to intense curiosity. I could tell that she was in her element. She picked up the dragon and turned it over, examining the etched marks that circled the statue. After a moment, she set it down again and told me she'd be right back. When she returned to the table, she carried with her a couple of oversized books and a notepad.

Not wanting to interrupt her, I glanced around the kitchen. On the surface, it was as homey and cozy as Mary seemed to be, but when I looked closely at the art on the wall, I realized that the prints were actually originals. What I'd thought were replicas of Depression glass also proved authentic when I cautiously lifted one piece and glanced at the markings on the bottom.

Mary flashed me a quick smile. "You like my collection? Everything here is authentic except the art on the walls. That painting up there—the one that looks like Norman Rockwell—that's my latest attempt at a re-creation."

Her attempt? "You painted that? You're talented!"

She laughed. "No, but I'm good at copying. My originals are about as eye-catching as a wet cat." She turned her attention back to the books she'd brought with her and jotted down a note on her tablet. A second cup of tea later, she sat back, tapping the page with satisfaction. "Got it!"

"You found something?" I straightened up. So far, all I knew was that Daniel had led an unhappy and tragic life.

"I don't know where you got hold of this statue, but the dragon's markings coincide with the description of a piece that was created during the time of the Emperor Wan-Li, who ruled during the decline of the Ming dynasty. A young sculptor made it for the emperor's birthday. He was supposedly one of the emperor's favorite artists."

Young sculptor? Emperor? Déjà vu. My vision. I had the sinking feeling I already knew the rest of the story.

She skimmed the page. "It says here that Huang Fu was an artist of rising fame who the Emperor Wan-Li had taken under his wing. Unfortunately, Huang Fu was caught with his fingers in the royal cookie jar, so to speak. That alone warranted a death sentence."

I looked at the little dragon. "You've got quite a history, bud. So Huang Fu was killed?"

"Well, yes, in the end," Mary said. "But before he was sentenced, Wan-Li discovered that Huang had been carrying on with one of his nieces and had gotten her pregnant. During interrogation, Huang admitted that he'd stolen the money so he could sneak off before he was caught."

"I can imagine," I said. If the sentence for thievery was death, I wasn't sure I wanted to know what the punishment would be for knocking up a royal niece.

"The emperor ordered Huang beheaded and imprisoned his niece. Before Huang Fu's execution, Wan-Li forbade priests from praying for the young artist, ensuring Huang would then wander forever as a ghost, lost and without direction."

"Good grief, he really wanted to punish him, didn't he?"

"Well, understand that Huang was supposed to be a friend of the court; he wasn't just some common thief. When he betrayed the emperor, it was a matter of honor."

I could see that. Betrayal was hard to bear; the emperor would have had to regain his pride in the eyes of his court. Cruel, yes, but par for the course as far as egos went.

"Right before Huang was beheaded, he was informed that the niece had been forced to miscarry. Huang called down a demon and invoked a curse on the statue. Any family possessing it would suffer grave misfortune. After Huang died, it wasn't long before the reign of Wan-Li fell into an abyss of corruption, and the Ming dynasty was tottering on its last legs by the time the emperor died. The statue disappeared at some point during the last years of his rule."

Good God! So that's what I was dealing with? A cursed statue? I stared at the dragon. Curses were usually just tricks of the mind, but both Kip and I had seen the dragon move, and I knew, I knew in my gut, that the story was true.

Somehow, Daniel had come across the artifact. His father had been murdered, his mother struck by lightning, Daniel had died in a tragic accident, as had his wife and twin boys. The hex was active, and now the damned dragon belonged to me. I sighed, letting my breath trickle out between my teeth. "Okay, so it's cursed. Do your books say anything about getting rid of the hex?"

Mary lifted one eyebrow but went back to poring over the book. After a moment, she glanced back at me. "No, but it does say that the curse will affect the entire family of the person who possesses it, and that getting rid of the dragon won't lift the curse. Apparently it just extends it to include the next owner."

I inhaled sharply. Wonderful. How many families had been destroyed by the bad luck this little statue seemed to magnetize? I toyed with the dragon. "And you're sure this is the same jade dragon?"

Mary closed her books and pushed them aside. As she removed her glasses, her gaze was troubled. "I wish I could say no, but I think they're one and the same. I don't know if I believe in curses or not, but I sure wouldn't want to own that little piece of jade, I'll tell you that."

Great. Now to find a way to break the curse on a jade dragon that was almost five hundred years old before it destroyed my family and me. And in the meantime, I'd have to protect it with my life, because if it disappeared, I'd never have a chance to break the curse, and we'd be doomed for sure. I slid the statue back in its envelope and spent another few minutes chatting with Mary before I thanked her and headed back to the cabin.

BY LATE AFTERNOON Miranda and Lori were arguing. I broke up their squabble and marched Randa down to the creek. We sat on a granite boulder, watching the current burble along as the whitecaps crested against the shore.

After she'd had a moment to cool down, I asked, "What's the matter with you? Why are you being so bitchy? I thought you were having fun."

She shrugged. "Yeah, we were, but then Lori told me she wants to run for secretary of the astronomy club. I wanted that job. It's the only one that they'll consider a teenager for, and I've been in the club a lot longer than she has."

"Verging on whiny, miss." I tapped her on the knee. "So you think that because you want the same job, she should bow out and not run."

"Well . . . yeah. She wouldn't even know about the astronomy club if I hadn't introduced her there."

Ah, self-righteous *and* possessive. My delightful daughter. I tried to help her find a way to deal with her anger. "You know, that's a big job. Why don't the two of you take it on as a joint project?" Her look told me just what she thought about that idea. "Did you ever tell her that you want the job?"

Randa squirmed. "Well, no, it hasn't come up."

"So you're mad because she wants a job that she doesn't even know you're interested in?" Good, we were getting somewhere.

Tossing a pebble in the stream, she sighed and crossed her legs, balancing on the boulder. "I guess that does sound stupid. Maybe we *could* do it together. That way it wouldn't interfere with homework."

Her logical nature was taking over, just as I'd hoped. "That's a good idea and will make it easier for you both to handle the job. You're a smart kid, you know that? Now, why don't you go find her and apologize? Talk things out."

She unfolded her legs and stood, giving me a quasi-apologetic smile before she went lithely bouncing across the river rocks that had been left behind when the glaciers swept through the area, great sheets of ice inching across the land, leaving massive alluvial deposits in their wake.

I leaned back against the boulder, staring at the sky. A hawk hovered in the distance, searching for dinner. Ancient energies haunted these mountains, reverberating through the canyons and rivers and streams, down into the valleys through which they had roamed for thousands of years. It was as if I could hear whispers from the past echoing in the breeze. I wondered if the spirits bound to this place could help me break the dragon's curse but shook off the thought. The statue belonged to a different land, a different culture.

Not wanting to leave but suddenly feeling in need of human contact, I made my way back to our cabin and joined the sing-along White Deer had started around the fire. Afterward, she told us legends about the volcanoes along the Cascade Range from the lore of her people.

After a dinner of pan-fried chicken and corn on the cob, I linked my arm through Murray's, and we strolled around the perimeter of the meadow, stopping to examine the early wildflowers that dotted the lea. "White Deer's really wonderful. She must have had quite an impact on your life."

"Yeah, she's pretty impressive, isn't she? I wish she lived here. I could use some guidance now, with the job and my lack of a personal life." She sighed, frustration tingeing the edge of her words. I kept my mouth shut; she just needed to vent.

We returned to the cabin, where I made hot chocolate before we turned in. Randa begged me to let Lori and her stay up late to stargaze. Barely able to hold my eyes open, I dragged a promise out of her that they would keep bundled up, stay by the picnic table, and be back in the cabin by midnight. I crawled in bed next to Murray and fell asleep the minute my head hit the pillow.

"Mom, Mom." Somebody was shaking me; muffled whispers woke me up. As I shook off the layers of sleep-induced fog, I realized that Randa and Lori were trying to rouse me. Murray and I sat up at the same time, waking White Deer, who was curled up in her sleeping bag on an air mattress. Kip wandered into the room, rubbing his eyes.

I pushed myself into a sitting position. "What's going on?"

"There's a bear outside. Near the picnic table."

Bear? A bear was prowling around outside our cabin? I glanced around; everybody was accounted for. "What time is it?"

Randa held up her watch. "Almost midnight. We were on our way in when we saw it over by the car."

We all headed for the living room. White Deer beat me to the window; she pulled back the curtain and peered out into the darkness. "Oh yes," she said. "That's a bear all right, and it's near your car. Don't turn on the light yet, I want to see what it's up to."

Murray was fumbling with something. I realized she was checking her gun. "The car? What's it doing near my car?"

White Deer suddenly opened the window and started shouting. Everybody stared at her. She yelled, "Turn on the lights. We need to chase it away, it's doing something to your SUV!"

I flipped on the lights and leaned out the window next to her. The bear was pawing at the tailgate on my Cherokee. The creature was huge. No way in hell was I gonna go outside to try to stop whatever destructive frenzy Big Boy had worked himself into. "You goober! You'd better not break my back window! Go away, you damn grizzly!"

White Deer looked at me, amusement playing over her face. "Black bear."

Black bear, brown bear, grizzly, or polar, I didn't care. The beast was four-legged, had long claws, and stood way too tall for my comfort. In the pale light of the stars, we could see its silhouette as it lumbered around the camp. Oh yeah, right at home. The wilderness belonged to bears and mountain lions, and I suddenly felt like an intruder, but intruder or not, I didn't want it messing up my wheels.

Kip shoved in between us and peered out the window. "Wow! He's huge! Is he going to tear up the Jeep?"

"I hope not, honey. The last thing I need right now is a car repair bill."

The bear raised its head and sniffed the air, snuffling as it tested the scents floating on the breeze. Then, with a grace I never thought possible for such a big animal, it turned and glided out of the meadow, heading for the woods. I slumped back on the bed. Beautiful, yes, but also dangerous. I hadn't seen any cubs nearby, so I assumed it was either a male or a lone female.

Murray found a battery-operated lantern and, once it was clear that the bear was gone, went out to check my car. When she returned, her face was set in stone, and I could tell she was trying not to laugh. "Okay, we thought we bagged all our garbage, but I found a package of marshmallows out there, and a handful of candy wrappers. That's what attracted it."

"And the car?"

"You'd better go have a look." She handed me the lantern and guided me out to the Jeep.

"I just hope Mr. Fuzzypants is gone for the night," I muttered.

We stopped in front of my car, where Winnie-the-Pooh's big brother had decided to gouge a long scratch along the side. I was looking at one expensive paint job, unless I decided to leave it as a conversation piece. I supposed I could use it as a great icebreaker. *"What'd you do*

*last weekend?" "Watched a bear tear up my car, wanna
see the scratch?"*

I returned to the cabin. "Okay, show's over. Everybody
get back to bed." The girls headed into their bedroom,
whispering about their close encounter. Kip trailed behind,
grumbling that he wished he'd been outside with them.
When the kids were tucked in, I slumped at the table, resting my chin on my hands. "When I think of the girls out
there alone . . . they could have been killed."

White Deer put her hand on my shoulder. "No harm was
done, except for your car. Be grateful for the blessings
instead of focusing on the negative, Emerald."

"I know," I said. "Believe me, I am grateful. I'm just—
we came up here to relax, and now the girls get into a tangle with a bear."

"You're exaggerating," White Deer cautioned me. She
was about to say more but then stopped as Murray shot
back inside. She'd been out gathering an armful of wood
and now she dumped it in the wood box and stoked the fire.

"Em . . ."

"What? Don't tell me the bear damaged anything else?"

"Not the bear, no. Do you have a spare tire?"

"Why?" I didn't want to hear the answer.

"You've got a flat; looks like you drove over a nail or
something and developed a slow leak. We'll have to
change the tire."

I flounced over to the bed. "It can wait until morning."

White Deer crawled back in her sleeping bag, and Murray stretched out after making sure the door was firmly
latched. I shoved my feet under the covers, flopped over on
my side, and pulled the covers up to my chin. If only I
could sleep for a week, maybe then things would start getting back to normal.

Ten

❦

IT WAS STILL early by the time we reached Chiqetaw, not quite nine-thirty. On the way through town, we dropped Lori off before heading home. We'd pick up the cats in a little while. Murray and White Deer had a busy day ahead of them; they just gathered their gear out of the back of the Cherokee and, with a hail of hugs, said good-bye. I asked the kids to unload the car while I took a bath.

As I trudged up the stairs, all I could think about was soaking in a mound of lavender-scented bubbles until every muscle in my body quivered like jelly. I was soft, I admitted it. Soft and cushy. No hard body here. But when I opened my bedroom door, all thoughts of a bath disappeared. My room had been ransacked; clothes were scattered all over my bed and the floor.

"Holy Hell—"

A trail of splinters led to my jewelry box, which had been smashed across the top of my vanity, splinters of wood gouging the top. Next to the bed, Nanna's trunk stood open, the padlock and one of the hinges broken. My heart in my throat, I peeked inside. Thank heavens! Though the contents were strewn on the floor, the false bottom and Nanna's journal were intact. That meant the thief hadn't found my heirloom dagger.

Kip's voice filtered up the stairs, startling me. Oh crap, the kids! The thief might still be in the house! I bolted down to the foyer, yelling for them to stay outside, but they had already inched into the living room. "Mom! Your treasures! They're gone!" Randa waggled her finger at the étagère. The glass doors had been shattered in an effort to reach my crystal collection. All my beautiful Faberge eggs were missing, along with a number of other expensive figurines.

Randa looked up at me, comprehension dawning. "We've been robbed?"

Numb, I hustled them out of the door. "I want you to get in the car, lock the doors, and wait for me." They obeyed without a word, edging out of the room while I took one last look before joining them. The front window was still intact, but the desk drawers had been tossed on the sofa. A bottle of ink stained the carpet next to the remains of the rolltop box in which I kept my fine pens. I had little doubt that the pens were gone, along with everything else. Thank God we'd gone camping; who knows what would have happened if we'd been home when the thief showed up.

Once I was standing next to the car, I fumbled with my cell phone and managed to reach Murray just as she walked through the door of her house. "He's been here, Murray. He's been in the house."

"Em, get out of there now! I'll call the station. Somebody will be over right away. I'll see you in a few."

The next ten minutes were a blur. I sat in the car with Kip and Miranda, waiting. They clamored, begging me to tell them what was going on, until I couldn't hear myself think.

"Hush!"

Sudden silence.

"We'll talk about it once the police get here. Right now, could I please have a little peace and quiet?"

Finally, Deacon Wilson and his partner pulled into the driveway. I hadn't seen him since Daniel's death. "Hey, Emerald," he said, patting me on the shoulder.

"Hey, Deacon."

"Murray radioed ahead; she's on her way. What happened?"

I gave him the rundown and, gun drawn, he headed into the house. By the time Murray arrived, he was back. "I checked every room and closet; the house is clear," he said. "I tell you, though, somebody sure did a number on your home. You've got one hell of a cleanup job ahead of you." We reentered the house, where they started dusting for prints.

Murray took my key and checked the shed to make sure no one was hiding there. She returned with a thumbs-up. The padlock hadn't been jimmied. She motioned to the table. "Sit down, Em. We aren't looking at random destruction here. Whoever did this systematically emptied every drawer in your house. All the actual damage appears to be focused on locked objects: the trunk, the étagère."

I shook my head. "I can't imagine what he wants. Everything I have of value is out in full sight." Thinking of the empty étagère, I added, "Or was. And how did the thief get into the house in the first place? The front door was locked when I got home."

"Does anybody else have a key to your house?"

"No," I said glumly. "But this clinches it. Tomorrow, I call Safety-Tech and sign up for a home security system."

Deacon left to file the report and to put out another APB on Jimbo. Nobody had seen him since the Roberts house had been hit; the police had assumed he had fled the area.

Now, though, it seemed likely that he was lying low, hiding out. I explained what was going on to the kids.

Miranda shuddered. "The thief went through everything we have?"

"Is it Jimbo?" Kip asked.

"We don't know for sure, but that doesn't matter. You and Randa need to be careful around *any* strangers."

I put in a call to my insurance agent, and he said he'd be right over but to make sure I didn't disturb anything until he got there. I sent the kids out back to play for a while so Murray and I could talk. After they left, I dropped into the recliner and rested my head on my hands. "I dunno," I said, "I feel like I've been catapulted into Bad Luck Central."

Murray nodded. "Have you done anything different lately? Are your protection charms up to date? Could another ghost be raising havoc?"

I shook my head. "I didn't tell you this yesterday because I didn't want the kids to hear." I filled her in on what Mary Sanders had told me about the dragon. "We're under a curse, and I'm really afraid of what might happen. I can't get rid of the dragon, because it won't stop the bad luck."

"Let me see the statue. You've never really shown it to me before."

I unwrapped the dragon and handed it to her. She held it for a moment, then abruptly gave it back. "I don't like it. Weird energy, but I can't pin it down. I have the feeling it's smiling at me with a big old toothy grin, and it makes me nervous."

"Yeah, I felt the same thing." I put the dragon back in my purse and told her about the visions I'd had. "One was right on the money, and I'm betting that the other is, too. This doesn't feel like a ghost, it feels . . . well, like chaos."

"I think you're right, and you'd better find an answer before it hurts you and the kids." She guided me out to the porch. "Let's sit on the swing. We don't want to disturb anything before your insurance agent gets here."

"I haven't the faintest idea of how to go about breaking the curse." A lump was growing in my throat as I talked. "This isn't fair! All my jewelry's gone, my Faberge eggs are gone, my house is torn apart! I've worked damned hard to get where I am."

Murray rested her hand on my shoulder. "Robbery's a violation, an invasion of privacy and personal space. You should think about talking to one of our victim's aid counselors. Too much has happened; they can help you handle the stress." She stood up. "I'm sorry babe, but I'm going to head out and write up the report. I've got a bunch of errands I have to get done before work tomorrow."

I walked her to the door just in time to greet Mr. Johnson, the insurance agent, camera in hand. He handed me a sheaf of forms, and I got to work filling them out as he went through the house, snapping pictures. Twenty minutes later, he reappeared in the kitchen. "I'm done. If I were you, I'd get a security system."

"Yeah, I'm going to. I imagine my premiums are going to skyrocket."

"Not necessarily, but many more claims, and Applewood will start getting suspicious. File these forms tomorrow, and we'll get started on your check." He shook my hand, and I saw him to the door.

As soon as he left, I called Harlow. "Harl, I have to get out of the house. I can't face looking at this disaster right now."

She told me to come right over. I grabbed the dragon— I wasn't about to leave it lying around where it might get stolen—and hounded the kids into the car. We'd clean up the mess later. When we got to Harl's, Kip and Miranda disappeared outside; Harlow had all sorts of nooks and crannies hidden on her property, with tiny gardens tucked away behind boulders and bubbling fountains and statues placed strategically through a miniature hedge maze.

She met me at the door, maneuvering her wheelchair like a pro. I followed her inside to her study, gratefully dropping into the chair by the side of her desk.

"You look wiped." She was wearing a pair of wire-frame glasses, very stylish.

"Where'd you get those? I've never seen you wear glasses."

"I usually wear contacts, but my allergies have gotten worse since I got pregnant. I wear my glasses on days when my eyes itch. What happened?"

By the time I finished telling her everything, she'd poured me a glass of sparkling water and added a chunk of lemon in it.

I took a long sip and almost spat it out. "Yuck! What the hell is this stuff? It tastes like chalk."

"Drink it," she said. "It's good for you. Replenishes your electrolytes."

"It better be good for me, since it tastes so bad," I grumbled, but finished the glass anyway. I didn't know whether my electrolytes needed replenishing, but I sure could use a pick-me-up. I held up the dragon. "Research time again."

Harlow reached for it, but I shook my head. "Nope, don't you lay one finger on this baby. Let me tell you what I found out." I outlined what I knew of Daniel's history and the curse on the dragon.

She jotted down a few notes as I explained what had been going on, and I noticed that, sometime in the past few months, she'd managed to learn shorthand. "You turning into a whiz kid?"

She beamed. "I never thought of myself as being very smart, but you know, I'm beginning to think that I should go to college. Get my degree in history, maybe. I love the work I'm doing for the Professor. What do you think?"

"I think it's a great idea," I said, happy to see her self-confidence rising. Harl never considered herself very smart, even though she had a natural brilliance that hid itself under all that golden hair. She fired up her laptop.

"Hold on." She brought up a browser and began to tap away, her fingers flying over the keys. Within a few minutes, she sat back and pointed to the screen. "Here we go. Information about Daniel's family that may explain why he had the dragon."

I leaned over her shoulder, glancing at the URL. We were looking at some history site I'd never heard of. "Where'd you find that?"

She handed me a steno pad and pen. "The Professor sponsored me for membership on a couple web sites focusing on antiquities and archaeological digs. The sites aren't public access, you have to be a member, and the dues are exorbitant."

"You sure get around," I said, chuckling. Yet another elite sector of society to which Harl owned a key. "So, what does it say about Daniel's family?"

She scrutinized the web page. "His grandfather was an archaeologist, of sorts."

"What do you mean, 'of sorts'?"

"You know, back in the thirties they would go on expeditions, rob graves, and call it archaeology. Despite their unsavory methods, those 'intrepid adventurers' made some important discoveries." As facetious as she sounded, I knew Harlow was dead serious. She scrolled down the web page, then tapped the screen.

"Okay, here we go, an entry for Terrance Barrington." She paused, deciphering the various charts and entries. "Terrance was Daniel's grandfather, and he was an independent archaeologist. Apparently, during 1935 he led a secret expedition into the outer reaches of China near the Mongolian steppes, where he found a cache of artifacts. He kept his favorite pieces and sold the rest on the open market. On a list of what he kept, one piece is listed as a *dragon carved out of jade, dating back to the Ming dynasty!*"

Bingo! "That's my dragon," I murmured, leaning over her shoulder. "Whatever happened to Grandpa Terrance? Daniel's father and mother met rather nasty ends." Come to think of it, so had Daniel.

After printing out the information about the dragon's discovery for me, Harl plugged in a few more words and another entry came up. She turned the screen so I could see better. "Terrance fell overboard during an expedition in 1937, and before they could throw him a life preserver, the sharks got him."

"Sharks?" The dragon didn't play around; that much was for sure.

She leaned forward, grimacing as she read. "Yeah. His crew tried to save him, but the group of sharks tore Terrance limb from limb. Says here in the ship's log that the water was so slick with his blood and bits of flesh that the crew couldn't eat meat for days." She looked up at me, blanching. "Ugh."

Daniel's family had been plagued with more carnage than a turkey farm on Thanksgiving. "Let's see, Terrance was eaten by sharks; Daniel's mother was struck by lightning; his father got axed to death; his wife and twin boys drowned. Daniel himself was the victim of a hit-and-run. Does it seem to you that this particular line of the Barringtons were destined for disaster?"

"Just a minute." Harl pulled up a second browser, and we were off to a London-based site, this one a genealogy site belonging to a church. She ran her finger down the charts. "Here are the records for Terrance's side of the family. Terrance's wife died in a tsunami in Hawaii. They had three sons, Trenton, Harcourt, and Charles. Trenton wandered into the path of an oncoming train. Charles . . . it just says he died accidentally when he was thirteen. Harcourt, Daniel's father, was murdered, but you already know the details about that. Harcourt was the only one of the three who had children."

"Can you find any information on Daniel's sister? Is she still alive?"

"Here. Look for yourself."

I studied the charts. Harcourt and his wife Molly had two children. Daniel was the youngest; his sister Deirdre was four years older. Deirdre had gotten married and had borne a stillborn daughter. Her husband was listed as dead. Again, an accident. He'd died on the same day Deirdre gave birth.

"Jeez, Louise!" I said, realizing the scope of what we were looking at. "One tragedy after another. Nobody seems to have lived past the age of fifty-five. His entire family was wiped out. No wonder Daniel was so depressed."

Wincing, not really wanting to see the line of bizarre deaths continue, I followed the family tree down to the bitter end. Three years after her daughter and husband died, Deirdre's death had been listed as accidental, with a notation in parentheses that read, "Suicide?" Which left Daniel the last of his line. And now, he had joined his ancestors.

"I guess that's it," I said, sighing. "There's nobody left."

"Look," Harl said. "Every single death listed in Terrance's family took place *after* he found the dragon." She gave me a wan smile. "Anything else?"

I stared at my notes. Gruesome. And now I was keeper of a five-hundred-year-old cursed jade statue. "I guess I just need to find out how to lift the hex." I glanced out the window. "I'd better take off. It's getting late, and I need to clean up my house. If you can dig up anything else, I'd appreciate it."

Harl snorted. "I make a good busybody, don't I? I'll find what I can." We headed outside, where I called for the kids.

They came running over, squabbling about who was the stronger, Superman or Batman.

"Superman is!" Randa argued.

Kip stuck out his tongue. "Nuh-uh, what about kryptonite?"

I herded them into the car. "This," I said to Harl, "is what you have to look forward to. Okay, gang, let's get moving." We took off for home, and when we got there, I found a note from Joe, saying he'd dropped by to say hello and check on us, and to please call him when I had the time. I stuck the note in my pocket, then headed inside. Time to sweep. Lately it seemed like all I did was clean up the trail of broken glass somebody else left behind.

MONDAY BROUGHT A respite, at least for the first hour of the day. I had been restless all night, tossing and turning until I was a bundle of knots. When the morning rays of pale sun crept through my window and drifted across my face, I tumbled out of bed, still tired but too nerve-racked to go back to sleep.

With a yawn, I opened the window, and birdsong filtered in on the cool spring breeze. Though it would be several months before it was warm enough to enjoy the weather, the buds on my maple tree were beginning to open, and little hints of green dotted the bushes all over town. Horvald's tulips shimmered from across the street, satin pink under the morning light.

What to wear? I decided on a pair of khakis, a hunter green tank top, and my espadrilles. I wound the ribbons up around my calves and tied them in pretty bows. A quick glance in the mirror told me I was beginning to look like Vampira's twin sister, so I added a touch of color with some coral lipstick that I liked to think made me a little mermaid-ish, then spritzed myself with my ever-present Opium.

Time to haul my butt down the stairs and into the kitchen. As I was grinding coffee beans and nuking a pocket sandwich, the phone rang. It was my banker, letting me know that they'd received a direct deposit to my store account from Applewood Insurance Company. He gave me the amount of the check, and I yipped for joy. Applewood hadn't been stingy! All my losses were covered, and I'd be able to restock. I just hoped they'd cover my losses at home, too.

"I love you, Mr. Conner!" I thanked him for the news and went back to brewing espresso. Maybe today wouldn't be a bust after all; I could begin restocking the store and be back in the running by next week. I put in a call to Safety-Tech and ordered a security system for the house, and they signed me up for a Saturday installation. Then I put in a call to Don Patterson, the locksmith, to get all the locks on our doors changed. He said he'd be out within an hour or so. Regardless of what else happened, I was determined that our home would be safe.

As I bit into my sandwich, the kids spilled into the kitchen. Kip fed and watered the cats while Miranda dug out the Cheerios. "You want cereal?" she asked, grabbing three bowls from the cupboard.

"Nah, thanks though." I held up my sandwich. They ate while I drained my chocolate-laced caffeine. Ah, that was the stuff! Damn good wake-up medicine. The world was growing more focused with every sip. "Safety-Tech's coming by on Saturday to install our security system," I told them. "And the bank got the check for the store." I glanced at the clock. "Off to school! You don't want to be late."

"Yes, ma'am." They saluted me, their eyes twinkling. "Anything you say, ma'am." I shooed them out the door and waved them across the street. I was on my second mocha, about to head out to work, when the phone rang.

Murray's voice came on the line. She sounded worried.

"Em, we've got a credible report placing Jimbo outside the Thai Market on Heather Street. That's damn close to your house."

"Oh hell. What should I do?"

"Keep your eyes open. We'll have a cruiser over there in a few minutes. Are the kids there?"

"No, they should be at school by now."

Time for a few chores while I waited for the locksmith. The garbage trucks had come down our street early in the morning, so I headed out to the curb to bring back the trash can when I heard the roar of a motorcycle behind me. An alarm went off in the pit of my stomach. I glanced around just in time to see Jimbo leap off the back of his Harley, and he was aimed right in my direction. The big man was quick and, even though I dodged out of the way, I wasn't as fast as he was. He grabbed hold of my wrist, leaning down to growl in my face.

"Listen, you bitch, get the cops off my back."

"Let me go!" I tried to twist out of his grasp, but he held fast.

"I didn't KO that broad, and I didn't steal nothing from her house. Why are you trying to pin this rap on me? I got a little drunk and smashed your window. No big deal, I'll pay the fuckin' fines. But I'm not going to jail for something I didn't do!"

No big deal? Anger replaced fear. "You oaf! You broke into my house and stole all my valuables. You destroyed my shop. What do you expect I'm going to do? Roll over and let you tear up everything I've worked for?"

Jimbo pulled back a little, and I sensed a flutter of puzzlement, as if he really didn't know what I was talking about. I took advantage of the brief interlude to give him a swift, sharp kick to the shin. Cussing like a drunken sailor, he let go of my arm, and I made tracks toward my house, where I could lock myself in and call the cops. He lurched forward, grabbing the air behind me.

"Oof!" I heard him fall as I raced up the porch stairs and into the house, slamming the door behind me. As my hands fumbled with the locks, the high-pitched keen of a siren told me that the police were out front. I ran into the living room to peer out the window. Jimbo's bike was still in front of my house, and there were two cop cars hedging it in, their lights flashing. Murray headed up the porch steps, smoothly taking them two at a time.

I unlocked the door and waved toward the back of the house. "He probably took off toward the alley."

Murray jerked her thumb toward the living room. "Get in there, and stay away from the window," she said, then raced back down the steps.

I obeyed, huddling in the corner behind the desk. *Let it end peacefully,* I prayed. *Let it end easy, without anybody getting hurt.* Shouts reverberated from out back, and then silence. I was steeling my nerve to go peek out the back window when Murray returned, pounding on the front door. I let her in.

"Everything's okay." She mopped her forehead with a bandanna. "We got him. He surrendered without a fight. Did he hurt you?" she asked, looking me over.

Adrenaline still pumping, I clutched my arms across my chest and perched on the edge of the recliner. Through the window, I could see Greg and Sandy hauling Jimbo to the cruiser. I rubbed my arm where he'd held it. The skin was a little tender, but there was no real damage. "No, not really. He says he didn't hurt Norma or steal anything."

"Yeah, he claims you're railroading him," Murray said.

I sighed. "Do you believe him? He admitted to me that he threw the brick through my window."

Murray sat on the sofa and leaned forward, her hands

clasped as she rested her elbows on her knees. She shrugged. "The thing is, criminals always claim they're innocent. The worse the crime, the more impassioned their plea, even when you catch them in the act. It's all part of the mind-set. Anyway, whether or not he hurt Norma, for now we can hold him on destruction of property because of your window, and assault, for accosting you out front."

There wasn't much I could say except "Thank you."

She shook her head. "What kind of a friend would I be if I let you down on something this big? By the way, Horvald Ledbetter called the police when he looked out his window and saw Jimbo pulling up on his bike. He recognized it from the other night when your window was smashed."

Good old Horvald! I'd have to give him a nice tea basket as a thank-you. "You sure got here fast."

"We were already in the vicinity because of the tip we got earlier. When Horvald's call came, we didn't have far to go—just a block or two. He's a good neighbor . . . a keeper." She glanced at her watch. "I better get moving, or Coughlan will be out here looking for me. He's all over my ass today." She gave me a weary smile. "I'll call you a little later. Meanwhile, I still think you better get that security system. We dunno for sure who ransacked your house yet. None of the prints turned up anything." She gave me a quick hug and took off.

I ventured back into the kitchen and made myself yet another mocha. When Jimbo had been holding on to my wrist, I'd been frightened, but when I really thought about it, I never truly believed he was going to hurt me. It was more like he wanted to scare me, and when I'd kicked him in the shins and ran, I had little doubt that he could have caught me if he really meant business. So why didn't he? Was he afraid someone—like Horvald—might see him? Something just didn't add up. Of course, I really didn't know what kind of person he was, not underneath it all.

A knock on the door announced the appearance of the locksmith. As I went to let him in, I thought that whatever Jimbo's beef against me, he'd have to take a number, because the dragon was holding the front of the line in the "let's make Emerald's life hell" marathon.

AFTER A DAY of ordering new stock and trying to forget all the crap that had happened during the morning, I came home to find that Miranda had made another stab at fixing dinner. This time, she'd limited herself to heating frozen lasagna and making a salad, and it actually smelled good. As we settled in at the table, she handed me a folder. "Here's the information about skipping grades that you wanted to see."

I bit into a steaming forkful of noodles and sauce. "Thanks, hon. I'll look at it tonight. Just put it on my desk, if you would." The cats milled around our feet, hoping for handouts, but finally slinked away, disgruntled. We were all too tired for conversation; the kids were especially quiet after I'd told them about Jimbo. Kip loaded the dishwasher while Randa fed the cats. Then she took off for her room.

Clear skies and good viewing, I thought. "Bundle up when you go out tonight!"

Kip grinned at me. "Someday she's gonna end up on the moon, you know?" He turned on the computer and loaded up SimCity while I settled on the sofa and flipped on the television. With Cathy Sutton on vacation, Jack Sullivan was out one party partner and probably wouldn't be cracking stupid jokes. Thank heaven for small favors. I sipped my tea and turned up the sound, wondering if they'd mention Jimbo's arrest.

"According to the medical examiner, the body is that of a male, Caucasian, between twenty and fifty years old. No sign of the victim's head or hands have been found, and there were no identifying marks. The police are asking anybody who knows of a man missing in the Vancouver area to contact them."

Lovely. Maybe a gang slaying or something.

"In other news, James 'Jimbo' Warren was arrested this morning when he accosted Chiqetaw resident Emerald O'Brien in front of her house."

Woohoo! Just what I needed, my name in the news again. I'd thought of taking out a late-night ad for the shop, but thanks to the local news station, I was getting plenty of free publicity.

The camera focused in on Jack's face. "Residents of Chiqetaw better start locking their doors. Over the weekend, police logged several burglaries. The suspect is believed to be a professional, and all of the stolen goods were small, expensive items. Eunice Addison, mother of prominent businessman Walter Mitchell, was one of the burglary victims." A picture of Eunice flashed across the screen.

I muted the sound and glanced over at the étagère. Well, if Jimbo was the thief, he'd better run once Eunice got wind of him. Walter's mother was hell on wheels, and I sure wouldn't want to be the culprit with her after me. Just then, Samantha galloped over, bounced, and landed on my stomach. I stroked her fur, letting the gentle purr from her throat relax me enough to send me into a light doze.

After a while, Kip woke me up. "Can I surf the net?"

Yawning, I gave Samantha a final pat and sat up. She bounded off my lap. "Okay, but check my E-mail while you're on-line." The beep-squawk-hiss of the modem signaled that he was in.

"Mom, Harlow sent you something. It's got the red exclamation mark next to it, so it must be important."

I took over the keyboard. Harlow wanted me to call her. I gave the computer back to Kip and picked up the phone.

"I think I've found some more info on your dragon," she said.

"Let's hear it," I said, too tired to do anything but listen.

"That vision you had about the dude caught in a snow-storm?"

"Uh-huh?"

"Think I found a reference to it. Looks like Daniel's grandfather wasn't the first person to dig this thing up. The dragon has surfaced several times throughout the past five hundred years; but each time, it ends up back in China."

A homing dragon, how delightful. "What about the people who found it?"

"In 1733, a Norwegian explorer unearthed a jade dragon with gilt etching northeast of Beijing; he was probably trying to follow the coastline toward Russia and then cross-country to his homeland. He and his traveling companions were on the way home when winter came early, and a freak snowstorm hit them. They got separated, and the explorer carrying the dragon was lost in the woods. Nobody knows what happened to him, but the others returned home, convinced the dragon had brought them bad luck."

"That matches my vision," I said. "Anything else?"

"No, except that this particular group of explorers were probably bandits. What are you going to do?"

"I don't know. Harl, a creature like the Chinese demon that Huang Fu summoned could wipe out astral meanies like Mr. B & U with a puff of bad breath. I have no idea of how to undo this kind of curse. I don't even know what kind of demon it is. The Chinese have more hells than you can count, and most have some sort of ugly sucker attached to them."

I wanted to believe it was all superstition. I wanted to believe that a little piece of carved jade couldn't possibly hurt me. Most people didn't believe that demons, ghosts, and curses existed. But I wasn't like most people; I'd spent my life working with spirits and learning how to use the psychic gifts I was born with. This curse was real.

"You there?" Harlow sounded worried.

I shook myself out of my reverie. "Yeah. Just thinking."

"It's true, isn't it? The dragon curse?"

I didn't have to say a word. Harl already knew the answer; I could tell by her silence. After a moment, I said, "Maybe I've known since I first brought it home. The statue moves, it turns in circles, its eyes glow red. We're talking a jade Linda Blair here, only it's not possessed. Just cursed. The question now is, what do I do? By the way, where did you find that information?"

"I traced Terrance's route through China, to where he found the statue. After that, it was a matter of digging through dusty old references relating to explorers who visited that area of the world from the latter Ming dynasty on. I haven't had much else to do the past few days, you know. And it's interesting."

"Resourceful," I murmured.

"So what's next?"

"Undo the curse. Try to dodge the bad luck the dragon's tossing my way. I need to hurry; I don't dare let it cause more havoc." I rubbed my eyes and yawned, then filled her in on the details of Jimbo's capture. We chatted a little longer before I hung up.

A wayward curse from an ancient dragon. Chinese demons. An artist-thief who impregnated the Emperor's niece and ended up on the chopping block because of his mistakes. I almost felt sorry for Huang Fu. Yes, stealing was wrong; but surely he shouldn't have paid with his life? And getting a girl pregnant wasn't a crime to die for. At least not now, not here.

His life struck me as more tragic than nefarious. No wonder the demon had taken pity on him and granted his dying wish.

"Mom, I'm going to bed." Kip broke into my thoughts as he came out of the kitchen. By the looks of the crumbs on his face, he'd been in the cookie jar.

"Okay, sleep tight." I gave him a distracted kiss. "I'll be up to check on you later." Samantha and the kittens followed him up the stairs.

I rummaged through the fridge until I found the cold lasagna. Cold pizza, cold spaghetti, I liked them all. Perched on the counter, fork in one hand, phone in the other, I pressed #1 on speed dial for Mur's home number. No answer. I tried her work phone. Nada. Where on earth was she? Curses, thugs, and thieves crowded my mind as I tried to sort out what was going on.

"You shouldn't eat that, Mom. It's late, and you'll get heartburn again."

Startled, I jerked around. Randa stood at the kitchen door. "Thanks, kiddo. I'll remember that piece of advice." I gave her a wry grin. She grabbed a fork, and we sat side by side on the counter, swinging our feet and munching cold pasta together.

After a few minutes, she asked, "Mom, is anything wrong? Things have been kind of weird the past week."

I sighed. I was going to have to tell them sometime. "You're right; a lot of strange things have gone wrong since that man died in front of my store."

"Maybe we're jinxed," Randa suggested.

I gave her a long look. Maybe it was time to fill her in. "You're not far off, kiddo. That dragon I brought home? The one Daniel gave me before he died? Apparently it has a curse on it." I told her about Huang Fu and the emperor, and the cursed dragon, but left out the gruesome parts.

Miranda rolled her eyes. "Great. More trouble. Mom, could you try sometime just being a normal mother? Maybe give the PTA a chance?"

I finished my side of the lasagna. "You'd like that,

wouldn't you? Of course, I'd have to take down your guard-railing because normal mothers don't let their teenage daughters go climbing around on the roof during the middle of the night."

"No! Anything but that!" She sobered. "Are we really in danger?"

What was I going to tell her? That everybody associated with the dragon had died in bizarre accidents and murders? I couldn't scare her like that, and yet I needed the kids to be careful. "Yeah, it looks that way. Watch your step the next couple weeks, okay?"

Randa raised her eyebrow and licked her fork. "Be sure to warn Kip. He's pretty careless. Have you had a chance to look through the material I gave you?"

Material? Oh yeah, the school information. "No, but I'll do it right now while you head up to bed." I gave her a quick kiss before she raced upstairs, then settled myself at my desk and sifted through the information she'd gathered. Straightforward and clear, the pamphlets and handouts presented both pros and cons of letting a child skip grades.

I knew why Miranda wanted this. Her schoolwork was a joke; she got A's in her sleep for most of her classes. And yet . . . to move her ahead, to stick her in with kids years older than she was. What would it do to her? I pushed the papers away. Who was I to hold her back? My daughter wanted a life that wasn't ordinary, and I owed her the opportunity. She was brilliant; she'd go far. I pushed myself away from my desk and stood, stretching so hard my back popped. Happy I'd made a decision on something at last, I was about to head for bed when the phone rang.

Eleven

❖

"EM, WHAT HAPPENED? What's wrong?" Murray's voice rang out over the line.

"Thank heavens you called back. You would not believe what I found out about the dragon and Daniel's family." I spilled out everything that Harl and I'd discovered in our quest for information.

Murray paused. When she did speak, her voice was curt, and I knew something was wrong. "Em, I thought you were in trouble, but you're obviously fine. I can't really talk right now. Why don't you call me tomorrow?"

Feeling guilty, I settled myself on the sofa. I hadn't meant to upset her. "I'm sorry. Is everything okay?"

"It's just been a hard day." She hesitated, then added, "White Deer and I had an argument. She went out for a walk, and I want to unwind before she gets home."

Argument? They never argued, as far as I knew. "You've got to be kidding! You told me you two never fight. What's up?" As soon as the words were out of my mouth, I knew I'd made a mistake, and I was right. The temperature in her voice went from chilly to freezer burn in a matter of seconds.

"If I wanted to talk about it, I would have called you." Murray seldom got angry, but when she did, she blew in a big way. "As it is, you're the one who called me. Again. Damn it, Emerald, do I phone you every time something goes wrong? Do I ask your advice on every little thing in my life? No, but you butt in anyway. Can't you be a little more supportive of my choices, even when that choice doesn't include following your advice? If you're not bitching about your problems, you're bitching about what you think I'm doing wrong. Give me a little peace, okay, and just back off?"

I stared at the phone, shocked speechless. What the hell was going on? I tried to smooth things over. "Murray, I'm sorry I bothered you. You *are* the one who suggested doing more research. When Harlow and I came up with all that wild stuff, I thought you might want to know about it, but obviously I was wrong."

She pounced on me like a tiger. "Couldn't it have waited until tomorrow? It's not like it's an emergency."

I took a deep breath and exhaled slowly, trying to remain calm. "I suppose to me, this *is* an emergency. My family's in danger. But hey, I won't let it happen again."

The Murray I knew returned for a moment, but just for a moment. "I'm not trying to discount what's happening to you, but Em, you always call me when you need something. Jeez, even when I'm off work, I'm always on call for you." Once again, her voice rose. "Sometimes I need time for myself, okay? Sometimes I need to be more than a cop or a shaman. Is that too much to ask of my best friend?"

Unsure just how to fix things, I shut my mouth and waited.

After a moment of silence, Murray said, "Oh, God." Her words came tumbling out, tripping over themselves as she rushed to mend the tattered conversation. "Emerald, I'm sorry. I didn't mean to go off on you like that. I've just been under so much stress."

I knew she meant it, but there was no going back. What was said, was said. And to be honest, she was right. I'd been too caught up in my own worries to realize just how upset she was. She had enough trouble on her own plate, without me adding to the menu.

"Don't try to explain," I said. The words came out a little too sharply but it was either that or bawl like a baby, and that would only make both of us feel like idiots. "You're absolutely right, and I apologize. I'll talk to you later, okay?"

"Damn it," she said. "Now I feel like a heel."

Before things could get any worse, I said, "Anna, I'm glad you called me on my behavior. Get in touch when you can. Take it easy, okay?" I eased the receiver back onto the cradle and headed for the downstairs bathroom. If I didn't find the antacids, and soon, I'd be up all night with the burgeoning ulcer I suspected was growing somewhere between my breastbone and my stomach.

Damn it. I hated arguing with friends, hated bickering in general. It always reminded me of the endless bouts with Roy and how I spent so many of our years together in tears.

Best buddies, Murray and I'd been there for each other through everything: Roy's betrayal, Murray getting her first job as a cop, ghosts and mayhem and family troubles on both sides. If it wasn't for Murray, I'd never have thought to settle in Chiqetaw. And now she was having problems with her job and her aunt and apparently, I'd trampled over her needs.

I numbly forced myself over to the computer and turned it off. As I started to trudge upstairs, the doorbell rang. *Oh God, what now?* Please don't let it be anybody who needed me to be even halfway coherent. I flipped on the porch light and peeked through the peephole. Andrew! Standing on my porch, a bouquet of yellow roses in hand!

"Andrew!" All thoughts of our bickering on the phone flew right out the window, and I leapt into his arms. He clumsily embraced me, trying to keep the flowers from getting squashed. "You're home! I didn't think you were going to be able to come back for another week or so. Why didn't you call me? I would have met you at the airport." The words flooded out as I realized how much I'd missed him.

He kissed me on the nose, then walked me into the living room and pressed the bouquet in my arms. I noticed he was wearing a new leather jacket, brown with suede patches on the elbows. In fact, his whole outfit was new; his jeans looked fashionably worn, but I knew what he had in his closet, and these were definitely a recent addition. He wore a silk shirt, the first three buttons opened to show a thin gold chain, and his ponytail was slicked back with some sort of mousse. There was something different about him, a spark in his eye that I didn't remember.

"Slow down a minute, Em. I'm just in town to get some files I forgot. I got in this evening, and I have to be at the airport tomorrow at ten in the morning." He stood awkwardly in the living room, as if he wasn't sure whether or not to sit down.

"You have to leave again?" Disappointed, I asked, "How long are you going to be gone this time?"

He gave a little shrug. "They want me to write the screenplay—"

"Wonderful—" I started to say, but he held up his hand.

"Let me finish, Em. I'll be gone at least three months. Maybe more." He seemed to be trying very hard to be nonchalant. I couldn't put a handle on what was wrong, but something felt off.

"Three months," I said slowly. "That's a long time. Will

you be able to come back for visits?" If he would only sit down. I wanted him to sit down and hold out his arm for me to go snuggle into, but he just stood near the sofa.

"Maybe, but I can't promise anything. It's a fast-paced world down there. Got to stay on top of things, keep my fingers in the pie. There are a lot of advantages, though. No driving over two hours just to find a decent store or restaurant. Sunshine every day. And, I met Zia Danes."

Zia Danes was one of the new crop of rising young starlets. She was too skinny and too blonde, and I didn't like the way he said her name. I studied my fingernails and edged myself primly onto the sofa, not feeling secure enough to relax. "I didn't know we didn't have any good restaurants or stores up here. Guess I'm out of the loop. So, you really like it there?"

He shifted. "I think so. Yes, I do."

Exhausted from the turmoil of the day, tired of pussyfooting around, I decided to go straight to the heart of the matter. "Are you mad at me?"

He cleared his throat. "Mad? No, Em, not at all. It's just that, well . . . how do I say this?"

I stared at him, feeling a chill spread across my heart. "Why don't you just come out and say it? That's usually best, right?" *Oh hell,* I thought. *Not another blow. Please let it be something easy, something stupid that doesn't matter.*

He studied my face. "Yeah, you're right. I owe you the truth, and you deserve it without me trying to pretty it up." He spilled out his news quickly, not giving me a chance to interrupt. "Zia's going to star in the movie. We've been working together since I got there, trying to develop her character. Em, we really hit it off and . . . well . . . she wants me to move in to her place when I go back. We've been sleeping together since the day we met."

A wave of shame flooded through me as my face flushed. I turned away, pressing my lips together as I fought against the rising anger and humiliation. I didn't dare speak, didn't dare look at him.

"I don't know how it happened," he continued, oblivious to my pain. "We just ignite each other like dynamite. We were sitting on the sofa one minute, talking about the story line, and the next—she was in my arms and I was ripping off her dress—"

"Stop!" My voice hovered in the room like a feather drifting on the wind. "I don't care how it happened. I don't care why it happened. I don't want to know the details." He leaned in as if he were going to take me in his arms. I held up my hand. "You'd better leave. You have a plane to catch tomorrow."

"Em, please, don't leave it like this. I never meant to hurt you."

Furious, I turned on him. "Liar. You don't give a damn about me, or you wouldn't have done it. You took less than two weeks to decide you wanted somebody else. Let me tell you this: I've had a lot of chances to sleep with Joe over the past few months, but never once have I crossed the line, because I respected our relationship. So don't give me that bullshit." Even though I'd fought this battle before, with Roy, I'd still been taken by surprise. So much for being psychic, I thought.

Andrew shuffled. "I just want you to understand. I don't want you to hold a grudge."

I looked up at him, and my radar clicked. "You just don't want me throwing a hex your way. That's it, isn't it? You're afraid of me?" He paled, and I knew I was right. "You really think that little of me? Thanks a lot."

He stammered. "I . . . I . . . didn't mean . . ."

I stopped him with an upraised hand. "Don't worry about it. I wouldn't bother. You're not worth the karma it would cost me. I have no interest in wasting my time and energy on you."

"Don't talk like that. We had something special together, please don't be so upset. I didn't mean to hurt you, I really didn't." He was pleading now, and I sensed that he really believed what he was saying, even though it reeked of denial.

I forced myself to stand, shoulders straight, and said in a dignified voice, "Apparently what we had wasn't special enough. If you need a starlet to make you happy, then I'm not going to stand in your way. I'm not going to beg, or plead, or anything else you might have been expecting. I learned the hard way that my dignity and self-respect are worth more than any man." I opened the door. "Good-bye Andrew."

He hesitantly stepped toward the outside. "You don't really need me, you know. Your life centers around your kids. I don't think you have any right to bitch since you've been too busy to pay me the attention I need."

What? I stared at him in disbelief. "You're using the fact that I care about my children to justify cheating behind my back?" Then, I stopped. He'd never get it. "No wonder you don't want to get married. You're just a spoiled brat in a man's body, and you can't handle reality. Well fine. While you were screwing Zia's brains out, I've been battling for my family's life. I think that's more important for me to focus on. Now, get your ass out of here."

As he passed by, I stepped aside. His car pulled out of the driveway, and I waited until the taillights disappeared, then took the bouquet of roses out to the backyard, where I tore the petals off, breaking one stem at a time. I dumped the whole mess in the trash can. Then, acting on autopilot, I returned to the house, locked the door, and forced myself upstairs where I fell into bed, too numb to even cry. The tears could wait until tomorrow.

* * *

COME MORNING, I was ready for a long, hot shower. Andrew's visit seemed like a nightmare. I could almost make myself believe that it had been a bad dream except the ache in my heart told me it had been all too real. But as I toweled off, I decided I meant what I'd told him: I couldn't afford to waste any energy on him. I knew we weren't a match made in heaven; last night had just confirmed it. Sure, my ego had taken a few bruises, but Andrew hadn't hurt me the way Roy had. I flipped through my closet and decided on a beige linen dress and my brown heels. Maybe if I looked professional, I could act the part and get through the day with as little distraction as possible.

I hauled out Nanna's trunk. Everything except a few odds and ends had remained intact when I gathered it up after the burglary, and I'd repaired the broken hinge without too much trouble. Luckily, the trunk itself was made of ironwood, and it would take a sledgehammer to dent that surface.

Dear Nanna. She'd taught me her folk magic, she'd taught me about my past and my roots, and she never let me forget that my mother's people were as old as the hills of Europe, as old as the Norsemen who worshiped Odin and Thor. Though she left some of her customs behind, she'd brought along her trunk when she came to the States, filled with charms and spells and bottles of incense and amulets. When she died, she willed the trunk to me, as keeper of the family heritage. I hoped that I was doing a decent job of it, though right now I questioned my judgment about a lot of things.

I hoisted out the heavy, leather-bound journal she'd kept, then closed and locked the lid. The writing was a mixture of German and English. I'd managed to learn enough German to translate most everything in the book, but I was cautious on the things I wasn't so sure about. I was all too familiar with the results of charms that backfired.

Tucking the journal into my tote bag, I got the kids off to school and headed out for the shop. I didn't mention Andrew's visit; no sense getting them upset before school. There'd be time enough later on; I'd just tell them that we'd disagreed too much and that we broke up. No sense showering them with the seedy details.

Cinnamon had arrived early. I set her to work on posters for the renovation sale that we'd use to let folks know we were back on track. She had beautiful handwriting with a real artistic touch; within an hour, she'd created some lovely signs. I admired the sketches of teapots and steaming cups of tea. "Very nice. We should be receiving some shipments today, so we'll spend the day uncrating merchandise, drawing up new ledgers and inventory logs, and shelving whatever stock shows up in the mail."

Before I got started, I retreated to my office to call Harlow. My first thought had been to call Murray, but after our fight, I didn't think I could handle another rebuff. Lost my boyfriend and my best friend in one fell swoop. Yep, good going, Emerald. The latter hurt far more than the former.

Harl answered, and I spilled what had happened with Andrew into her waiting ear. She was agreeably outraged, and her anger made me feel better, especially since I didn't have the energy to throw a tantrum myself. Maybe I could manage a little wail, if pressed, but even that seemed overwhelming.

"I can't believe he did that to you! You were right when you told me you weren't sure about him. I'm so sorry. I was the one who introduced you guys." Her voice spired, fueled by pregnancy hormones and guilt. "I feel so awful, and you know James is going to hear about this. Andrew's on my shit list."

Oops, she was angrier than I thought. I should have known she'd take it personally, and I knew that Andrew's reputation would be dead meat if Harl got mad enough. I was furious, but not enough to ruin his life, which Harl could do with a few well-placed calls. "No, please. I really don't have the energy to retaliate. Just don't invite the two of us to the same gig, okay? Though, with his new life down in Hollywood, I doubt if he'll be spending much time up here for the next few months." New life, new woman, I thought. Can't wear old clothes to a blue-blood party, right?

"That idiot has no idea what kind of life he's getting into. I've been there. They'll eat him alive and spit out the bones, and when they're done, I can guarantee Zia Danes isn't going to stick around to put Humpty-Dumpty back together again. I know her type; they never change." Harl's voice was edgy; I knew her days as a supermodel still haunted her.

She continued her rant. "I can't believe he turned out to be such a louse. Why the hell are you protecting him?"

"I'm not protecting him, Harl. . . . I just don't think it matters that much. Not considering what I'm facing with that damned dragon."

"Maybe you're right," she said after a minute. "But I can still make him regret treating you this way, and I will. And don't worry, you'll always take precedence over *his sleaziness* when it comes to invitations to parties and soirees."

Feeling vindicated and just a little bit guilty, I thanked her and hung up, feeling better than I had all morning. Time to get busy. I opened my tote bag and withdrew Nanna's journal. Flipping through the aged pages, I looked for any mention of removing curses. Of course, Nanna would never have heard of the jade dragon or the curse attached to it, but maybe there would be something that might help. I hovered over the vengeance-for-straying-mates spells, then forced myself to pass them up. Nope! Not a good idea. By noon, I'd scoured every page and come up empty-handed, except for a single charm that might, or might not, do the trick.

If only I knew something about Chinese magic and folklore. I put in another call to Harlow. "What are the rules for a community member who wants to use the library at the university?" I asked.

"You have to purchase a community access card in order to check out material. I suppose you're hunting for ways to break that curse?"

I sighed. "Keeps my mind off the other stuff." I broke down and told her about my fight with Murray. "Last night sucked rocks all the way around, tell you that."

"Jeez, what the hell is going on with your biorhythms? Maybe your stars are out of alignment?" She paused, and I thought I heard the sound of a match striking up.

"You aren't smoking, are you?"

There was a hasty noise as she jostled the phone. "No, no . . . just . . . lighting a candle." I waited until she added, "I put it out, okay?"

"Okay, then. You know it's better for the baby—"

"Hey, I sympathized with *you*." Another pause, then, "Yeah, I know. Anyway, regarding this curse. I suppose you've already looked in Nanna's journal?"

"Ahead of you there. I found a few hex-breakers, but I have an uneasy feeling that they're gonna do squat. We're talking Chinese demon magic here." I took a swig of diet cherry Coke and leaned back.

Cinnamon poked her head around the corner. "Excuse me, but there's someone here to see you."

I told Harl I'd call her back and headed out to the front counter. White Deer was standing there, a stern look on her face. Not sure whether to be grateful or worried, I invited her into the tearoom. I'd managed to pick up new chairs and tables, and Lana was in the process of refinishing the sideboard from which we served the tea and pastries. It had been damaged during the orgy of violence that had played out in my little shop.

White Deer looked around at the sparsely furnished shelves and the half-finished renovations. "Someone left a shadow here, Emerald. If you don't clear it, you won't draw customers back in. We can help you do that." When I didn't immediately answer, she added, "I know all about your argument with Anna."

I poured tea for us and fetched a couple of sandwiches. "That's okay, I'll do it myself. I've got to stop asking Murray to help me so much. I hurt her feelings, and I didn't mean to."

White Deer's face was placid, almost stoic, as she commanded my gaze. "You aren't good at playing the martyr. Neither is Anna. I told her the same thing I'm telling you. This anger that has come between you wasn't spawned by your friendship. You need each other; you nourish each other's soul, and if you two insist on being stubborn jackasses, that old trickster spirit Coyote's going to be on your ass like white on rice and make things worse until both of you learn to laugh at yourselves and let go of your self-righteousness."

I stared at my hands. Stubborn? Murray and I were as stubborn as they come. "You're right," I said. "I'm not sure what to do about it, but you're right."

She snorted. "Exactly what Anna said. I've always believed the two of you are twin souls. You walk different paths and practice different traditions, but you share the same vision. Now, should you call her, or should she call you?"

White Deer's questions were never as simple as they sounded, and long ago I'd learned not to blurt out a frivolous or snappy comeback. As much as I wanted to snatch up the phone, if I called Murray right now, I wouldn't know what to say. She needed to sort out all the crap going on at her job, while I needed to focus on my own life, on the breakup with Andrew, and on the dragon.

"This problem with her job is one she'll have to work out on her own," I finally said. "She doesn't have any energy to spare, and neither do I." I looked at White Deer as she waited patiently. "She'll call me when she's ready. Until then, I have to be patient."

With a satisfied nod, White Deer motioned to Cinnamon. "Bring us some more tea, please. Emerald and I need to have a little talk." Then she asked me to tell her about the dragon, and I understood that I'd earned a new confidante, at least for today.

THE TALK WITH White Deer did me a world of good. She sympathized with me over the situation with Andrew, encouraged me to get the security system for my house, and reassured me that I wasn't being overly paranoid. She also set my mind at ease about my friendship with Murray.

"You haven't lost your best friend," she said. "Just give her some time. Meanwhile, you need to use your intuition more. I think you tried to wall yourself off after Daniel died. Tune back in to the otherworld; if you don't, you'll risk short-circuiting your psychic powers. You know that just as well as I do." She stood up and placed her hands on her hips, arching her back as she stretched. About to leave, she stopped and flashed me a curious look.

"What is it?" I asked.

She tilted her head. "Just a hunch. Emerald, when the chips are down, don't be afraid to ask for help, even if you have to swallow your pride. Even if you have to ask for help from somebody you don't want to ask." With a hug, she was gone.

After she left, Cinnamon, Lana, and I spent the rest of the afternoon organizing the stack of crates that had been delivered at noon. I grabbed the crowbar and got to work opening cases. "Oh, how lovely," I said, holding up a beautiful black lacquered teapot. A matching set of teacups and saucers followed. We sifted through the packing material and began the job of inventorying the new stock.

By closing time, the shop looked rejuvenated. It felt good to wander around and poke through the shelves and not be able to see every item with just one sweep of the eyes. I was dusting off a porcelain ballerina when the phone rang, and Cinnamon held it out to me.

It was Harl. "Can you get the Internet at your store?"

"Um-hmm," I said. "I brought an old computer from home to use here until I get the replacement for the one that was stolen." That was one good thing my marriage to Roy had provided: a steady stream of computers coming through the house. I had several spares in the shed. I knew they were outdated by now, but they'd work in a pinch, and this was a pinch.

"What's your E-mail at the shop?"

I gave it to her, and she told me to check my in box right away. "I think I found a solution to your curse, but I don't think it's going to make it any easier on you."

My heart skipped a beat. "Why? What's wrong?"

"Take a look. I just sent you the info." With a rushed "Bye," she hung up. I settled myself behind my desk and logged on. Sure enough, an E-mail slowly downloaded into my in box. I clicked on the attachment and found myself staring at a page copied from some site, referring to various forms of Chinese curses. I quickly skimmed the information, and sure enough, there was a mention of a jade dragon carved during the Ming dynasty.

Holding my breath, I began to read through the information. Most of the story I already knew, thanks to Mary Sanders, but what caught my eye was a brief sentence at the end of the article. According to legend, the only way to break the curse was to bathe the dragon in the blood of a thief.

Oh goody! Blood rites! And not just any blood, but the blood of a thief. It made sense, in a twisted sort of way, but just where was I going to find a thief willing to fork over a pint? Maybe Murray would let me go over to the jail and bleed one of their convicted thieves. I could go all the way and use leeches! Or I could tell him I was a research doctor, and we needed his blood for an experimental treatment. Yep, this was going to be a piece of cake—break your foot, heavy as brick, fruitcake.

"Great! Just great, now what am I going to do?"

Cinnamon peeked around the door. "Are you okay?"

I shook my head. "I dunno. I just want to go home and crawl into bed and stay there until everything's okay again." I waved her off again and took the dragon out of my purse, where it lay snuggled in a handkerchief, looking for the world like the cat that ate the canary. I set it on my desk. "So, you need a bath? Wonderful. I'm really looking forward to that."

The dragon didn't say a word. It just stared at me, eyes unblinking.

"Why did you come into my life? I didn't need you. I didn't ask you to show up. And now, I'm supposed to go break into the jail and play vampire?"

Again, not a word. This conversation was a little one-sided. I wanted to call Murray, to tell her what I'd found out, but then I remembered that we weren't speaking. *Shit;* I tucked the dragon away.

Cinnamon and Lana were finishing up the unpacking. Six o'clock. Time to close. "You girls go ahead and take off. I'll stay for another hour or so. I need to get these new ledgers finished." I called the kids and told them to nuke frozen dinners for themselves or to eat sandwiches and that I'd be home before eight.

The Chintz 'n China's accounting system ran off both hard-copy ledgers and a computer inventory tracking system. It was a damned good thing that I was as compulsive as I was. I'd kept a zip disk of every scrap of digital information on the shop, and on Tuesday nights, I took the info home with me until the next week, when I updated it again. Because of my diligence, the chipheads down at Compu-ER would be able to load all the old info off those backups onto my new laptop, which I would take home every evening for safekeeping.

After a solid hour and a half of work, I held my breath and armed the security system. I was still jumpy; it would be just like me to punch in the wrong numbers and have the cops breathing down my neck, but it proved easier to handle than I thought. Maybe this wouldn't be so hard to get used to.

I climbed into the Cherokee, fastened my seat belt, hit the ignition, and took off for home. The engine knocked loudly. Maybe I'd better call the auto shop tomorrow. I'd been putting off getting the bear scratches looked at, but with the engine clanking, I didn't want to take any chances.

Home wasn't far away, fifteen minutes by car, but as I turned onto Elmhurst Street, the Cherokee shuddered and died. I rolled to a stop near the curb.

Hell and high water! What now? I tried the ignition again but got only a bare rumble. When I dug out a flashlight and shone it on the dashboard, I knew exactly what my problem was. Dry as dust. Not a drop of gas left. Dandy! I'd forgotten to fill the tank after our trip to Mount Baker. Maybe I was self-destructing, I thought, as I hunted for my cell phone. Or maybe I should just write it off to stress and not worry about why it happened. That sounded good. Now, all I had to do was call Triple A, and they'd bring me some gas.

That is, they'd bring me some gas if I could find the

damn phone. I emptied my purse on the passenger seat and sifted through the contents. Nope, nothing resembling a cell phone amid the gum and lipstick and receipts and M&M's littering the bottom of my handbag. Had I left it at work? No, I was pretty sure about that. Home? Maybe. I got out and dug my way through the car, but either I was getting old and my memory was fading, or I'd be receiving the Space Cadet of the Year award.

I must have left the cell at home. Okay, that meant a nice, brisk walk. Not a bad thing, I reassured myself. My house was only about ten blocks away. I could call Triple A from there and have them pick me up and drive me back to the Cherokee with some gas. Though this wasn't a part of town that I frequented, comprised of old buildings and even older houses, I knew where I was.

I tucked my bag over my shoulder and slipped my keys between my fingers the way they'd shown us in self-defense class. If some jerk came at me, he'd get a face full of metal tips fueled by my frustration. After making certain the car was locked, I set off on foot, teetering on my high heels. From now on, I'd carry emergency sneakers in the car along with the first aid kit and a spare bottle of water.

Twelve

❖

EVEN THOUGH WE were into April, the days were still getting dark early. The temperature had managed to hit fifty-five today, but now it was dropping, and I pulled my blazer tightly around my shoulders. My feet hurt, and I wished again that I'd chosen flats this morning. Harlow could waltz around in spikes without a problem, but me? Nope, as pretty as they were, I looked like a cat trying to walk on its hind legs when I wore any heel higher than two inches.

I passed an abandoned corner grocery store and then one of Chiqetaw's many moldering houses, shivering as I glanced up at the old Victorian. I'd nearly lost my life in Eunice Addison's white elephant last December; it had looked remarkably similar to this one. Give me a new house any day, tidy and neat and compact.

A low hooting startled me; an owl in the tree I'd just passed was waking for the night. I stopped, gazing up at it as it eyed me silently. While some cultures considered the owl a bad omen, others thought it wise and magical. I preferred the latter version. "Are you telling me something?" I whispered. The bird slowly closed its eyes, then opened them again. Observant. The owl watched everything, looking for the smallest signs of scurrying rats and mice. Maybe that's what it was trying to tell me—to keep my eyes open, to pay attention.

. Which brought to mind White Deer's advice. If I was honest with myself, I knew she was right; I'd shut off my inner senses, blocking my intuition, and I wasn't sure why. Maybe Daniel's death frightened me from looking too closely at the future. Maybe I felt some misplaced guilt that I had contributed to his death. One way or another, I'd flipped the switch to dim, except for when the dragon had hurtled me into the midst of its visions. I had enough experience to know that psychic power could be dangerous when repressed. Time to open the floodgates.

Eight blocks from home, I tentatively reached out, listening with what I dubbed my "astral radio." After a moment, during which the night felt so ethereally silent that the very brush of air on my skin spooked me, I began to sense turmoil; there was an argument going on somewhere on the other side of the street, behind the closed curtains and locked doors of a house. A few houses later, a wave of intense grief washed over me, and tears sprang to my eyes, threatening to crystallize and spill over. Someone was mourning the loss of a loved one.

Six blocks from home, as I passed what was obviously a teenage hangout; waves of party-hearty energy assailed me. Music was blaring from inside. Somebody was stuck in the eighties, I thought, watching as the spinning lights from a disco ball flashed through the window. A vortex of laughter and sexual energy flooded my mind, and I was suddenly aroused, flushing as I quickly broke contact. The party had enough booze and funny cigarettes making the rounds to light up Chiqetaw. Enough for one night. I was ready for TV and a bowl of soup.

I crossed the street and paused at the next corner. If I took the shortcut through the vacant lot in front of me, I'd end up in the alley that ran behind Ida's house. I could then slip through her yard and shave two blocks off my route. My feet decided for me. They were tired and sore; I decided to go for it. I scurried down the alley, trying to keep from stepping in a hole. I kept center of the dirt track until I recognized the back of Ida's lot, but as I headed toward her fence, I tripped on a downed branch and stumbled, falling against her garbage can and knocking it over.

Stunned, I caught myself, using the fence for leverage. It was a wonder that Oliver didn't hear the crash and come out to see who was bumbling around his back gate. I shook my head to clear my thoughts and began to gather up the trash; I wasn't the kind of klutz who hit and ran without cleaning up my mess. I'd almost finished when I picked up one last bag and the plastic ripped. Oh yeah, just what I needed. Praying that I wouldn't be reaching into a handful of old spaghetti, I closed my fingers around the batch of garbage and stopped, stock-still. I was holding a necklace. A crystal one, by the feel of it, and a familiar feel, at that.

I hesitated. It was probably nothing, really. Maybe I should just ignore it and get moving. I mean, a lot of people wore polished quartz necklaces, didn't they? I knew, though, that I was going to fish out my flashlight and take a closer look at it. I couldn't go home and sit and wonder.

Even with splatters of unidentifiable trash on it, the polished spikes were familiar down to the cracked one on the end. This was one of my necklaces. I searched through the rest of the bag: matching earrings, gold hoops that weren't real gold; another necklace, this one low-grade carnelian. None of the pieces here were worth much, but they'd been in my jewelry box along with the valuable pieces when the house was robbed.

I glanced up at Ida's house. No lights; Oliver must be out. His rental car wasn't in the driveway, so I was probably safe. I played the light around the inside of the trash can, contemplating whether I was going to dig through the other bags to look for anything else that might be important. The roar of a car engine from the far end of the alleyway answered my question. I switched off my flashlight, glancing up as headlights flickered; the car was making its way onto the narrow dirt track. Even from this distance, I knew—absolutely, without question—that it was Oliver.

Yikes! I had to get moving. I dropped the lid to the garbage can and tried to grab hold of the necklace again but it slid out of my hands, onto the ground. No time left! I clambered over the gate into Ida's yard.

Had Oliver seen me? I couldn't be sure. As I snuck along the hedge, hurrying as fast as I could, my heel caught in a mole hole, and I went sprawling to my knees again. Oh joy; I was batting a thousand. This time the heel snapped when I went tumbling, and I frantically pulled off my shoes as I scrambled to my feet. I tested my ankle—no real damage, just a bit of a skinned knee.

The headlights had reached the back gate, and the car rumbled to a stop. Oliver parked in the alley, as did a number of people who lived in this neighborhood. I pushed closer to the hedgerow and hurried to the front of the lot. A glance over my shoulder showed a light flickering on in his living room. Afraid he might come out on the porch, I looked frantically for something to hide behind, but the front yard was well-groomed, and there weren't any overgrown bushes here.

If I raced directly across the street, I would run headlong into the bramble-covered lot. Even the sidewalk was scattered with the thorny vines, and I wasn't wearing shoes. Nix that idea. But if I dashed kitty-corner across the street, I'd be on the edge of Horvald's double lot. There were plenty of flower bushes over there that I could hide behind. I could catch my breath without being seen, and not terrify the kids by racing panicked into the house.

I charged across the street and up the incline leading to the rose garden. As I pushed through the bushes, I dropped to my knees and crawled behind the biggest one, a monster of a rosebush, already heavy with swelling buds. I peeked around the edge, cautiously looking back at Ida's house. Sure enough, Oliver stood on his front porch, looking around as if he was searching for something. After a few minutes, he turned, went back inside, and shut off the porch light.

I fell back, sprawling on Horvald's lawn. So much for a simple walk home. From now on, no more shortcuts. Of course, now I had a pretty good idea of who'd been in my house, robbing me blind, but I wasn't sure if I'd been ready for that tidbit of information. I liked it better when I thought Jimbo was my nemesis. At least he was up front about his feelings. I could handle a biker tossing a brick through the window easier than an friend's nephew stealing my beloved possessions.

As I lay there, catching my breath, it occurred to me that if Oliver really was the one who'd ripped me off, he might have robbed my store, and he also might be behind the recent spate of burglaries. If that was true, he might have been the one who attacked Norma Roberts, and that made him dangerous.

"Emerald? Are you okay? Emerald?"

The voice penetrated my thoughts, and I forced my eyes open. Horvald hovered over me, a concerned look on his face. I struggled to sit up, realizing I must look a mess. I was wearing an expensive dress covered with smudges of garbage, I probably smelled pretty ripe, my feet were bare, and I had a pair of broken heels in hand.

"Uh . . . yeah . . . I think I scraped my knee, but I'm okay." I felt like an idiot; how was I ever going to explain what I was doing sprawled in his flower bed?

Horvald reached down and helped me to my feet. He eyed me up and down and shook his head, then draped an arm around my back and helped me into his house. "You can call your youngsters from the house and let them know you're okay. No offense, Emerald, but you aren't looking your best tonight."

As he deposited me in a rocking chair, I started to slump back, then stopped, realizing I was covered with flecks of garbage, dirt, and grass stains. I kept my back rigid, not touching the cushion. "I'll be all right," I said. He handed me the phone, and I punched in my number and told Randa that I'd be home in about ten minutes, but until then, under no circumstances was she or Kip to let anybody in. "Nobody at all, do you understand? If Murray or Joe shows up, call me over at Mr. Ledbetter's house." I pointed to the number printed neatly on the phone and looked at Horvald questioningly. He nodded. "His number is 555-8442."

When I was done, Horvald sat down in the chair across from me. "Before I forget, I was outside in the garden this morning and saw somebody on your porch. He looked like he was fiddling with the door. I didn't know whether or not he was a friend of yours, so I yoo-hooed at him, and he took off and ran around the side of your drive and up the alley. I didn't get a clear look at him. Like a damned fool, I left my glasses inside."

Somebody messing with my door? Cripes! Thank heavens I'd called the locksmith. "Thanks, Horvald. I don't think it was any friend of mine. Next time you notice something like that, call the police, would you?" He nodded and then disappeared, probably to get me a roll of paper towels and the 409, I thought.

I dropped my shoes and the broken heel on the floor. So somebody was trying to break into my house again. Could it have been Oliver, back for another round? What the hell was left for him to steal? Maybe he'd had second thoughts and wanted my computer, the television, and Randa's telescope. Damn it! If only I'd managed to keep hold of that jewelry, I could prove he'd been in my house. Thinking of him prying through my dresser drawers made me queasy, so I tried to shake the thought out of my head. I'd deal with the whole mess once I got home. Right now, I just wanted to get some of this muck off me.

A noise from the kitchen brought me out of my thoughts, and I glanced around. This was the first time I'd ever been in Horvald's house. The living room was a masterpiece of tidy organization, just as I'd expect it to be. No clutter anywhere, but the room felt far from sterile. No, it felt like a museum, almost; like a tribute to passive beauty. What few knickknacks he owned were artfully arranged with careful precision. A menorah graced the mantel, and a few jade plants added color to the room. Horvald returned with a mug of mint tea. I sipped it gratefully and, as I set the cup on the end table next to the chair, noticed a lovely cobalt box with a Star of David on the lid.

"What a pretty box." I could feel a wave of emotion wash off Horvald as I spoke.

"Thank you. It belonged to my wife." He pulled up an ottoman and sat next to me. "Are you feeling better?"

I nodded. "I had a bit of a run-in with a dog. Ended up being chased through a couple of yards, and yours looked like a safe place to hide. The dog took off when he couldn't see me anymore." It sounded plausible and would account for my appearance. I needed to talk to the cops before I started spreading any rumors around. "I ran out of gas and had to walk home." Then, because I couldn't help myself, I asked, "You're married? I don't think I've ever seen your wife."

"You never met her," he said. "Ruthie died ten years ago, long before you arrived in Chiqetaw." He retrieved a photograph from one of the console tables near the fireplace. The woman in the picture was in her forties, with dark curly hair that tumbled past her shoulders. Her smile blazed out at me. If she had found me in her rose garden, she would have welcomed me in and tucked me in bed and made me chicken soup. She wasn't a beautiful woman in the traditional sense, but the radiance in her eyes lit up the room, even through a photograph taken long ago.

"She was beautiful, Horvald,"

He gazed at the picture. "I miss her. The garden was her pride and joy, her fairyland. I try to keep everything up the way she would have liked, but it's not easy. I'm sixty-three, and don't always have the energy I used to." His voice broke, and I suddenly felt sorry for the older man.

Regretting every joke I'd made about his late-night jaunts out to weed his flower beds, I laid my hand on his arm. "You loved her very much."

He rested his hand on mine. "She was killed by a drunk driver. I didn't even make it to the hospital in time to say good-bye." His grief eddied through the room, gentle waves rocking against the shore.

I sniffled. "I'm so sorry. Thank you, though, for trusting me enough to tell me about her."

"I haven't talked about Ruthie to anyone in a long time." He straightened his shoulders. "You shouldn't be worrying about an old man like me. Back to business, young woman. How are you feeling?"

I considered the question seriously. How *was* I feeling? Scared out of my mind, but he didn't need to know that.

"Filthy and in need of a shower. Skinned knee's going to bruise, but I've had worse. I should get home to the kids, though."

"Why not wash your face and hands first?" He pointed out the bathroom and handed me a dark green washcloth. Good, I wouldn't leave visible stains on it. I shut the door and turned on the hot water, then pumped a handful of soft soap and lathered my face and arms. I squinted into the mirror. Gluck. I looked like I'd fallen into a Dumpster; which—when I thought about it—was pretty much what happened. My dress would have to go to the dry cleaners and even then, I had the sinking feeling the grass stains were here to stay. Maybe I could dye it bright green. Like shopping for new clothes, without the hassle of going to the mall.

I rinsed the dirt off my skinned knee and found that Horvald had left a small bottle of Bactine on the counter, so I sprayed the scrape with the medication, hoping to stave off any nasty bugs. Finally, as ready as I was going to be, I wiped down the counter and returned to the living room.

Horvald walked me to the door. "You go home, check on your children, then come back when you've changed clothes. I've got a gas can, and we'll go get your car running. Bring the youngsters with you. That girl of yours is always out on the roof with that telescope. I'll bet she's told you some tales about me working in the garden in the middle of the night?"

I couldn't help but break into a big grin. "Well, yeah. She's quite the little voyeur, that's for sure."

He laughed. As he stood in the doorway, waiting to make sure I got home okay, I spontaneously turned and gave him a huge hug before heading across the street. The moment my arms slid around his husky shoulders, I knew that here was a grandpa without any grandchildren.

* * *

MIRANDA AND KIP stared at me as I slipped into the house. I shook my head. "Don't ask. I'm going to go take a shower. Lock the door, and don't let anybody in unless it's Joe or Murray." After I showered, I picked up the phone, then stopped. Murray and I were still on the outs. I'd call Greg at the station about the jewelry as soon as we returned, but I really wanted to get my car home safe.

We piled into Horvald's sedan. Within minutes, he had Miranda chatting about astronomy and Kip, about bikes. "How about some ice cream?" he asked.

I grinned at him. "You don't have to do this."

He waved off my protest. "Oh, let me. I love a good cone as much as the next person, and the Shanty Barn is right up ahead."

The kids leaned forward from the backseat expectantly, and I broke down and accepted. They cheered as he turned right and entered the drive-through. After we ordered soft-serve twists, Horvald headed to Mike's Service Station, and within half an hour, the Cherokee was back in action. We waved good-bye and pulled out away from the curb.

Miranda watched Horvald's car disappear in the rearview mirror. "I like Mr. Ledbetter. He seems nice."

I glanced at Kip in the rearview mirror. "What about you? What do you think about him?"

"He's real," was all Kip said, but it was enough to make up my mind.

"Kids, if you need help from now on when Mrs. Trask is gone, I want you to go to Mr. Ledbetter's house. Don't *ever* go over to Oliver's again unless I'm with you. I'm serious." They asked why, of course, and I fed them a line about not bothering him, knowing that they probably knew I was lying but too tired to address the issue.

After we got home, I put in a call to Greg and told him

about the stranger Horvald had seen, the necklace, and my suspicions that Oliver was behind both incidents. "The necklace and earrings were stolen with the other things. He had to be the one."

"The problem is, I don't think that I can get a search warrant based on what you've told me; at least not tonight. Since the garbage is still on his property, you were really going through his possessions. I doubt if Judge Heinz would give us the time of day, the hard-nosed old coot. He'd have my head if I bothered him for something that wasn't an emergency. Now, I could come out and dust for prints on your door, but I doubt if anything will turn up."

"What if I did have the necklace?"

Greg sighed. "Then you'd give it to me, and I'd do some poking around—legal poking around—but I'd see what I could find out."

I stared at the floor. That meant going back over to Ida's house and rooting through the trash can again, all the while hoping that Oliver wouldn't see me. Delightful. Oh yeah, just the ticket for a fun evening. "Okay, I'll see what I can do." Greg reminded me to be careful. I thanked him and hung up.

The kids told me about their day as I made myself a sandwich and nuked a cup of soup. Randa hopped on the counter, twirling her jump rope. I was glad to see she was finally getting some sort of exercise besides stargazing. Her raven hair glimmered under the light. "Mom, have you decided about the tests?"

At least I could give her a clear answer on that. "Yeah. Remind me to call your school tomorrow and make arrangements for you to take them. I warn you, though, if you do get skipped ahead, we're going to have a serious talk about all the responsibilities I expect out of you. And you will *listen,* not just brush me off."

Randa leapt off the counter and danced around the

room. Naturally, Kip wanted to know what was going on, and she burbled along to him like a fountain gone amok.

Her sudden switch into teen motormouth status jogged my memory. "You wanted some new clothes. How about I let you go out this weekend and get them? You can get your hair done, too, but I want you to call a salon. I'd rather pay extra for a good cut than take a chance on an inexperienced beautician." She gave me a quick hug and raced off for her room. Kip shook his head and disappeared into the living room.

I checked my voice mail. Safety-Tech had called to reschedule; they couldn't send out anyone until Monday, which meant we had almost another week to get through without any protection. Peachy, but there was nothing I could do but wait.

The second message was from my sister Rose. She wanted to talk about our parents' thirty-ninth anniversary. The affair wasn't until early September, but she was starting to plan for it now. Typical. Rose was so tight that you could wind her up like a top and let her go and she'd never run down. We called her the Energizer Bunny when I was a kid. Since we'd grown up, we seldom spoke; it wasn't that we didn't love each other, we just lived in vastly different worlds, and she preferred her own set of friends and lifestyle. She'd fallen under Grandma McGrady's spell, just as I'd fallen under Nanna's. And so the War of the Grandmothers, as we'd called it since childhood, had also divided the granddaughters.

I put the kettle on for tea and sat at the kitchen table, scribbling notes. So Oliver was a thief. Jimbo had been telling the truth about not robbing my house. Was he telling the truth about the shop, too? And what about the manager's wife? We knew Jimbo had thrown the brick through my window, but if he wasn't behind the burglaries, then he couldn't be the one who attacked her.

Oliver, on the other hand, had managed to get into my house and go through my things. I thought back, trying to figure out when he'd had a chance to snoop around without me knowing about it.

Bingo! He'd been alone here when I asked him to watch for the window pane to be delivered. Joe wasn't around; I'd been on my way to pick up the kids from Harlow's. Oliver would have been able to go through the house at his leisure then.

Another thought struck me as my gaze fell on the Peg-Board that held the key to the shed and the spare key to the front door. What if . . . I jumped up and pulled open the junk drawer, rummaging around until I found the old spare house key. I turned it over in my hand, examining it closely. There—little flecks of a pale substance clung to the metal of the house key. White, dry . . . powdery almost. I closed my eyes. What did it remind me of? Flour. It reminded me of the dried dough on my hands after I made cookies. And what was like dough? Clay. Sculpty, maybe, or Fimo. Damn, he'd taken an impression of my house key! That's how he'd gotten in when we were gone on our vacation to Mount Baker, and that's why the door had been locked when I got home.

Damn squirrel, I thought, trying to push away images of him pawing through my stuff. Here was Ida, giving him a second chance at life, and he was ripping off her friends. I wanted to wring his filthy neck. I tossed the key back in the drawer. Trouble was, would the cops be able to act on what little evidence I had?

The kettle whistled, and I fixed myself a pot of tea. I poured the water over orange spice tea bags and hauled out a package of Oreos. Now what?

One thing was for sure: I needed to retrieve the necklace and earrings from the trash can. Tomorrow was garbage day, so I'd have to do it tonight before the evidence disappeared on its way to the landfill. That meant I had to wait until Oliver was asleep, then sneak back to the alley behind his house, a thought I didn't relish. I toyed with the phone; if I could just call Murray, she'd bolster my courage. I let go of the receiver. Not a good idea. White Deer? She was more of a listener than a cheerleader, and a cheerleader was what I needed. Murray and I'd always encouraged each other on in the face of overwhelming odds.

I finished my tea and wandered into the living room to stare at the dragon, the lone inhabitant of my now bare and broken étagère. "Are you behind all of this?" I asked. "Did you summon all of our bad luck? And now you're waiting for a bloodbath that I don't know how to provide."

The dragon sat poised, almost breathing. I lifted it up to the light. Jade was a peaceful stone, a lucky stone, and placing a curse on an object made out of it was like handing Pandora the key to the forbidden box.

"Whatchya doin', Mom?" Kip was staring at me from his perch at the computer desk. "Did the dragon move again?"

"No," I muttered. "No, it didn't move again."

"Have you tried using Nanna's book to remove the curse?" Kip didn't talk much about the journal anymore, not since December, when he'd gotten himself in trouble for trying to work charms he didn't know how to control. He'd made our life hell and had paid for it by being banned from helping me with anything magical for six months.

I didn't want to tell him what I'd found out; it seemed too gruesome, even for my Ninja-video-game-playing son. "I suppose I can try." Though I doubted if it would work, at least I'd be doing *something*. I took the dragon and my tea and went back to the kitchen, cautioning Kip to stay off the Internet and out of the kitchen unless I called for him.

I opened the journal to what seemed like the strongest charm Nanna had written down. *Breaking Curses.* Hmmm.

Digging through my stash in the pantry, I hauled out the components that the journal called for. Salt and crystallized sulfur. Holy water, for which I substituted Florida water, a Voudoun concoction that worked just fine. Nanna's pewter star pendant. A large piece of quartz crystal, and a silver ring with a polished cabochon of amethyst in it. I slid the ring on and draped the pendant around my neck, then cleared a space on the counter.

Sprinkling a circle of salt around the statue, I chanted, "Depart, all spirits evil and wayward energies. Flee this dragon, flee this house, and never return." Channeling the energy that ran through my hands, I focused it around the statue. Flickering, the faintest of lights emanated from my fingers to engulf the dragon. I placed the amethyst next to the dragon's right side and held the quartz crystal in my left hand, point aimed directly at the statue. I was about to complete the second part of the spell when a flash startled me as the page of Nanna's journal that I was reading from burst into flames and flew into the air, showering me with ashes as the dragon slowly pivoted to stare at me.

"Holy crap!" *Put the quartz back on the counter and step away from the statue, ma'am.* I rubbed my hands to stop them from tingling with the backlash of energy. I checked the journal to make sure it was okay. There was no obvious damage, other than the crisped page. I turned back to the dragon. So, obviously basic hexes and charms weren't going to work. "Damn you, don't you mess with Nanna's book again." Exasperated, I snatched up the statue and stared at it. The dragon mutely eyeballed me back, a snarky look on its face. I shoved it into the broken étagère and headed upstairs to change into dark jeans and a black sweatshirt. Time to play garbage man. Lucky me.

Thirteen

❖

AFTER MAKING SURE I had my flashlight, I
paused at the phone. I knew I should call somebody
to go with me, but all my logical cohorts were out of reach.
Harlow was still in a wheelchair, and Murray wasn't talking to me. I tinkered with the receiver, then picked it up
and dialed the firehouse. The dispatcher on duty told me
that Joe was out on an emergency call and wouldn't be
back for some time. I thanked her and left a message for
him to get in touch with me as soon as possible. So that
was it; I had to get over there before morning, and apparently I was going to do so alone.

I finally settled for leaving the kids a note. If they woke
up and I wasn't back, they were to call Officer Greg and
tell him that "Mom went after the necklace and isn't back
yet." If he wasn't around, they were to call Murray.
Chances were, they'd never know I'd been gone.

Locking the door, I slipped quietly into the shadows.
Although the night was clear, the moon was a sliver, barely

visible, and the only light came from the stars that formed a glittering canopy overhead. I turned right at my front gate, hightailing it around the block. I approached the alley from the far end, where I figured I'd be well out of Oliver's sight.

I matched my breath to my steps, moving carefully to avoid stirring up any sleeping dogs or other such denizens of the night. Give me a ghost any day over an angry homeowner who might think I was a thief attempting to break into his house. A scurrying movement stopped me, and I froze, listening as some creature skittered through the tall grass that was growing alongside the dirt alleyway. Cat, skunk, or raccoon, whatever it was disappeared, and I was once more alone.

As I approached the back of Oliver's house, I paused, hiding behind the gatepost. So far, so good. No lights in the kitchen, no lights upstairs. I didn't have the faintest idea of what he'd do to me if he caught me. He was obviously short a few cards in the deck, and I didn't particularly want to know which ones were missing. After a few minutes, when there was still no sign of anybody stirring in the house, I cautiously approached the garbage can. It had been righted, and the lid was back on.

Not so good. He'd noticed the mess. I lifted the lid to find the can empty, the mishmash of garbage gone. Had he seen me? Or had he come out to empty more trash and found things in disarray? If that had been the case, why hadn't he just shoved the trash back in the can? Then again, with the necklace right on top of the pile, he might have gotten spooked.

I looked around. Tomorrow was garbage day. If I were looking to hide a bunch of smelly garbage until then, where would I put it? The house? No, he was a neat freak. Maybe the car? I turned off the flashlight and snuck up alongside Oliver's car. With another glance at the window to make sure nobody was watching, I shone the light in the backseat. Nothing. Clean as a whistle, just like the house. Maybe the trunk? Feeling rather foolish, I bent over and sniffed the back end of the car. Nothing but the faint residue of exhaust.

Damn it! I leaned against the car, trying to think. If only I'd grabbed the necklace when I had the chance, but I'd been too startled. Maybe I could sneak into his house? Have a look around? Uh-uh . . . nix that idea. A confrontation with Oliver was the last thing I wanted, especially when I wasn't sure just how dangerous or screwy he was. Nope, nothing left to do but go home.

About to retrace my footsteps, another thought struck me. What better place for garbage than a trash can? And there were trash cans lining the alley, since tomorrow was garbage day. I peeked in the one belonging to Ida's next-door neighbor. Nope . . . the next was a bust, too, but on the third, I saw a familiar bulge. Oliver had managed to get all his garbage into a neighbor's half-empty bin. Smart boy, very smart. But not as smart as me.

I burrowed through the bags, and though I couldn't find the earrings, I did find half the necklace; the strand had broken, but I managed to confiscate the remaining crystals and clasp. I pocketed them and was about to take off for home when there was a movement behind me; a soft *click* warned me that I wasn't alone.

"Put your hands up, nice and slow." *Oliver.*

Oh shit! I took a deep breath and slowly raised my hands. "Don't hurt me," I said, wondering if he really had a weapon.

He answered my question by jabbing a gun barrel between my shoulders. "Be a good girl, and you'll do fine. So, I see you've found what you were snooping for. Now you're in on my little secret. I wonder what else you know?"

Not knowing what to say, I kept my mouth shut, waiting for his next move. I heard him fumble around for a moment, then he gave me a little push toward the gate leading into his yard. "Start walking. We're going back to your place. If you do what I say and don't scream or run or try any stupid tricks, I won't hurt you."

That's what all the bad guys said in the movies, then they ended up blowing the brains out of their victims. "Can't we just talk this over? I won't tell anybody—"

He snorted. "Nope, you've got something I want, and I doubt that you're carrying it in your pocket, though knowing you, I might be wrong. Move, and don't try to get away, because I won't hesitate to shoot. This gun is equipped with a silencer. Nobody would even know you were hurt until it was too late."

I obeyed, slowly leading the way across his front lawn as he maneuvered us into the shadows. We crossed the empty street and, before I could clear my thoughts, we were standing on the front porch of my house. Could I make it inside, slam the door on him before he could follow? I considered the possibility as I fumbled with my keys but decided it wasn't worth the risk. As I unlocked the door, I turned to him and said, "Kip and Miranda are sleeping. I'll do whatever you want, but if they get hurt, you're mincemeat, gun or no gun."

He just snarled and pushed me through the door, where he motioned me into the living room. "Sit down and be quiet." He kept the gun trained on me while he backed over to the étagère. "Aha! There you are!" He reached through the missing glass to grab the dragon.

Comprehension flooded my brain. "The dragon? You've been after the dragon?"

"Hell yes, the minute you showed this to Ida and me, I knew what it must be worth. I can get a good price for it on the black market. If you hadn't played hide-n-seek so well when you said you were taking it to the store, and then again when you went camping, I'd have it now, and you wouldn't be in this mess." He slid the figurine into his pocket. "The question is, what do I do with you?"

His eyes flashed, and in their reflection, I caught a glimpse of Norma Roberts, lying unconscious on her floor, and I knew Oliver was the one who'd hurt her. Startled, I almost slipped and said something but managed to stop myself before it was too late. If I kept my mouth shut, maybe he wouldn't realize how much I knew. "Just leave; take the dragon and leave."

"Well," he said, perching on the arm of the sofa, "I can't just run off and leave you to call the police. Maybe . . . if I had insurance that you'd keep your mouth shut . . ."

I broke out into a cold sweat. Something about the way he said "insurance" scared the hell out of me. "Really, just tie me up if you want, then leave. I promise I won't call the cops, and I won't tell Ida when she comes home." Like hell I wouldn't.

He cocked his head and gave me a cunning smile. Squirrel, yep, and a rabid one, at that. "I got a call this morning. Ida's coming back next week, and somehow, I think it would be best if I was long gone. I would love to thank her for her hospitality and the nice assortment of trinkets I found in her house, but don't think she'd appreciate my gratitude. Maybe you can thank her for me."

I was about to say something when he pointed the gun at me. "Quiet. I need to think. Hmm," he mused. "Let's just get you trussed up and gagged for a start." He looked around, then spotted Randa's jump rope coiled in the corner where she had left it. "This will do—" The phone interrupted him, startling us both. "Who's that?"

"I don't know, but if I don't answer, you can bet somebody will be over here. I'm never out late, and I always answer the phone, even when I'm in bed." Maybe this was my chance.

He pointed the gun at me. "Okay, answer it, but not a

single word that will make me inclined to pull this trigger. Understand?"

I nodded and picked up the phone, swallowing. Please, oh please, be Murray or Greg. Luck was with me for once. Greg's deep voice boomed across the line. "Emerald, we thought you might want to know that Jimbo's just posted bail. One of his buddies managed to come up with it."

I forced myself to remain calm. "Thank you, I appreciate the warning. I'm scared Jimbo might come back, though." I prayed that Greg would catch the hint and come over, but he seemed oblivious. Oliver, however, shifted, and I felt the gun graze the back of my neck.

"We've thought about that, too. I'm going to have Deacon swing by your house every couple of hours. You call us at the first sign of trouble. And about the necklace—I'll look into it tomorrow morning. If I stop the garbage truck right after they pick up at his house, then I can go through the bags without a problem. So don't you go getting yourself in trouble by going over there again, you hear?" Greg said a quick good night and hung up.

I listened to the ringing dial tone, kicking myself for not catching his attention. Oliver reached around from behind and took the receiver from my hand, gently replacing it on the phone cradle. "Good girl. Now get your butt over to the sofa, lie facedown, and put your hands behind you."

Shaking, I obeyed. Oliver looped the rope around my feet, then yanked them back so my knees were bent. He hog-tied me, winding the cord around my hands, binding them so tightly to my feet that I wanted to scream. Then he twisted a scarf that I'd left on my desk into a long, taut rope and forced it between my lips, tying it at the back of my head. I started to choke, and he loosened the knots but left the gag in place.

"There we go. You won't be going anywhere. Now, for some insurance . . ." With a snap of his fingers, he took off

upstairs. Shit! He was going after Kip and Miranda! I
rocked back and forth, terrified.

A few minutes later, Oliver returned, dragging the kids
by their arms. Kip was the first to see me, and he broke
away and raced over to my side. I couldn't see everything
that was happening, but I heard Kip yelp and then Oliver
said, "Get over by the fireplace, you two. Do as I say, and I
won't hurt your mother."

I tried to turn my head to get a better view, but my arms
were so strapped by the bindings that I couldn't twist
around. A stabbing pain drove between my shoulder blades,
and I forced myself to relax until the cramp passed. I
wanted to tell the kids to do what he said, to keep him calm
and not make him angry, but the scarf seemed to expand in
my mouth, and it was all I could do to keep from choking.

Oliver ordered Randa to sit in the chair. Petrified, I held
my breath, wondering what he was doing, but then he said,
"Don't get your panties in a wad, Emerald. I'm just tying
her up so she won't feel the need to play Wonder Woman."

Randa spoke up quickly, her voice shaking. "Why are
you doing this to us? What's happening?"

"Tell your mother what I'm doing so she doesn't kill
herself trying to see that you're okay," Oliver said gruffly.

After a pause, Randa spoke again, sniffling, but sounding a little calmer. "I'm okay, Mom. He's just tying me up
in the rocking chair."

She was frightened, but I could tell she was telling me
the truth. With panic one step away, I knew I had to calm
myself, to conserve my strength. I tried to breathe evenly
and slowly through my nose. Inhale . . . exhale . . . slow
and easy.

After another moment, Oliver knelt near me. He was
clutching Kip's wrist, and by straining to the side, I could
just make out the petrified expression on my son's face.

"Here's the deal. Kip's coming with me, and we're

taking your car, so don't even think about calling the cops when you finally get free. I'm meeting up with my buddies, and we'll drop the kid on the side of the road before we hit the border. He'll be safe with me as long as you don't call the police, but if I even *think* I smell a cop car, he's history, dead in a ditch. Got it?"

"N-n-nooo . . . ." Kip stuttered.

Oliver cuffed him on the side of the head. Furious, I struggled against the ropes, but they immediately dug into my skin. Kip threw himself at me and begged me to stop. "M-m-om, your hands are turning white. S-s-top! You'll hurt yourself."

"Knock it off!" Oliver's voice rang through the room. Kip sniffled and looked up at him. "If you behave, your mother and sister will be safe. If you don't do what I tell you to, I'll call some of my friends and have them come over and slit their throats. Do you understand me, boy?"

Pale, Kip nodded, his lip trembling. He looked down at me, and I gazed into his eyes, praying that he'd be safe, that he'd have some chance to escape. Oliver was dangerous. No way did I trust him to keep his word.

"Good," he said, then pushed Kip toward me. "Kiss your mother and say good-bye. You behave, and you'll be back home by tomorrow afternoon."

Kip leaned down, he looked in my eyes and, with a single glance, we said so much. Dashing the tears from his eyes, he gave me a brave soldier smile and whispered, "I'll be okay, Mom." He kissed my cheek and turned back to Oliver. "I'm ready," he said. And then, they were gone.

AS SOON AS they left, I started to struggle, but the ropes began to cut off my circulation, and I remembered that hog-tying somebody pretty much insured that if they tried to escape, the ropes would automatically tighten. I slowed my breathing, trying to calm my thoughts. Could I somehow get off the sofa, knock the phone off the hook, and dial 911 with my nose? The scenario seemed within reason until I tried to shift around, only to discover just how ridiculous the stunts in those action movies are. Barring the miraculous discovery of a jagged metal edge nearby on which I could cut the ropes, I was trussed up like a pig on butchering day.

I did, however, manage to squirm around enough to see Randa. She caught my glance and held it, her eyes waging a war between fear and anger. Yep, she was my girl all right. Oliver had tied her arms to the arms of the rocking chair and gagged her, but her feet were free. I gauged her strength. Could she tip the rocking chair forward enough to land on her knees and crawl to the phone? Nope. The chair was solid oak, and while it wasn't upholstered, it was a heavy son of a bitch. I hoped to hell she didn't get the same idea because, knowing Randa, if she thought of it, she'd try it.

Samantha came padding into the room and stretched up against the side of the sofa to stare at me. I glared at her. Silly cat. Kip was right. We needed a dog. Lassie would be perfect. *Emerald's tied up on the sofa, you say? Come on girl, let's go rescue her!*

Out of ideas and rapidly losing hope, the tears were beginning to well up. Uh-oh. Not a good idea when I had a gag in my mouth that could choke me if I got too much phlegm in my throat. Not a good idea when my nose might get all stuffed up, and I couldn't breathe through my mouth. Focus on something else, I thought. Focus on . . . on . . . my eyes caught sight of the corner of the étagère. The dragon! Oh shit. Oliver had stolen the dragon, and even if I was able to get free and save my son, we'd still be doomed. If Oliver got away with that figurine, I'd have no chance of breaking the spell.

How had I been so stupid? Going after that necklace

without somebody there to back me up was insane. I'd been so preoccupied that by the time I'd sensed Oliver behind me, it had been too late. On the verge of panic, with no other hope, I decided to try contacting Nanna. If I could transcend the pain from the ropes, maybe I could slide out on the astral and call for help.

A noise at the front door startled me out of my thoughts. What the hell was going on now? I couldn't turn my head, but I saw Randa's expression shift, her eyebrows raising as she stared at the archway leading from the foyer into the living room. Then, after a brief pause, a man's voice echoed through the room.

"You are the weirdest freakin' woman."

It wasn't Horvald or Joe or Andrew. Who else did I know that would show up at this time of night? One of Murray's buddies, maybe? With a hopeful heart, I tried to speak through my gag, but it came out as garbled gibberish. A few seconds later, the cloth fell away from my mouth and I gasped, breathing as deeply as I could.

"What the hell are you up to now?" The deep reverberation of his voice triggered off my memory. Then I caught a glimpse of black leather and smelled tobacco.

Oh, no, it couldn't be. "Jimbo? Is that you?"

He snorted. "Oh, yeah. It's me all right. My, my, my, isn't this convenient, you all tied up and waiting for me?" With a chuckle, he slid down on the floor next to me. Grinning with delight, he raised his hand and traced along my face, over to my nose where he lightly bopped me. "Looks like you had quite a party, babe."

I'd been exhausted, but this new turn of events sent a fresh rush of adrenaline through my veins, and I let out a shriek of frustration, with a little fear thrown in for good measure. "Shut up! Shut up and untie me, you goon! This isn't funny. My son's been kidnapped."

That wiped the smirk off his face. In less than a minute,

I was free from my bonds, and Jimbo was untying Miranda. I leapt to my feet and immediately fell back on the sofa, dizzy. "I have to go after him. I know he's headed toward the border."

"Who?" Jimbo pocketed his knife and folded his arms, looking puzzled. A red bandanna covered his hair, which was held back in a long braid, and his beard nearly reached his chest. Made me think of ZZ Top, now that I looked at him more closely.

"Oliver—my neighbor's nephew. He robbed me and kidnapped my son to keep me quiet." I glanced out the window. "Oh hell, he took my car."

"Mom, shouldn't we call the police?" Randa was crying, her eyelashes shining with tears.

I pulled her close and kissed her on the head.

"He's gonna hurt Kip, isn't he?"

"I don't know if he's going to hurt Kip, honey." I looked at the bewildered biker. "What are you doing here? I mean, thanks for untying us, but why are you here?"

Jimbo shrugged. "You know, it was the weirdest thing. I was headed to Reuben's to get stewed, when I stopped to gas up my bike, and this old woman comes out of the shadows near the station. She looked like something out of *Heidi,* you know? She told me to get my ass over here pronto, and then she vanished. Made me think of my granny. I got back on my bike and aimed for Reuben's, but damned if I didn't end up in front of your house. I saw that your door was open, and I decided to come on in."

Nanna? It had to be her! Unable to comprehend the bizarre happenings, I turned to Randa. "Go upstairs and get dressed. Don't screw around, I want you to hurry."

As soon as she took off upstairs, I turned back to Jimbo, gauging his mood. White Deer's advice echoed in my memory, and I cringed. How could I ask for help from someone I despised? The very thought set me on edge, but

I had no choice. I didn't trust Oliver to keep his word, and every minute that passed put more distance between me and my son. I swallowed my pride.

"Jimbo, I need your help. Oliver's got Kip, and they're in my car. He's headed for the border, but he said that he has to meet some friends first. Do you have *any* idea of where he might be? If you do, please tell me. My baby's in danger."

Jimbo stared at me for a moment, the gruff machismo in his eyes giving way to a slightly softer glow. "How old is your boy?"

"He just turned nine last month." I held my breath. "Please, please help me. Help Kip."

"I had a little brother," he said, distracted. Then he sighed. "Oh, for chrissake. Okay, I've got my chopper out front. You sure you don't want to call the police in on this?"

I glanced at the clock. We were wasting time. "Randa can do it after we leave."

She came running down the stairs and looked from Jimbo to me, then back to Jimbo. "What should I do?"

I grabbed the phone and dialed Horvald's number. He answered, sounding a little sleepy. "Horvald, I need your help. If I send Randa over, will you watch her until I get back? She'll tell you what happened. Please, Kip's in danger, and I'm going after him."

Horvald stammered out an "Okay," and I thanked him.

I gave Randa a long hug, then kissed the top of her head. "Go. Once you're safe in Horvald's house, I want you to call Murray and Greg. Tell them what happened. And . . . be my good girl, okay?"

She nodded, pale and drawn, then scurried across the street to where Horvald was standing, his front door open as light streamed out onto his lawn. As soon as she was safely inside, I turned back to Jimbo. "Let's ride."

He shook his head. "I can't believe I'm doing this. Have you ever ridden a motorcycle before?"

"Years ago," I admitted. "One of my boyfriends owned a Yamaha, and he used to drive me around town on it."

Jimbo let out a strangled cough. "*Yamaha?* Whoa, boy. Okay, listen up, babe. When I lean to the side, you lean to the same side. Hold tight to my belt at all times. Don't jerk around or freak out on me. If the dude is meeting some friends before heading toward the border, I'm pretty sure I know which route he'll be taking 'cuz I got buddies who do border runs on a regular basis. There's a field along the way that they party at during the summer. Easy to get to but not easy to spot from the main road. Good hideout material."

I didn't ask him why his buddies made border runs. I didn't want to know. "There's something else," I said. "If we're able to catch him . . . he took something of mine that I have to get back. It's a little statue of a dragon." I considered Jimbo's questionable nature and record. "It isn't worth much, but I really need to find it."

He shrugged. "Right now let's focus on your kid." He swung a leg over the chopper and scooted forward. Feeling awkward, I clumsily crawled on the back, wincing as my thighs stretched wider than they had in a while. Damn, it was a big bike!

"Hold on," he said over his shoulder. "And put this on." He reached back, handing me his helmet. It was too big, almost covering my eyes, but I wasn't going to complain. Motorcycles made me terribly uncomfortable, and I prayed we'd get through this without an accident. "What kind of car you got?"

"Grand Cherokee. Green."

He nodded, revved the engine, and we shot off like a bottle rocket. I leaned forward, tucking my arms around his sides as I grabbed hold of his belt. Holding on as if my life depended on it, I clenched my teeth as the road raced by beneath us. The wake of cold air that blasted by sent goose bumps up my arms; I should have brought a jacket.

Kip . . . Kip . . . Kip . . . the sound of the engine seemed to chant out his name as we roared along. Would Oliver keep his promise? Would he let my son go if he didn't see the cops behind him? Or would he take a sadistic delight in hurting my child? I thought back to Huang Fu and the curse he'd called down on the dragon, and found myself wishing that I could command the spirits like he had, that I could summon up some demon or spirit to spiral into Oliver's path and destroy him, leaving my son unharmed. The tendrils of anger coiled against my tailbone wound together, rooting into my being, blossoming up to overwhelm every sensation I felt except for the worry for my son. The next thing I knew, I shot away from my body, my spirit connected to my physical form by a silver cord stronger than steel. I was out on the astral realm.

I hovered in a gray mist as a current of energy rumbled below my feet. And then, the jade dragon was there. Perhaps it was the spirit of the stone from which it was carved; most assuredly it was the essence of the carving. The dragon curved and coiled, eyes glowing red as it leaned down to meet my gaze. Not flesh, not in the sense that a bird is flesh, but a spiral of energy and form, one of the mysteries of the universe better left untouched.

"Help my son, and I'll free you of the curse!" My words were feathers on the breeze, wafting aimlessly as they hovered for a second, then vanished. The dragon turned, coiled again, reaching out to graze me with long cat whiskers. They twitched, agitated, and I repeated my request, not caring whether I was speaking to the demon who cast the curse, the spirit of the dragon statue, or just the residue anger that Huang Fu had poured into the statue. "Help my son, and I'll free you of the curse!"

The dragon reared back to cover the sky. The gray mist that seemed to stretch on forever shuddered, looping in on itself in waves. I shuddered as the mist became clouds became a vortex sucking me in. Wanting to scream but somehow managing to remain in control. And then . . .

And then, I was on the bike again, my cheek pressed against Jimbo's back as I clutched at his belt. I shook my head to clear my thoughts, looking around for the dragon, but it was gone. An incredible surge of energy and strength raced through my body. I was ready for a fight.

Jimbo seemed oblivious to what had just happened, which was just fine. I cautiously probed his aura; nope, nary a speck of psychic energy, which was probably a good thing, considering his predilection for causing mayhem and trouble.

The night sped past as we traversed the back road, and I was beginning to wonder if we were going the wrong way, but the roar of the bike and the feel of the big man's girth between my arms was oddly comforting; I let myself reach out again, breathing slowly to regulate my jump onto the astral.

No dragon awaited this time. I searched for Kip's energy, for anything that would tell me we were on the right track. There—in the distance, a little spark that I knew was my son. His aura was usually bright, flickering with strength, but now it was pale, fear overwhelming his ability to trust his intuition.

Once again, the connection vanished, and my head whirled with the roar of the energies that had raced through my body and engulfed my mind. And yet, regardless of all the psychic abilities in the world, I was afraid. Could I trust my instincts? Could I trust the visions that, for so long, had seemed simply another one of my senses? Could I trust that my son was still alive?

As I struggled to hold on to the remaining confidence I

had, White Deer's advice came rushing into my ears. *"Tune back in to the otherworld; if you don't, you'll risk short-circuiting your psychic awareness."* I believed in White Deer's powers. And if she believed in me, then I had to believe in myself as well. I took a deep breath and let it out slowly. Kip was alive, and we were headed in the right direction. And the dragon? I didn't know what would happen, but I had touched its core and had faced it square on.

Jimbo slowed down and pulled off to the shoulder. He pointed to a turnoff ahead. "There," he said. "I'll bet you anything that he's in there."

I closed my eyes again, reaching out once more. There. Again, a tiny spot, a Kipling-spot, faint but alive, faint but breathing, faint, but undeniably my son. "They're there, all right. Okay, what do we do now?"

Jimbo gave me a lurid grin. "Sneak in, grab your kid, and see what havoc we can cause. Are you ready to rumble?"

The energy that had filled me moments earlier reeled up, making me dizzy. I nodded. "Ready as I'll ever be."

"Then let's go bag us a bad boy and see what we can do to him." Without another word, he pushed the bike off the road before anybody spotted us, leading me into a thicket of ivy and fern.

Fourteen

✤

JIMBO LEANED HIS chopper against a nearby cedar and motioned for me to follow him. The turnoff was a few hundred yards ahead. "We'd better cut through the woods," he said. "If we go in on the main road, they'll see us for sure."

We huddled in the shadow of the trees while he got his bearings.

"Do you know which way to go?" I asked.

He snorted. "Babe, I know my way around the woods better than anybody in this godforsaken town. I've lived and worked out in the forest for years, so don't get a bug up your butt. You big-city broads are all the same. Soft as a creampuff."

Big city? If Jimbo considered Chiqetaw a big city, I'd hate to see what he thought of Seattle. "I just thought, since it's dark and all . . ." My voice trailed off, and I had the feeling I'd made him mad. Hell, I couldn't afford to lose his help; but when I glanced at him again, his eyes twinkled, and I knew he was just spouting off.

He motioned for me to follow him. "Keep quiet, don't scream or shout, don't go all wacko on me. If a cougar or bear wanders in, I'll sense it before it senses us." He gave me an appraising look as he plunged into the undergrowth. "Can you move any faster than that?"

"Cocky, aren't you?"

"I got reason to be. Come on, your kid's in there waiting."

I followed him, struggling over the vines and branches that cluttered the forest floor. The temperature must have been hovering around forty; without my coat to keep me warm, I was finding it hard to keep up with the big man.

Jimbo glanced back to see what was holding me up. He must have noticed that I was shivering because, without a word, he took off his jacket and tossed it back to me. I silently wrapped it around my shoulders. Engulfed in the folds of leather, I wasn't sure which was worse—the cold or the smell of smoke-laden, sweat-soaked cowhide.

The huckleberries crowded in between trees, snagging us on their thorns, and ferns rose knee-high, obstructing every step we made. Jimbo went slowly, pointing out branches and sticks along the path that were big enough to trip me up. Grateful, I stumbled along, barely able to see his silhouette in front of me.

After a moment, he stopped, raising his hand. I froze and listened. Voices, coming from somewhere up ahead. Jimbo leaned down to whisper in my ear. "We still got a ways to go. My plan is this: we head to the north, then swing to the west and sneak up on them from behind. They'll be watching the main road, not the forest itself." He motioned for me to get moving. "Keep your mouth shut, and don't scream if you fall or bump into anything. I have to concentrate on the path, so don't screw up."

"Uh-huh," I said, swinging in behind him. The night

took on a surreal glow as we fought our way through the tangle of brambles and vines. Though I wasn't a girly-girl, I'd never really been out in the woods like this; I'd always stayed sheltered within my tent or my cabin and kept to the paths when I went hiking. Now, thrust into uncharted territory, I had no idea of where we were, or which way we were going.

As I glanced at the forest canopy, a pale light glimmered as it haloed the treetops. *The spirits of the trees, the very essence of the forest.* I inhaled deeply, and the clean, crisp scent of the cedars and firs cleared my head. Nearby, water drops trickled, an ever-present force in these mountains as they dripped off trees and bushes in rivulets, carving long snakelike fingers through the forest floor. As I pushed through one of the thigh-high ferns, a frond snapped back, slapping my face, and I could taste the wet, gritty tang of fresh earth.

I was so wrapped up in my thoughts that I bumped into Jimbo when he came to an abrupt stop. With an irritated grunt, he pushed me into a crouch behind a fallen log, holding his finger to his lips for silence. I leaned against the stump; it was as big around as my kitchen table and covered with moss. A sour smell rose from it, one of decaying mushrooms mingled with the acrid scent of the soil. My nose began to itch. A handkerchief was sticking out of one of Jimbo's pockets, and I took a chance and wiped my face with it.

Sudden laughter filtered through the trees from our left. We had looped around, all right. Jimbo had managed to lead us through the inky forest until we were hiding right next to the clearing. *Please let Kip be there. Please let him be safe.*

"Stay here while I check out things." Jimbo took off, bending low as he scuttled away. Within less than a moment, he was out of sight, and I was alone. My eyes had adjusted to the night, but everything was still bathed in indistinct shades of black and gray. I pulled his jacket close around my shoulders and shifted so I was sitting on the ground with my back against the stump. Oliver had sure done a number on my legs; they still ached. I'd never again truss up my Thanksgiving turkey without thinking of him. I rubbed my calves, trying to get the circulation going, but my blood felt like it had been thickened with molasses.

Where the hell was Jimbo? How long could it take to peek out into a clearing? I glanced in the direction from which we'd heard the voices. Was my son really over there, or was it just a group of Jimbo's friends, on one of their border runs? I knew in my heart that Oliver wasn't going to let Kip go, and I prayed that they were the ones in the meadow, that we had actually caught up to them.

A brief notion of following Jimbo danced through my head, but before I could seriously entertain the idea, I came to my senses. He was right; I wasn't trained for guerilla warfare. If I traipsed off by myself, I'd probably end up giving away our position. Digging at the ground with the heel of my sneaker, I forced myself to wait until the brush rustled with Jimbo's return. He let himself down on the ground next to me, sitting cross-legged.

I leaned close to him so we wouldn't be overheard. "Are they there? Is Kip out there?"

"He a short, strawberry blond haired, scared looking little runt?"

"Runt?" I sputtered. "He's not a runt, he's just small for his age!" Then I realized what he was telling me. "Kip! You saw Kip? Is he okay?"

"Shush. He looks fine, just tied up and a little scared." Jimbo pulled me to my feet and dragged me away from the encampment until we were out of earshot. There, under the frozen starlight, he laid out what he'd seen.

"There are four or five men there, besides your kid. I didn't see your car."

"Okay, so how do we get my son away from them? Oliver's dangerous, and he's got a gun."

Jimbo shrugged. "That so? They don't look so tough, but if one's packing, I'll bet they all are—"

I interrupted him. "Packing?"

With a disgusted sigh, he said, "Carrying weapons. Are you going to let me finish or not?"

I shut up.

"Anyway, there's an old van there, beige. I'm not sure what's in it, but I don't think we're going to have time to find out. We nab the kid and get out of there."

"I've got to get hold of that dragon that Oliver stole." I wished I could just let him keep it, to pass the bad luck from me to him, but I knew that it didn't work that way. Until I broke the curse, my family was in danger.

"What's so special about it?" Jimbo narrowed his eyes. "Don't try to bullshit me, either. Unless you tell me why we gotta take down a man with a gun for a little piece of plastic, then you're going to have to make do with getting your kid back."

I just wanted to move, to get in there, get Kip and the dragon, and go home, but Jimbo obviously wasn't going to budge until I told him what he wanted to know. Maybe if I resorted to tears? Nope . . . one look and I knew that he'd just hand me the hanky and wait for me to blow my nose. "You're going to think I'm nuts."

"Tell me something I don't know." He grinned.

I glared at him. "Yeah, yeah, funny man. Fine, you want to know what's going on? Here's what's going on: that dragon has a curse on it. Unless I get it back so I can break that curse, my kids and I are dead meat."

He paused, stroking his beard, and I resisted the

impulse to suggest that he braid the tangled mop. "You remind me of my granny."

"I'm not that old." Gee, I hadn't been insulted this much since I last talked to Roy.

He gave me a withering look. "She's a hoodoo woman, down in Louisiana. Breaks hexes and cast spells for people all the time. My mother moved us up here when I was seven, but before that, Granny used to tell me stories about the bogeys in the swamps down there. And I tell you, I've seen plenty of weird shit out in these woods."

I realized he had accepted my story without so much as a blink. "So, you believe me?" This day had been just full of surprises, too many surprises. Right now, I'd happily settle for routine as usual.

Jimbo shrugged. "People around town say you're a witch, but I just thought it was some cockeyed way to make money. Either that or their spelling ain't so hot." Another grin. "Okay, so we go after the dragon, too. Which dude is their leader? What's he look like?" I quickly described Oliver. "Yeah," he said, "the guy with the cigarettes. He *does* kinda look like a squirrel. So, here's the deal: Kip—that's the name of your boy, ain't it—he's sitting on a log near the back end of the field, tied up. The gang's got a fire going in the fire pit, and I think they're arguing about something. It doesn't look like they're ready to head out yet."

"We need some sort of distraction, something to divide their attention so we can get to both Kip and Oliver," I said, leaning against the nearest tree. My adrenaline rush was at low ebb, and I was feeling woozy and tired.

"Excuse me? So *we* can get to Oliver? Sorry to bust your bubble, babe, but you couldn't even take on the Easter bunny. I'd lay ten to one odds on the rabbit."

I held my breath and counted to ten. "Fine, you've made your point. Do you have any suggestions?"

Jimbo thought for a moment and then snapped his fingers. "You said we need a distraction. I know just what to do, but I'll have to go back to the bike to get a few things. Wait here. Don't move and don't say a word."

Before I could speak, he had turned tail and disappeared into the gloom. Great. Alone again and still waiting. We'd be lucky if Oliver and his gang didn't decide to take off before we got in. If they were arguing, it probably had something to do with money or whatever else they'd managed to get their hands on. I hoped to hell they weren't debating over what to do with my son.

Jimbo was back in less than five minutes, carrying a plastic bag that he must have grabbed out of his bike's saddlebags. He was missing his bandanna, though, and when he lifted the trash bag, the odor of gasoline overwhelmed me. "You got a gun in there?" I asked, hoping for once that he would be true to stereotype and be "packing" himself.

He looked at me like I was crazy. "I just got out of the slammer tonight. You think I'm going to cart a gun around while I'm up on charges? Charges *you* brought against me, I might add?"

"Oh. But you *were* justified in smashing my window? Yep, you're a real force unto yourself, aren't you?"

He snorted. "You know you're pretty when you're fired up?" I glared at him but kept my mouth shut. "Okay, down to business. What I have in this bag will keep 'em so busy they won't have time to think about the kid, let alone their getaway plans."

"What are you talking about?" If he didn't have a gun, just how did he expect to keep them from hightailing it out of here? "Knockout gas?"

"Not quite," he said, pointing to a large tree about fifteen yards from us. "Get behind that tree, and try not to fall over anything."

I cautiously picked my way through the undergrowth,

ignoring the soft brush of moss against my face; it dripped off the tree limbs like lace. A rustle near my feet startled me, and I froze as something slithered over the tops of my shoes. A snake. Shit! I closed my eyes, pretending it was Sid, one of Murray's boas. Sid was a nice snake. He liked me. He would never hurt me. As the reptile tickled my ankle and disappeared into the undergrowth, I let out a deep sigh. At least we weren't east of the Cascades, where the rattlesnakes roamed. Over here in western Washington, we were civilized. All our wild snakes were harmless.

As I crept to the spot behind the tree Jimbo had pointed out, I found myself peeking through a narrow opening in the forest into the clearing. Flames flickered in a ring of stones, lighting up the glade, while a circle of trees protected the meadow from view. A beige van was parked near our hiding place. I looked around for Kip.

There! On a fallen log toward the back of the meadow. My baby was perched on the trunk, knees drawn to his chest. He rested his forehead against his knees, encircling them with his arms, which were bound at the wrists. A rope trailed along the ground, from the bindings over to where it was tied around a tree stump near the fire. Yep, Oliver had made certain he couldn't run off into the woods. I searched but couldn't see any obvious signs of injury. The adrenaline kicked in as I stared at my son. Oliver needed a good thrashing, and that was just what he'd get. Nobody messed with my babies and walked away clean; I was going to make him so sorry he ever laid eyes on me that he'd be begging the cops to cart him away.

Four men huddled around the campfire, arguing over what appeared to be a pile of loot near the flames. Oliver wasn't with them. I craned my neck, trying to pinpoint him. After a moment, he emerged from behind a bush on the opposite side of the fire, zipping up his fly.

"That's him, that's Oliver," I whispered, trying to keep

my voice as low as I could. Jimbo nodded. He squatted down and opened the plastic bag, taking out a half-burnt candle and a lighter. A moment later, he was up again, peering back through the trees. Then he pulled his missing bandanna from the bag. The cloth was soaked with gasoline.

He grinned at me and whispered, "Gonna be a hot ol' time for those boys tonight. You see that van of theirs?"

I glanced at the van and nodded.

"It's got mag wheels."

I shrugged. "So?"

He handed me the candle and lighter. "Hold these. Mag wheels have magnesium alloy in them." I must have looked as blank as a fresh canvas because he gave me a look of frustration that mirrored how I felt. "Don't remember your high school chemistry, do you? Magnesium is highly flammable." He pointed at the van. "I'm gonna make that baby blow like crazy."

Whoa! I managed to stop myself from shouting as I began to understand his intentions. "You're going to blow up their van?"

With a wink, he snickered. "Yep, but first, I have to get out there and file a few scrapings off one of those wheels. That, wrapped up with this candle and bandanna, will give us a wick to ignite whatever's left in their gas tank. That should do the trick. The tanks on those old vans usually drop down directly below the gas cap. I'll light this baby and toss her in there, then run like hell, 'cause when she blows, she's gonna blow big."

"Will anybody get hurt?"

Jimbo shrugged. "That's a possibility, if they're close to the van. Your choice—you want your kid, or you want to let them cart him off in that thing?"

I'd never been party to deliberate wholesale destruction before, but when he put it that way, I didn't have much choice. They had my son, and I'd do whatever it took to rescue him. "What else do you need?"

"Time. The dudes around the fire seem pretty caught up in whatever they're doing. I don't think they'll give us too much of a problem. It's Oliver I'm worried about. He seems to be keeping a close eye on the whole camp." He took the candle from me, wrapped part of the bandanna around it, then tied it in a loose knot. Then, pocketing the lighter, he took another look at the encampment.

I considered the situation. "What if I sneak up behind Kip and grab him? If I time it right, they'll come after me but not be able to catch me before I'm back in the woods. They'll be hunting for us, not paying attention to the van. Will that give you the time you need?"

Jimbo raised his eyebrows; he nodded ever so slightly as he thought about my proposal. "That would work. If you could give me five minutes, that would be enough. Once it goes, they'll be back in that meadow in a flash, and then I can grab this Oliver dude when he comes back out of the woods. Trouble is, can you get over there on your own, snatch your kid, and dodge back into the forest without getting shot? I don't think you can do it without getting your butt blown to smithereens. And trust me, a bullet wound ain't a whole lot of fun." He pulled up his shirtsleeve, and I saw a scar across the top of his bicep. "I know."

He was probably right, but those men were going to kill Kip. Even supposing Oliver kept his word, the other members of his gang wouldn't leave my son alive. He could identify them. Kip's life was on the line.

"I can do it," I told Jimbo. I dusted my hands on my jeans, then stopped and looked back at him. "Hey . . . thanks, you know?"

"We'll get your kid back safe," he said, then stretched out his hand. I lightly grazed his fingers with my own. "Just a minute," he added. "You're going to need a knife to cut the ropes. Here, I brought back an extra, just in case."

He handed me an ominous-looking weapon. The trigger made me grin. A switchblade, just like the one I'd carried around in high school to attract the attention of Jimmy Salver, one of the bad boys. I'd never had the guts to even open the thing, but now? I'd learn fast. I flicked the button, opening and closing it a couple of times, then rested the hilt in my hands, searching for the blade's center of balance before slipping it into my pocket.

Crouching as low as I could, I picked my way around the perimeter of the field, staying as close to the edge of the forest as possible so as to not be seen. I kept my eyes on the movement in the camp, pausing as I came to one of the fallen logs covered with moss. It was huge, with a hollow space beneath it where the rain-soaked earth had washed away. Good hiding place, I thought as I clambered over the tall timber. Once I rescued Kip, we'd have to hole up somewhere. There was no way in hell I could haul ass back through the woods while leading a frightened little boy out of harm's way. Not with a gang of desperate men following me.

After what seemed like an interminable amount of time, I came to the edge of the clearing, directly in back of my son. He was about five yards away, staring at the men, and I was close enough to see that they were divvying up a stack of money. Oliver was leaning against the van, drinking a beer and smoking a cigarette. He was looking in the other direction, watching the entrance to the field, thank heaven. I steeled myself. It was now or never.

A drop to the forest floor brought me face-to-face with a mound of rotten debris. Yuck! And I'd thought Oliver's garbage can was bad. With a deep breath, I sprawled out on my belly, using my elbows and feet to push me forward. Sheesh, everything in the movies looked so easy, but this slithering stuff was for stunt men, not for normal people like me. I was out of breath before I even got near Kip's perch. I stopped, trying to keep myself from panting. What if they heard me? What if they shot me right in front of Kip? Oh hell, what the fuck were we doing here?

It was all the fault of that damned dragon. The root of everything that had happened, the statue had drawn one nasty surprise after another to my life. I shook my head. Whining was getting me nowhere; I had a job to do. I had to rescue my son.

Before I moved on, I readied my knife. No sense in losing any time, though I doubted that I could stop a bullet with it.

A moment later, I reached the back of the log. Bless his heart, Kip must have sensed my presence, because he gave a quick glace over his shoulder. I held my finger to my lips and, cool as shrimp on ice, he casually returned to resting his head on his knees. Now to free him and get both of us back into the forest before they shot us. Using my son as a shield from prying eyes, I slowly pulled myself up so I was barely peeking over the edge of the log.

Oliver polished off his beer. He crossed the camp to where an ice chest sat near the fire, grabbed another, then headed toward the woods opposite the van. The minute he stepped into the shadow of the trees, I eased my arm around Kip's waist, and he swung his legs over the log. The men still hadn't noticed. Kip faced me now and, trembling, I sliced through the ropes around his wrists.

I grabbed Kip by the arm and, in a low crouch, we raced toward the trees. As we neared the edge of the forest I stood up, breaking a branch as I did. Shouts erupted from the camp; we'd been spotted. I grabbed Kip and pulled him along, racing for the tree line, where we dove into the welcome embrace of the foliage. "Listen to me," I said as I dragged him over stump and branch. "We have to hide before they get here."

The sounds of shouting were closer now, and I knew that the men had reached the edge of the clearing. I frantically looked for the tree with the hiding spot. There! "Scramble under there and be quiet, no matter what you hear."

"What about you, Mom?" Kip clutched my hand, panic washing across his face.

"Don't worry about me," I said as I gave him a fast peck on the cheek. "I love you. Now go! Do as I say and remember—keep quiet no matter what until I call you!" He crawled under the tree and vanished from sight.

I shuddered; probably a spider-filled hellhole under there, but still better than what awaited if Oliver and his cronies got hold of him. I took off in the other direction, making enough noise to draw their attention. I plunged through the forest, flailing at the low hanging branches that slapped against my face. Unable to see more than a few feet ahead of me, I tripped and went sprawling when my toe caught on a branch. Up again, no time to assess damage, no time to think, only to act.

As I straddled a log blocking the way and rolled over it to the other side, an ethereal silence descended to cloak the trees around me. Everything settled into a peaceful fog, even the pounding of my own heart. Mute, I stopped short; there was a light shining from a small stand of trees. The glimmer emanated from the roots on up to the branches, so faint it was almost undetectable. I reached out to touch the energy housed in the long white trunks, and an undertow swept me into the current that flowed through the copse, surrounding me with a feeling of safety and welcome. These trees were offering me a shield. I slipped into the midst of the birch stand and waited.

"Where'd they go? Damn it, find them!" Oliver, his voice angry and fueled by fear.

"Who the hell is she?" One of his cronies, no doubt.

"The kid's mother," Oliver shouted.

They searched all around the outskirts of the thicket, but not once did they set foot inside. It was as if the trees created an impenetrable barrier. I leaned my head against one of the cool trunks, grateful to whatever woodland spirit was protecting me.

The next moment, a huge explosion rocked the forest, and a fireball billowed up from the clearing. I flinched but managed to keep my mouth shut. Jeez! Jimbo hadn't been kidding when he said he was going to shake things up!

Immediate pandemonium erupted from the group of thieves. All four men headed back for the clearing, but Oliver remained, still nosing around the copse. Damn it! What was I supposed to do now? I held my breath. He was less than a yard away. And then my cell phone in my back pocket rang. Hell and high water! I fumbled with it, but not before Oliver had honed in on the noise.

"Emerald? Emerald? You might as well come out now. I know you're in there." His voice showed no sign that he'd been shaken by the explosion. "I'm going to find you in a few minutes; it'll be easier if you just come out now." He was edging into the copse of birch when the sound of sirens began to wail in the distance. Murray, I thought. It must be Murray! Without a doubt, I knew she was on her way, but could she make it in time?

"Shit!" I could see Oliver turn toward the clearing, listening to the sirens, and it dawned on me that he probably had the dragon with him. This was my last chance. If he escaped, we'd be stuck with the curse. So would he, actually, but that was of little comfort. I leapt out of the trees, aiming directly for his back. He let out a sharp grunt, wavered a moment, then fell with me right on top of him.

"What the fuck—" he twisted around, shifting position under me. I knew he had a gun, but I couldn't see if it was still in his hand. I tried to pin his arms, to hold him facedown, but his muscles were wiry, and he managed to roll over, taking me with him. His hands were empty; the gun must have been knocked out of his grasp when I hit him.

"You wanted me to show myself. Well, here I am!" I rammed my knee toward his groin, but he was too quick, moving aside as I aimed my leg straight toward his blue boys. Before he could grab me again, I rolled and came up into a crouch. Wow! Sometimes the action hero stunts actually worked!

"Don't make this hard on yourself or the kid." Oliver was on his feet, too, skirting the perimeter of our tree-lined arena.

I circled with him, gaze darting to the forest floor. Where the hell was his gun? If he found it before I did, he'd kill me and then go after Kip. And then I remembered; I had a weapon! I yanked out the switchblade and flicked it open. So I didn't know how to use it, at least it might make him think twice about jumping me.

Oliver saw the glint of the blade and hesitated. That brief pause was all I needed. I plunged at him, screaming. He dove to the side and immediately started scrambling forward on his hands and knees, gaze fastened on something near one of the maidenhair ferns buttressed up against an ancient fir tree. The gun, there, a few yards in front of him. Maybe I could get it before he did. I tossed the knife away and threw myself toward the base of the tree, sailing through midair to land on my belly, right next to the revolver.

"No you don't!" Oliver was almost within reach as I grabbed the revolver and scrabbled to my feet. He came up, eyes blazing as I whirled and took aim. I'd never held a gun before, never even wanted to hold a gun, but now I homed in on him and waited as he charged.

He caught sight of the revolver, targeted at his heart. As he flailed, trying to stop, his boot caught on a branch, and he went sprawling to the ground, screaming as he landed.

Not sure just what had happened, I cautiously circled him until I was far enough away to avoid his hands but close enough to be sure the bullet would hit him if I had to shoot.

"You'd better stay right where you are, because if I have to pull this trigger, I might just hit something a little more important than your leg. Now, where's the dragon?" The sound of sirens whirred into the clearing. "Tell me! Now!"

Oliver moaned and forced himself into a sitting position. The switchblade was jutting out of his shoulder, embedded deep in the muscle. Blood poured down the side of his shirt, soaking his clothes and pooling on the ground below. "In my pocket." He grunted, doubling over with pain.

I motioned for him to move his hands away from the knife. "Don't touch that knife! Leave it right where it is, or that stab wound will feel like a walk in the park next to a bullet hole."

A sudden movement diverted my attention as Jimbo stepped into the clearing. Oliver snatched the opportunity and fumbled for the knife hilt. He had barely closed his fist around the handle before Jimbo was all over him. The biker grabbed the blade and yanked it none too gently out of Oliver's shoulder.

Oliver was no match for Jimbo, and the fight was over in seconds as Jimbo pummeled him into the dirt. Moaning, the thief sat up, grimacing in pain. Besides the self-inflicted knife wound, he sported a double shiner and a broken nose. Jimbo looked relatively unscathed, except for singed eyebrows and a substantially shorter beard than he'd had half an hour ago. I knew *that* little makeover hadn't come from the fight.

The smell of smoke filtered through the forest, and I coughed, trying to clear my lungs. How bad was the fire? Was it coming our way? "Give me the dragon!" I waved the gun at Oliver.

Oliver cautiously reached into a blood-soaked pocket and pulled out the jade dragon. Jimbo grimaced as he took it and handed it to me. The statue was covered in warm, sticky liquid. "Eww," he said. "You sure you want this?"

I nodded, accepting the blood-soaked statue. I tried to give Jimbo the gun in exchange, but he wouldn't touch it.

"You gotta be kidding," he said. "If I'm packing when the cops get here, they'll be all over my butt."

I was about to answer when a sudden flurry of wind swept through the stand of birches as a tree limb sailed past my head. I ducked as the bough crashed next to Jimbo. Another gust sent a second branch skyward, and a low roar began to echo through the forest. The noise rebounded off the trunks of the trees to form a cadence, a *rat-a-tat-tat* of thumps that sounded like nothing less than a machine gun. I stared at the dragon; it had begun to vibrate. I tried to keep hold of both it and the gun, but a brilliant shaft of lightning shot forth from the eyes of the statue, and I flung the dragon to the ground and covered my face from the blinding flash.

The wind howled as I peeked through my fingers, my eyelids still dancing with spots from the afterglow of the fiery light. Jimbo was on the ground, holding Oliver down to make sure he didn't get away, but the biker's eyes radiated with fear, and I didn't know how long he'd last before he bolted.

As we stared at the spot where I'd thrown the statue, a sparkling crimson mist coiled up from its jade eyes. The mist hovered for a moment, then drifted out to encircle the tree-dappled arena, tendrils aiming toward us.

"Don't breathe, don't move," I whispered. Jimbo caught my gaze and nodded just enough to show that he'd heard me.

The mist traced a line along my cheek, silken fingers searching, probing for a host. I remembered a game I'd played with my sister when we were children and willed myself to become a living sculpture, a queen of ice in this woodland kingdom. Just as Rose and I'd played for jelly beans when we were children, now I played for higher stakes. I thrust myself out on the astral. There it was—not a living being, but an energy, searching for a new home. Whoever moved first, lost.

One minute stretched into five. I could see Jimbo and Oliver, both frozen, staring terrified at the crimson haze. My muscles were throbbing, I didn't know how much longer I could stand like this; another moment, and I'd lose control. A second cramp rippled through my calf, and I clenched my teeth. Hold on, hang on just one more minute. Focus on my breath, breathe in with the cramp and exhale the pain.

And then, just as my strength began to waver, the mist pulled back. Unable to locate a proper host, it twisted into a vortex and began to spin. The miniature tornado whirled faster and faster, and then—with an ear-piercing shriek— spiraled into the sky. The blood on the dragon sizzled to a boil and burst into flames. Just as quickly as the fire appeared, it vanished, leaving only a fine ash to cover the jade. The breeze racing through the copse caught up the ash and it, too, soared into the night and was gone. I slumped to the ground, every muscle in my body aching. It was over. The curse was broken.

"What the fuck just happened?" Oliver asked, his voice laced with pain.

I let out a tremendous sigh. "Something that should have happened five hundred years ago."

Jimbo's gaze never left my face. "Shit! You'd give my granny a run for her money. You really *are* a hoodoo woman, aren't you? Remind me not to mess with you again!" He pointed toward Oliver. "If the show's over, we could use some rope to truss this guy up. Isn't there some out where they tied up your kid?"

My kid. Kip! I called out, "Kip! Kip! It's okay, you can come on out now." Within seconds, my son answered as he found his way over to the birch grove. I raced to him, dropping to my knees as he threw himself in my arms. "Kip, we're safe now, honey. Everything's going to be okay!"

His eyes grew wide when he took in the scene, with Jimbo holding down Oliver, and the dragon back in my hands. Another round of sirens sounded from the clearing. "It's all over?" Kip asked. "Really?"

I nodded. "Yep, it's all over, bud. It sounds like the police are out there, doesn't it? We caught Oliver, and I broke the dragon's curse. The statue's clear."

He buried his face in my shoulder, and we stood there for a moment till Jimbo cleared his throat. "Not that it matters, but my arms are going to sleep."

"Oh! I'm sorry, of course."

I started back for the clearing, but at that moment, my cell phone rang again. This time, I answered, and Murray's voice rang out, loud and clear. "Em, are you okay? Where are you? We're out here in the meadow. We've found the van, but where are you?"

"In the woods." Feeling an ambiguous mix of relief, exhaustion, and bewilderment, I gave her our approximate position. "Hurry up, and don't forget your handcuffs."

"We'll be right in."

Within minutes, Murray led Sandy, Greg, and Deacon through the woods. She eyed our motley group and quizzically turned to me. "You look like a mud rat."

In the glow of their high-beam flashlights, I glanced down at myself. Yep. Wearing Jimbo's oversized black leather jacket, covered with dirt and branches and moldy old leaves from my scuffle with Oliver, I looked like I'd just emerged from some highland bog. My ankles were beginning to itch; I'd probably lucked out and landed in an anthill.

Utterly exhausted, I leaned against the nearest tree I could find as Kip raced over to Murray and threw his arms around her, mouth running full steam as he poured out his story. She listened for a moment, then gently hushed him. "You keep track of what happened, okay? We have to take a statement from you, but we'll do that down at the station in a little while."

Kip wrinkled his nose. "Cool. Hey, Mom broke the curse on the dragon!"

Murray glanced at me. "Did you really?"

I nodded. "I don't ever want to go through that again." Now my hands were stinging; I rubbed them on my jeans, but it felt like little barbs of fire were digging in to the flesh.

"I wish I'd been here," Kip said, pouting a little.

She put her arm around his shoulder and walked him over to Deacon. "Well, how about you tell me the whole story in a little bit? Right now I need to talk to your mom, okay? Deacon, can you take Kip out to the cruiser and get him into a warm blanket?"

Deacon motioned for Kip to take his hand. "C'mon buddy. Can you walk or do you want a piggyback ride? You've had a hard night." Kip took his hand and they headed out toward the clearing.

Murray walked over to Oliver as Greg and Sandy were handcuffing him. She searched in his pocket until she found his wallet. "Take him out and read him his rights."

Before I had the chance to thank him again, Jimbo blew me a kiss and winked as he followed them. "See ya later, babe. You put on one hell of a good show. Maybe you're all right after all."

Murray raised her eyebrows and looked back at me.

"Hmm, interesting." Then she opened Oliver's wallet and flipped through it. My stomach twisted, and I began to feel a little dizzy. "Just as I thought," she said, her voice echoing as if from through a long tunnel.

"What? What did you say?" I could hear her words, but they didn't make sense to me, they were full of static.

"This guy isn't Oliver."

"What? Of course it's Oliver." What was she talking about? I didn't understand.

She shook her head. "No, Em. Oliver's dead. They found his body down in Vancouver."

"Dead? That can't be. If Oliver's dead, then who the hell just tried to kill me?" Confused, I tried to focus on what she was saying. Something was very wrong. "Murray?"

"Em? Em? Are you okay?"

I couldn't see her anymore, the forest was spinning around, and I was at the center of the twister. "Murray, I think I'm dying," I said.

"What? Em, what's going on?" Her words fluttered on drifting leaves, and everything began to cave in on itself.

And then, the world went black.

Fifteen

❖

I OPENED MY eyes to find myself stretched out in a
hospital bed, florescent lights glaring down at me. My
legs burned; or maybe they itched. I couldn't tell which by
this point. "Kip, where's Kip?"

Murray leaned over me, eyes narrowed as she examined
my face. "He's okay, Em. He's fine. White Deer took both
kids back to my place. They'll stay with me until you're
feeling better."

"What happened?" I was having trouble staying focused
long enough to speak.

She rested her hand on my shoulder. "You had a bad
allergic reaction. You landed in a patch of stinging nettle
while you were fighting Ced . . . Oliver. When the toxin hit
your bloodstream, it sent your blood pressure plummeting.
You fainted."

I tried to pay attention to what she was saying. "Am I
going to be okay?"

"You'll be okay. You just need to rest. The doctor gave

you some medicine, and it's making you woozy. The kids are just fine, so you go back to sleep now. Okay?"

My mouth didn't want to work. I nodded. *Blink* . . . back to the darkness again.

THE CLOCK ON the wall read one P.M. as Doc Adams peeked through the door. He checked my blood pressure, temperature, looked at my chart. "You're going to be just fine. You gave us a little scare, but a good shot of antihistamine took care of it. The welts on your legs are shrinking. Looks like the nettles were too much for your system, and you overdosed on the toxin. Allergies are often hereditary; since Randa has an allergy to shellfish, I want you to make an appointment in a week so we can check how these hives are healing and to schedule a set of diagnostic tests for you. Better check out Kip while we're at it."

Boy, that sounded like a load of laughs. "I'll call Tissy next Monday and set up the appointments," I said, leaning back against the pillows. "May I leave now? I'm so ready to get out of here. I want to see my kids."

He signed the chart and draped his stethoscope around his neck. "Last night was quite a free-for-all, wasn't it? Detective Murray told me what happened. She also asked me to remind you that she took your children home, and that both of them are fine as fiddle ferns. She's out in the waiting room. I'll let her know you'll be ready to go in a little while. Why don't you take a shower first; that way the nurse can reapply the cream on those sores before you go."

He paused at the door and, with a grin, added, "I recommend you start working out if you intend to make a career out of crime fighting. You could use a little more muscle on those bones."

I huffed, but he'd already disappeared, so I padded to the shower. The welts on my legs were about the size and shape of inflamed mosquito bites, and some of them were oozing a little. My hands were covered with weals the size of pencil erasers. It occurred to me that, if the hives had already started to shrink, I must have looked like death warmed over when they brought me in the night before. I scrubbed away the mud and dirt, letting out a shriek as the soap hit the hives. Damn, felt like I'd fallen into a wasps' nest! Hopefully the walls in the bathroom were sound-proof.

After I managed to catch my breath, I lathered the smell of smoke out of my hair and climbed out of the shower and toweled off, cautious around the open sores that covered my calves. The mirror affixed to the wall beckoned. Wincing, I dropped the towel and peeked. Jeez! I looked like some deranged Dalmatian, covered with red bumps, and black and blue bruises. No short hemlines anytime soon, that was for sure.

As I pulled on the flimsy robe the hospital provided and stepped out into my room, I found Murray, sitting on the bed, waiting. She jumped up, a smile creasing her worried face. "Em! You're okay! Oh, I am so glad to see you up and around, girl. We were worried."

I grabbed her, holding her tight. "Mur, I don't ever want to go through a night like last night again. Doc said you have the kids?"

She nodded. "Yeah, they're at your house with White Deer right now. Kip is fine, honey. So's Randa. They know I'm here to get you." She handed me a tote bag containing clean underwear, a long, loose gauze skirt, and a T-shirt. "I took your other clothes with me. White Deer's trying to wash all the nettle out of them."

I started to pummel her with questions, but she shushed me. "Get dressed first. Kip and Randa are champing at the bit, waiting to hear *you* tell them you're okay." She sat on the bed while I got dressed. "Hey, Em . . . before we head out, there's something I have to get off my chest. I want to apologize for the nasty things I said during our argument." She gave me a tight smile, and I could tell she felt pretty awkward about the whole situation.

I flopped down on the bed next to her and let out a big sigh. "Umm . . . you know, let's just leave it in the past? White Deer and I had a long talk, and she helped me understand what happened, on both sides."

"Then, we're friends again?" Her eyes were shining. "I was so scared last night when you fainted. I thought you were going to die."

I choked back my tears. "Mur, you're my best friend. I'm sorry I wasn't more supportive. I let you down, and I sure didn't mean to. You're my best buddy, you know?"

She wiped her hand across her eyes. "Stop it, you're getting all maudlin, and you know I don't do mushy. C'mon, goose. Let's get you home."

I stood up and threw my bag over my shoulder, wincing. A twinge, most definitely a twinge. I'd need to slather on the Biofreeze for a week or two. The nurse loaded me up with antibiotics for the hives, and cortisone lotion for the itching. I signed the release papers, and we were finally free to leave.

The ride home felt surreal. As we pulled into the driveway, I saw that it was empty. "Mur, when can I get my Cherokee back?"

She put the car in park and turned off the ignition. "I hate to tell you this, Em, but we have no idea what they did with it. My bet is that they left it at some local chop shop where it's being parted out. That's the easiest way to dispose of a stolen vehicle."

She had to be joking. "My car's gone?"

She nodded. "Probably."

"For good?"

"I'm sorry, Em. Really."

I digested the news. My beloved SUV was history. Probably forever. A parting shot from the dragon, no doubt. When I realized I'd have to put in yet another claim to my insurance agent, I cringed. I'd be lucky if Applewood didn't politely request me to take my business elsewhere.

"What about all the stuff I lost? Do you think you'll ever find any trace of it?"

Her frown deepened. "Truth is, Em, we think it was all in the van. At least that's what they told us when we interrogated them."

I closed my eyes. "The van that Jimbo and I blew up?"

"Yeah. Honey, you helped blow up your own antiques."

I gave her a hopeless look. "Mother fu—"

She held up her hand, suppressing a smile. "I know, I know, but hey, you and Kip are alive, and that's what counts. C'mon Em, it's all water under the bridge now. I have to admit, you and Jimbo sure did a number on that baby. Impressive, but please, don't do it again?"

I glared at her. "I hadn't planned to make it an occupation, you know."

"Well, good, I'm glad to hear that. By the way, we think that van may have been the one that hit Daniel, but we'll never know for sure unless somebody confesses, and I doubt if that's going to happen."

I tried to find some bright spot in the whole mess. "At least you'll get the credit for solving this case. Coughlan can't do much to you after this, at least not directly."

She snorted. "Uh-huh. We'll see. I hope you're right, though. You'll never guess who's going to interview me later today."

I cringed. "Not Cathy Sutton?"

Murray nodded. "Yep, one and the same. She tried to get an interview with Jimbo, and he mopped the floor with her; told her just what she could do with her microphone. Talk about blazing cheeks, she looked like she fell in a bucket of red paint." She laughed. "It was pretty funny, I'll have to admit. You would have loved it."

I snorted. "You're right, I would *love* to see Cathy go up against Jimbo. Talk about no-win scenarios. At least you'll get some well-earned recognition out of the whole mess."

"By the way," Murray continued. "I forgot to congratulate you on your new friend. Jimbo's one hell of a guy." With a wicked grin, she poked me in the arm. "Em and Jimbo, sitting in a tree . . . blowing all the cars to smithereens!"

I glared at her. "Hey, he *did* help me save Kip."

"Yeah, he did, all right, and I figured you'd want to drop the charges, so I've started the paperwork." She gave me an odd look. "Em, just don't forget, Jimbo's the bad boy. Always has been, always will be."

I eyed her suspiciously. "Don't even think it—no way. He helped me out, I'll drop the charges. There's nothing more for you to worry about."

"Good. Now, you've got a houseful of people waiting for you. Let's go." We climbed out of her car and headed into the house.

Harlow, Joe, Horvald, and my children were gathered around the kitchen table. They cheered as I walked in. Randa and Kip crowded in, wrestling me into a chokehold. "Mom! Mom! You're safe!"

Throwing my arms around them, I relished the feel that they were safe under my wing again. I kissed Randa's forehead, then tipped Kip's chin up so he was meeting my gaze. "How you doin', bud?"

"I'm fine," he said in a hesitant voice. "White Deer took good care of us. Mom . . . I was scared you were dead. They carried you out on a stretcher an' everything." Relief over my homecoming must have pushed away worry, because he broke into a mile-wide grin. "I can hardly wait to tell all my friends how you kicked that guy's butt and saved me! You were like Lara Croft, running through the trees and using that big ol' knife an' everything!"

I suppressed a laugh. Lara Croft I'd never be, but if my son saw me as the action queen of the world, then I'd happily leave him with his fantasy. At least he wasn't looking at me like an old mother hen. "Well, we had quite an adventure, didn't we?" I turned to Randa. "And you . . . you called Murray, didn't you?"

She nodded. "You told me to, but before I could, Officer Wilson stopped by to make sure everything was okay." Her words flooded out in a rush. "I told him what happened, even though you said to call Murray first. I'm sorry! I was just so worried about you and Kip."

I sat down and pulled her onto my lap. She rested her head against mine. "Randa, you made a good decision. Thank you. You helped save our lives."

It was then that I noticed the dragon in the center of the table, polished and gleaming, sitting next to a vase full of maidenhair fern and tea roses. In fact, everywhere I looked, bouquets of brightly colored tulips overflowed their jars and vases as the kitchen blossomed with the fresh scent of springtime. I flashed a smile at Horvald, and he lifted his glass of lemonade in salute.

After the initial buzz died down, Murray motioned for my attention. "Can I talk to you a minute, please?"

Harlow joined us, wheeling out of the kitchen door with our help. We stepped into the backyard and strolled over to the plot of earth I had every intention of turning into a vegetable garden. As we neared the overturned soil, the bitter tang of moist soil was all too familiar; I could still taste it in my mouth. Maybe I'd fill it with sod and flower bushes instead.

"Let's talk about Oliver," Murray said.

I glanced over at Harlow. "I suppose you already know what's going on?"

"As always," she said with a strained smile. "I wish I didn't, though. It's pretty gruesome."

I turned back to Murray. "Last night you told me that he was dead. That's about all I remember."

She sighed. "Yeah. He is. Did you catch the news a few days ago when they discovered the man's body down in Vancouver, the one missing both hands and head?"

My stomach twisted. Oh no. "Oliver?"

"Uh-huh. Some guy was out for a walk, his dog ran off in the woods and led him to a shallow grave where he discovered the . . . rest of Oliver. The warden identified Oliver's remains."

I took a deep breath and crossed my arms across my chest. "Then who the hell was the guy who kidnapped Kip?"

"His name is Cedric Anderson. He and Oliver were cell mates."

"Cedric." The name felt strange on my tongue. "What was he in prison for?"

"Stalked his ex-girlfriend, found out she was engaged, and hit her with a car. He ended up with a seven-year sentence for vehicular manslaughter. He had a long history of burglary and theft, but most of it was as a juvenile, so he got off easy. Oliver ended up assigned to Cedric's cell."

I thought of Ida and how excited she'd been about Oliver's impending release, and my heart dropped. She was going to be devastated. "I take it they were let out on the same day?"

"Yup. Cedric must have found out about Ida and the money she inherited from her sister. He got the idea to run a scam on her and take the town for a ride while he was at it. He learned everything he could about Oliver, then the day they were released, killed him and took his place. Cedric was the same height, build, hair color. Since Ida hadn't seen Oliver for thirteen years, the one day they spent together didn't ring any alarm bells."

"Poor Ida," Harlow broke in. "This is horrible. But why was Cedric on the run if he'd been planning on scamming her?"

Murray rubbed her temples. "He told us he got cold feet. When Ida was called out of town, it seemed the perfect opportunity for him to take what he could and hightail it before she got back. When you showed him the dragon, he figured that alone would bring in several thousand. Along with everything else, he and his buddies—who he contacted before he left jail and told them to meet him up here—managed to take in nearly $30,000 worth of small, high-ticket items."

I coughed, fighting the urge to scratch my welts. I could see the next few weeks were going to be delightful. "Ida's going to need our support, all right. Anybody know when she gets back?"

"Actually," Harl said, "Murray called me after your little adventure. Randa found Ida's number for us, and I got in touch with her late last night. She should be pulling into town right about now. She's coming directly here."

"Well." I wasn't sure of what to do next. After all the chaos of the past few weeks I suddenly felt deflated, like a balloon that had just been popped. "I guess that pretty much takes care of that. I wonder . . ." Harl and Murray waited. "It's just that the dragon drew all this bad luck to me. How much of this would have happened if I'd never picked it up? What if Daniel had never come into my shop? If he hadn't been hit by that car? Would Oliver still be alive? Just what all was set in motion by the curse?"

Murray shrugged. "I don't think we can even begin to guess, Em. The dragon drew the bad luck, but it didn't make Cedric kill Oliver, it didn't force him to rob your house or destroy your shop. It was simply a magnet, I think, for the winds of ill fortune."

We turned back to the house, and I watched Harl slowly traverse the lawn. I rushed up to her, made her stop, and gave her a huge hug. "I'm so happy you're part of my life."

She stuck her tongue out at me. "Wait till you get my bill for the hours I spent on your research," she said, then broke into a wide grin. "Psych! Hey, guess what? I get rid of this four-wheeled monster tomorrow! I get my cast off! Now, come on you twit, let's get back inside to the party."

When we reentered the kitchen, there was Ida. She ran up and, for the first time I'd known her, threw her arms around me, sobbing. "Emerald, I almost got you killed by letting that monster into my house. How can I ever make it up to you?" The tears streaked down her face, and I knew she was crying for her nephew Oliver, for the lost hopes and dreams.

I gave her a gentle kiss on the cheek. "Ida, please, don't ever think I'd blame you for what happened. I'm just concerned about you and how you're going to weather this."

She shuddered, then wiped her eyes with a lace-edged handkerchief. "My dear, I've gone through far worse. I'm still in shock, I suppose. My poor, sweet Oliver, he never had a chance. I hope they give that monster just what he deserves."

Horvald moved in and took Ida by the elbow. "Let me take you out back where you can get a little air." He gave me a weary smile as they edged out the kitchen door.

From then on, the kitchen rang with a waggle of tongues. The kids clamored for my attention, and White Deer seemed certain that the night's events had drained me to the point of starvation. She kept pushing cookies on me until I felt ready to burst. Everybody was talking at once, and I was starting to feel the need for a little fresh air when Joe leaned over and asked if he could speak to me alone.

I tucked the dragon in my pocket, and we wandered out to the front porch. I turned to face him. "So . . ."

"So, Randa said that you broke up with Andrew." He questioned me with his eyes, and I knew he was waiting for my next move.

I took a deep breath and let it out slowly. "Yeah, he decided he wanted to be with a starlet down in Hollywood more than he wanted to be with me. It wasn't all his fault though; I really don't think we were meant to be together, except maybe as friends."

Joe planted himself on the banister. "Dare I ask where that leaves me? Us? You and me?"

He looked so hopeful that I didn't know what to say. Was I ready for another relationship? Was he old enough to handle my needs, my expectations? "I don't know," I said slowly. "I love spending time with you. We have a lot of fun, and you're caring and kind and . . . and awfully cute." I grinned at him, and he grinned back. "It's just that the past two weeks have merged into one big, painful blur. Can you give me a little while longer to sort out everything that's happened?"

He touched my arm lightly, avoiding the worst of the bruises. "Em, you know I think you're fantastic and that we'd rock as a couple, and I think your kids are great. You also know that I meant what I said: I'm your friend, no matter what happens. Take your time. Take all the time you need. I'm not going anywhere." As he leaned down toward my cheek, I turned my head, brushing his lips with my own. We shared a long, luxurious kiss, and then I gently untangled myself from his touch.

"I hope you don't mind," I said slowly, "but I could use a few minutes alone."

He stroked my cheek, then took off for his truck. As he started the engine, he waved and blew me a kiss.

I leaned against the newel post as the breeze filtered

through my hair. So much had happened that I couldn't even begin to assimilate it yet. If only I'd listened to my intuition. If only I hadn't been so afraid after Daniel died. If only I'd been able to stop Cedric before he kidnapped Kip. If only . . . if only I'd seen it all coming.

A familiar presence jostled my elbow, and I looked up to find Nanna standing beside me, glowing with that gentle golden hue that always surrounded her.

"Nanna!" Trust my sweet Nanna to know when I needed her. "Oh Nanna, it's been one hell of a ride." I dropped to the porch swing.

She laid her hand against my cheek. Her fingers left no marks on my skin, no weight to tell me she was actually present, but a wave of energy rushed through me, and I closed my eyes, basking in the knowledge that we could still connect, that I could still reach out for her when I most needed her presence. We might be separated by a veil stronger than any mortal's power to scale, yet our bond remained, and her love echoed into my heart from that distant land she now called home.

Her energy buoyed me up, and I found myself breathing deeply, letting go of the fears that had controlled my every waking moment the past two weeks. As much as Nanna loved me, I knew that this time, she didn't have any answers. I would have to figure out things on my own.

A brisk wind sprang up, and I stared out at the yard, at the new leaves blowing on the trees. Sometimes chaos swept into life and sucked everything up into a vortex, spitting it out willy-nilly, and then we had to pick up the pieces the best we could. Sometimes, our best wasn't good enough. I hadn't been able to stop Oliver's murder or Daniel's accident or Cedric's burglaries. I'd simply done the best I could under the circumstances I'd been given, but my best had been fraught with mistakes, miscalculations, and bad luck. But maybe a stumble or two was okay. Life happened, and it wasn't always fun or pleasant or even safe. Sometimes we needed to remember that we were only human.

And yet . . . Kip was unharmed; he might be frightened for a while by the kidnapping, but he'd be okay. Ida would mourn her nephew and move on. Murray would tackle her boss when she was ready, and she would do so on her own terms. Regardless of what the school decided about her studies, Miranda would never lose her passion for the stars. White Deer would continue to play the lynx, teacher of secrets. Joe would become a part of my life, as a lover or friend or both. And Andrew would follow his path to fame and fortune.

We would all meet and surmount the obstacles in our lives, whether they be from a cursed dragon or from the hand of fate. We would grow and learn from our mistakes and our troubles, hopefully becoming stronger for the effort.

I looked up at Nanna's spirit, longing to throw myself in her arms. "Am I doing a good job carrying on the family traditions?"

She threw back her head, and her laughter tinkled like crystal bells. With a wink and a nod, she began to back away, and I knew she had to go. I reached out, but she faded and then was gone.

As I wandered out into the yard, I thought about Huang Fu and Daniel and wished their spirits peace. One man had been an artist, searching for a new start. The other man, cursed from birth, had been looking for a way out. I knew now that Daniel had been on his way to the Pacific in order to dispose of the dragon for good. He probably planned on sending the statue to a watery grave, figuring to be its last victim. He might be destined to die, but the curse would never have affected anybody else again.

Huang Fu and Daniel, men from different times who

both died in the presence of the little jade statue. Neither one had really ever had a chance.

The sky was darkening; we were gearing for a storm. The clouds rolled in from the west, heavy with rain from the ocean. I raised the dragon up to the light and examined the milky green of the jade. Everything was as it should be, the dragon a creation of beauty and art and no longer a harbinger of death.

A chaotic kaleidoscope had taken over our lives and, even though this little dragon had been the cause of it, I couldn't help but think how incredibly beautiful it was and how much love Huang Fu must have put into it. Maybe even thieves had their good points. Maybe, in our journey through life, the cycles of sorrow and confusion were just storms along the way.

The wind was whipping briskly now and, suddenly invigorated, I raised my face to the sky and let out a shout of joy. Yes, we would have rain and high gusts before nightfall, but Kip, Randa, and I'd weather the storm without a problem. Charms for good fortune? Who needed them? We had each other, and that meant we'd already found our pot of gold at the end of the rainbow.

Salt and Herbal Breaking-Bad-Luck Spell

❖

Here's an easy charm to shake up negative energies and move them out of your house. If you've had a run of bad luck lately and can't seem to find out what's causing it, give this a try. For each room in your house, you will need:

1 cup sea salt
2 ½ cups bottled spring water (or water from a clear stream, lake, or river)
1 teaspoon dried rosemary
1 teaspoon dried lavender
½ teaspoon cayenne pepper
juice of one lemon

You will also need:

A spike of quartz crystal (you will be able to reuse this, but don't use your favorite if you're worried that it might fracture)
A bowl for each room (glass or plastic; don't use metal)

Wait until the day before the new moon. First, clean your house, clearing out cobwebs and dust (this is important: negative energy and chaos thrive in dusty areas).

In a large stainless steel or enamel pan (don't use aluminum) mix the water, rosemary, lavender, and cayenne. If you are making enough for several rooms, you don't need to make separate batches; just put all the water and herbs in one big pot. Bring to just below a boil and simmer for ten minutes. Cool to room temperature and strain.

Add the lemon juice and the salt. Stir clockwise with a wooden spoon to dissolve salt. Add crystal and let sit at room temperature for thirty minutes. Remove crystal and divide liquid into the number of bowls needed. Place one bowl in the middle of each room that you wish to cleanse. Leave uncovered. Rinse crystal in lukewarm water and set aside.

If you have children or animals, put the bowls where they can't be reached. *Do not drink this mixture*. Leave the herbed water overnight. Salt water absorbs negative and chaotic energies. The herbs act as an extra booster, since they are used in magical practices for purification, clarity, cleansing, and protection.

The next morning, pour the water down the drain and run cold water after it for a few moments to flush it out of your pipes. Do this only if you are on a sewer system. If your house has a septic tank, take the water to the nearest body of running water (a river, stream, ocean), or way out into a field or forest, and dispose of it there. Don't pour it onto any plants; the salt won't do them any good.

Wash the bowls with soap and water. I do this regularly every month or so to keep my home free of chaotic energy, which attracts bad luck and negativity. And remember—sometimes we are the ones who make our own bad (and good) luck. Always pay attention to what you might be doing to cause an uncomfortable situation, and also be on the lookout for opportunities to bring new and wonderful changes to your life.

Bright Blessings,
The Painted Panther
Yasmine Galenorn